Nox tucked her body tight when she hit the ground. The sand was burning hot and scrapped the flesh from her elbows and ripped her pants.

While the world spun around her, another bullet whizzed past and shattered a rock. Nox could do nothing about it.

The next shot could well be the last.

Mechanic

By

E. R. Torre

Please visit my website:

www.ertorre.com

Comments or questions? Email me at:

atrocket@aol.com

Special thanks to Ray Villarosa for coming up with the name of *Yoshiwara's* favorite band, "Virgin Slayer," as well as the lyrics to their song.

ISBN: 978-0-9729115-4-2

Library of Congress Control Number:
2009924680

First came the flashes. They were bright like lightning but low to the ground and continuous. They were followed by roars far louder than thunder. When it was finally over all was dark and you couldn't escape the smell. It was acrid; a mix of burning rot and seared flesh.

If you survived long enough, you heard the screams.

If you survived just a little longer, you heard the cries.

Prologue

The exhaust panel snaking out from under the *Betty Lou* 5032 Reconnaissance Tank's grav track belched a thick gray plume of smoke. Gears hidden deep behind fortified plating shifted down and the tank's engine howled like a caged beast. The vehicle's massive bulk slowed to a crawl before stopping.

"See anything?"

Sara Desola, the tank's pilot, wiped the sticky sweat from her forehead. Her eyes locked on the monitor before her and the hazy black and white shapes that flickered to life on them.

"Nothing, yet," she replied. Her eyes scanned each image as it appeared on the screen. "What was the estimated population?"

Ellis Howard, the navigator, reached for a sheet of paper.

"Intelligence estimated a couple thousand," he said. "I think it was like six, seven."

"Can you give me a little more accuracy?"

"Like it really matters now?" he said, pointing to the devastation before them.

The devastation was complete. There was nothing left of the small town but blackened sand. No corpses, not even fragments of corpses. Regardless, Ellis scanned the paper.

"Ok, here we go. Seven thousand eight hundred. Give or take a hundred."

"Fuck me," Sara muttered.

Ellis smirked and opened his mouth to say something.

"Keep the snide comments to yourself," Sara said. "That's the largest population estimate yet. You sure?"

"Feel free to take a look," Ellis handed Sara the paper. "E-mailed straight from the top."

"What's the time frame on this estimate?"

"It came in yesterday with the other Intel."

"Which means all these numbers aren't even a week old," Sara muttered. The ghostly images flickered before her, each zone as devastated as the last. Two hours before, the two man crew of the *Betty Lou* released a dozen robotic drones into the air. They were pre-programmed to circle specific sections of the village until recalled. The tank's occupants knew the images would be grim. Now they wondered how long these images of such utter destruction would haunt them.

"This ain't war," Ellis sing-songed. "This is genocide."

Sara cleared her throat and looked away from the monitor.

"Better them than us," she said. She tried to sound neutral, but couldn't quite manage the feat. "At least we don't get our hands dirty."

"Agreed. It's *so* much better to sit outside the slaughterhouse and wait until the shit settles."

"I'd rather count the dead than join them. The quicker we kill these fuckers, the quicker we get home."

"As long as we're in the right," Ellis mumbled.

"Don't give me that crap. We're not the monsters. They are."

"What's left of them."

Sara rubbed her chin and took a moment to examine her navigator's face. There were deep black circles under his eyes. Though she couldn't be sure, she suspected Ellis was hooked on Quick. The illegal drug was the military underground's favorite. And why not? It made people feel happy, even euphoric. Such feelings were in great demand in these parts. If Ellis was using, he wouldn't be the first. Nor the last.

"You know what the worst thing about all this?" Ellis asked.

"What?"

"I've forgotten just what the hell we're fighting for."

Sara opened her mouth to say something. *Don't you remember? We're here because...*

The answer didn't come.

All she knew was that the Nations Army were in their twenty sixth year of the occupation of the Arabian Deserts. Their original role was to be a police force while tempers –and ancient and new hatreds– simmered. The monetary and humanitarian impact proved a fatal blow to that old political system. As it withered and died, the Big Business Conservative stood ready to rush into the power vacuum left behind and assume control. Just as they did the police action, in the past few weeks, turned into outright war.

To those who cared, there was great irony here: It was the Corporations, in their infancy, who were the loudest to push the old Democracy *into* the police action. Afterwards, it was Corporations who promised to end the whole mess. Few realized, or even cared about, the profits to be made from a long, drawn out conflict. Few but the Corporations.

"I see something," Sara said, changing the subject. She reached for the controls and pushed a joystick forward. The image on this monitor zoomed in until it was a distinct form, a shadowy figure of a person. According to the readout, the figure was a little over a mile away.

"By the Gods. It's one of them."

"A villager?"

"No. *Them.*"

Ellis leaned in for a closer look. The figure sat on a shattered concrete pillar in the middle of a field of rubble. He – she? – was dressed in black and carried an impressively bulky Shock Rifle. The figure's eyes were hidden behind reflective goggles. The sophisticated eye ware was red hued and thick enough to resist the impact of shrapnel. Over the figure's head was a thin alloy helmet. It was scratched and dirty and carried more than a few dark stains. On its side was a drawing of a crude skull's head. To its side were three light blue vertical lines, each one thinner than the one before it. It was a logo, complete with a trademark symbol.

"One of ours," Ellis whispered, as if fearful the figure so far away might hear his words. "I see call letters. BB 1003."

"Blue Brigade. What's he doing?"

"Absolutely nothing."

"Is that unusual?"

"Very much so. They don't just sit back and do nothing."

"Maybe he's injured?"

Ellis shook his head.

"Not possible. If injured, they're programmed to—"

"Programmed?"

Ellis eyed the tank's driver. Sara pointed to the figure.

"That's *not* a machine,"

"They may be flesh and blood," Ellis admitted. "But they're far from human."

A chill passed through Sara. Though it was the first time she actually saw a member of the Blue Brigade, she recalled vague rumors people at home base told about these soldiers: They were tough and unimaginably cruel. They were also damn near unstoppable.

"What were they trained to do?" Sara asked.

Ellis grinned.

"Trained, right," he said. "If they're immobile, they're *trained* to self-destruct and take as many hostiles with them as possible."

Sara grimaced. It was an irony of this war that those who so harshly condemned the techniques of our enemies discovered advantages in emulating them and fighting at that level. The enemy used torture, so the allies sanctioned and mastered its use. The enemy used suicide bombers strapped to improvised explosives, so the Blue Brigade equipped their people with low level nukes.

"Maybe wiping out an entire village wore him down," Sara said. "Maybe he just needed to catch his breath."

Ellis shook his head.

"They don't rest. They move on until they're ordered to stop or until they *can't* move anymore. This soldier clearly isn't dead and I can't see any other members of his squad in the area."

"Maybe he was abandoned."

"No way. They'd take him out before that."

Ellis licked his lips. The figure on the screen remained frozen in place.

"How about we go in, get a closer look?" Sara asked.

"Are you crazy? Do you see the weaponry he's carrying? If he's malfunctioning and thinks we're the enemy, he'll peel this crate open like a paper bag."

"He might need medical attention."

"Do you remember what management said about interacting with these guys?"

"Management says a lot of shit. They told us we'd be here only a couple of years. That was way back in '55."

"You want to get close to a God-damned killing machine, be my guest. I'll wait behind."

Sara considered this.

"All right, what if he *is* malfunctioning? What if his...his internal programming locked up? He stays right where he is, a nice little target for the enemy. Now suppose they find and capture him. The bastards are crafty. They get hold of one of our super soldiers and the next thing you know, we're facing *their* version of a super soldier."

"Sara, I really wish you didn't talk so much damn sense."

"I'll call headquarters, see what they—"

Her words were cut off in mid-sentence. The figure on the screen rose to his feet.

"He's moving!"

The figure scanned his surroundings as if seeing them for the first time. When the figure was done, it looked up, directly at the drone's camera.

"He sees us?"

Sara shook her head.

"The drone is a foot long and hovers over a mile in the air. No way he sees us."

The figure on the screen, however, continued staring at the camera. After a while, it turned away.

"Now what?"

The figure's face, the part that was visible, darkened. The figure turned back, looked directly at the drone...

...and waved!

"No *way*," Ellis muttered.

Sara eased back in her seat.

"Do you think he...do you think he knows where *we* are?"

"Could be," Ellis said. "Let's see what—"

Ellis' words died. The figure on the monitor made an urgent motion and pointed to the west.

"What's he doing?"

"Trying to tell us something. There might be something going on to the west. What do the drones see?"

Sara hit a series of buttons on the computer before her. Images of destruction transmitted from the other drones appeared on the side monitors.

"Nothing."

"At all?"

"Village rubble ends in roughly five miles. After that we've got desert. Scanners aren't picking up any hostiles or enemy machinery."

Ellis thought for a few seconds.

"Maybe he doesn't mean the immediate vicinity. What's the nearest city to our west?"

"There's only one city to the west. Sada-bir. You know that."

Sada-bir was one of the last of the major cities in Arabia. It was designated a neutral zone years before by the Corporate Guard and boasted a population of several million. Most were refugees: Children, women, the elderly. There were small elements of the enemy's military staff hidden within the city too, just as there surely were in the other four major cities. But Sada-bir was a safe haven, the place where the idea of an eventual peace between the cultures was planted.

The figure on the monitor once again looked up and waved wildly.

"What is he saying?"

"I don't—"

The figure broke into a run.

"He's coming our way!"

"He's gone crazy!"

Ellis and Sara furiously pressed the buttons before them. It would take several minutes for the tank to initiate its defensive measures. The grav tank's engine roared and Sara forced it to make a sharp turn. In the middle of that chaos, an internal speaker with the cabin came to life, sending static throughout the cramped compartment.

"What the hell?" Sara yelled. "Did you turn that on?"

"No," Ellis responded.

"Sada-bir is going hot," a deep, calm voice said. It was a female voice. "Lock the vehicle down. Now."

Ellis and Sara looked at each other, then at the figure on the monitor.

"It's...it's the Blue Brigade soldier. She's a woman," Ellis said.

"How did she get on this channel?"

"How the hell should I know?"

"What should we do?"

Ellis bit his upper lip. The figure on the monitor ran toward them at full speed. A lone woman, yet one capable of single-handedly destroying the Corporation's finest recon tank.

"If we lock down, she catches up to us."

"She's one of ours."

"That's not enough reason—"

"She's *one of ours*," Sara insisted. "Lock it down."

"But—"

"Lock it down. It might be too late already."

Sara stared into Ellis' eyes.

"I hope you're right."

"You're not the only one."

Sara shut the grav tank's engine. Ellis hit a series of keys and the tank touched the ground. Heavy spikes shot from the tank body and embedded themselves ten feet deep into the rock below. Inside, the tank vibrated wildly before all was still. On the monitor, the lone figure approached fast. She was only a couple of hundred feet away.

"I'll aim the guns at her," Ellis said. "Just in case."

"You'll get no argument from me not to," Sara said.

Ellis reached for the weapon control. Before he could push a single button, however, a brilliant flash and a bone crushing tremor rumbled throughout the area. The *Betty Lou's* monitors abruptly blinked off, leaving the cabin immersed in total darkness. A second later hurricane force winds and a wall of debris smashed against the tank's side, threatening to rip her from the ground and send her flying.

"Son of a bitch," Sara yelled. "Nukes detonated."

"Sada-bir is dust," Ellis whispered.

"We don't know that," Sara said. "Get the sensors online. Try the emergency generators."

In the darkness, Ellis fumbled with a series of buttons. The computer monitors winked on and off. It took several seconds before they were fully engaged. Afterwards Ellis read each display, cycling through the various scanner readouts. Sara did the same. After a while, she lowered her head.

"You're right. Sada-bir is gone."

"H... how many?"

"We'll... we'll never know."

"What about... what about the other major cities?"

For now, there was no answer to that question.

It took the winds a few minutes to die down. When they did, the tank's monitors winked on and remained on.

"Engine's power is at forty percent," Sara said. She pressed a series of buttons. "Defensive weaponry is shot. All but two drones are down."

"She saved our lives," Ellis said. "If she hadn't warned us..."

Sara nodded.

"Is she...is she still alive?"

Ellis stared at the ghostly images before him. The previously devastated terrain before them now looked wiped clean.

"No one could survive that."

Sara sent the remaining drones into circular patterns. It took only a few seconds to lock on to the last spot they had seen the figure.

"She's not there."

"Radiation levels are spiking," Ellis said. "Can we move?"

Sara re-routed the drones and focused on releasing the spikes from the ground. The tank vibrated and a bone rattling squeal filled the cabin.

"Damn!"

Ellis anxiously eyed his pilot. The tank wasn't moving. Not at all.

"Fuck," Sara yelled. She slammed the palms of her hand against the computer. "We're stuck."

"How long?"

Sara pressed several more buttons.

"I'm activating the repair droids. They'll cut the spikes and free us."

"How long?" Ellis repeated.

"The outer spikes should be easy enough to cut. No more than a day. The inner spikes...that could take a couple of days."

Ellis leaned forward. The monitor before him was giving off a series of warning lights and readouts.

"Radiation levels continue rising."

"Our shields can handle it."

"For a while. Three days. Any more than that..."

"Call in for help."

Ellis hit a button, then another. He bit his upper lip and tried to contain the rising panic.

"Radio transmitter and long range antennae were fried in the explosion. I'm afraid we're on our own."

"Terrific."

Ellis leaned back in his chair.

"Let's hope the drones—" Ellis' voice faded. "Sara?"

"Yeah?"

"Take a look at monitor three."

Sara looked at the monitor. Her mouth swung open in surprise.

"Holy shit."

The black clad figure was there, no more than a hundred feet from the Betty Lou. She walked with a heavy limp toward the tank. Her body armor was ragged from the blast and her helmet, as well as most of her weaponry, was gone. Her face was red with welts. A trio of vertical blue lines, tattoos, were on her forehead and over her right eyebrow. Her shock rifle still hung from a strap on her shoulder.

"She's alive!"

"And armed," Sara muttered. "She's coming at us. What should we do?"

"We're not going anywhere, Sara. Let her in."

The tank's outer door opened and the dark figure walked into the sealed decontamination compartment. Low level lights flashed as the air within was cleansed of all impurities. A wave of chemicals then blew in and flooded the cramped quarters. All remaining hazardous materials were removed while the proper aerosol medicines were applied.

The figure within the compartment lowered her shock rifle and slid down to the floor.

Sara and Ellis watched the images sent in from the decontamination compartment. For the first hour, the figure remained deathly still. The only movement coming from her was her chest, which rose and fell with each labored breath. She was either unconscious or in a very deep sleep. She stirred a couple of times afterwards and even let out a faint groan. It was obvious she was in a lot of pain.

"We need to get her to a hospital."

"She's beyond medical help," Sara said. She eyed the radiation levels within the compartment. "We go in there, we're just as dead as she is."

The next day, the woman in the decontamination compartment stirred some more. The irritating noise from the repair drones had, perhaps, awoken her. She rose to a sitting position and stared at the opposite wall.

"I can't believe she's still alive," Sara said.

Ellis didn't comment. Together they watched the monitor of the decontamination chamber. The soldier tried to stand. She couldn't. She eased back to the floor and lay very still.

Two hours later, the soldier stirred once again. She groaned in pain and unzipped the front of her suit. Taking it off proved an excruciatingly painful chore. The flesh below the suit was red and covered in bloody welts.

"By the Gods," Sara said when the soldier was fully nude. "She's a little girl. She can't be more than fifteen years old."

Ellis didn't look surprised.

"Did...did you know?" Sara asked.

Ellis nodded.

"I saw a couple of them back at the base. I thought they were someone's kids. I thought..."

Ellis didn't finish his statement. For a while, silence descended upon the cabin.

"Have we come to this? Sending children into a warzone to fight and die for us?" Sara asked.

"Someone told me they were clones. No family, no ties. As I said before, they're *programmed* to fight and die and nothing more. That's why they're so effective."

Ellis pressed a button before him and talked into a microphone. His words were broadcast into the decontamination chamber.

"Soldier, we can't go in there to help you. Your clothing and weapons are irradiated. If you can, please throw them in this slot."

Ellis pressed another button and a metal drawer opened to the girl's side. It took a great effort, but the soldier was able to put the clothing and gun into the drawer. The drawer shut and the irradiated items were vaporized.

"That makes me feel a hell of a lot safer," Ellis said.

"She's done fighting," Sara replied. She turned to the microphone. "Are you hungry? Thirsty?"

The girl gave a weak nod.

"We'll send in some food."

Sara shut the microphone off.

"The least we can do is make her last hours a little more comfortable."

The girl ate little of the food but drank all the water. Sara sent along more liquid but was not surprised to find the girl soldier once again drifted off to sleep. Ellis turned from the internal monitor display and looked at the view of the outside area. For many hours now the sun was unable to penetrate the thick cloud of dust that lingered for miles around them.

"How are the repair drones doing?"

"Progressing. Schedule's tight, but we'll make it."

"Then there's little to do but rest," Ellis said. He rose from his seat and stretched. It occurred to him that neither he nor Sara had slept in over thirty hours.

"It's done," came a voice over the speaker. It was low and weary.

Ellis' eyes returned to the monitor. The girl soldier was awake.

"What was that?" Ellis said into the microphone.

"The war... it's over," the girl mumbled.

"How do you know?"

"Sada-bir. The other major cities. We... we made them – the enemy– think they were safe havens... neutral zones. All the refugees went there, seeking peace. In time, the military leaders hid out there, too. We kept track of their movements and left the cities alone for years. We waited for the right time. When they were all there..."

"It was a trap?" Sara gasped. "It was *always* a trap?"

"Blue, Orange, and Black Brigades were ordered to infiltrate and surround each city," the girl continued. "They were ordered to detonate."

"How could anyone convince a group of children to willingly sacrifice themselves?"

"It wasn't our choice. They... they controlled us."

"And you?" Ellis asked. "Why didn't you...?"

"Never was good at taking... taking orders."

She closed her eyes and Ellis shut the microphone off.

"Genocide by remote control, performed by children strapped to nuclear devices," Sara said. "I was wrong."

"About what?"

"*We're* the monsters."

The next day, the girl ate all her food and the repair drones reported progress over and above their estimated completion time. The tank would soon be free. The tank's pilots, however, kept their focus on the decontamination chamber and their guest. Sara was the first to note the change in the girl's condition.

"Her skin's not quite as red as before," she said.

Ellis hit a switch and the decontamination chamber's camera zoomed in on the girl's back. It then tracked right and left, providing a close up view of her entire body. When he was done, Ellis sat back.

"She does look better."

Sara pressed a series of buttons and the monitor displayed several readouts. Sara read the information before her. Her eyebrows rose with surprise.

"I don't believe it. The radiation within the compartment is lower. The level's still lethal, but significantly lower. And..."

Sara shook her head.

"It can't be."

"What?"

"A... at this rate of degradation, the chamber –hell, the girl herself– will be free of all radioactive contamination in... in three days. That's just not possible."

"It is," Ellis said. "The girl's Blue Brigade. *Nothing* stops them."

The cursed war ended as it began, a mix of pointless destruction and very real despair. Taxed economies were fully exhausted. Massive famine and political upheavals followed. The planet, polluted and sick, roared her displeasure. Ice flows melted and temperatures rose. The desert lands spread, until they were found on every continent...

1

Twenty years later...

The sandstorm came out of nowhere and sent a cloud of red dust billowing over the area. Like the storms typical of this time of the year, she barreled on, like a freight train uninterested in whatever stood in her path. The occupants of the Octi Corp Survey Group 4 camper watched in awe as she raged in the distance, just a few miles from their position. Had they been more interested, they could have charted her progress with their bare eyes.

There were five of them scattered in a semi-circle around the shiny silver camper. In each of their hands was a Geiger counter. The Geiger counter remained stubbornly silent, to the consternation of the men and women carrying the devices.

One of them, a woman wearing a floppy beach hat, struggled to shade herself from the burning sun. Like the others, her face and all exposed body parts were swathed in heavy white sunscreen. And like the others, a close look at her face revealed blistered and deep red skin. Her clothing was coated in a thin layer of desert sand but it didn't bother her. The only thing bothering her was her silent Geiger counter.

She swore and turned it off. Beyond the group and the sandstorm, the sun faded.

Another wasted day.

She swallowed her frustration and arched her back. Scouting the area was both tedious and draining, but what kept her and her group going were the rewards for those who succeeded. She laughed at this thought. Right now, a decent shower was a pleasant enough reward. If the others heard her laugh, they didn't react. Emotional outbursts were the norm when you spend this many hours each day under these conditions.

A bearded man in the center of the group also noted the setting sun. He eyed his wristwatch and said:

"Let's wrap it up."

There was no need to repeat the instruction. The three remaining members of the group stored their gear and headed back to the van and a much deserved rest. They were part-timers and worked only as long as they were contractually obligated to do so. They walked past the lady in the floppy beach hat. The bearded man stopped at her side.

"What's the matter, Mary?" he asked.

"Nothing," Mary replied. "Just admiring the view."

"What view?"

Mary shrugged. By this time, the others were already inside the camper.

"The place has its beauty," Mary said. "If you look."

The bearded man spotted the sandstorm, now tiny in the distance. It soon disappeared, blurring the last of the sunlight into a bloody red cloud.

"I suppose you're right," the bearded man said. For several minutes they admired the dimming lights and the rapidly cooling breeze. Unlike the others, this was their element, this was their world. The bearded man wrapped his arm around Mary and gave her a soft kiss.

"How about dinner?" he asked. "We've got Jambalaya ready to go. My treat."

"And I thought we were eating Octi Ration 8a."

"You say tomato..."

Mary chuckled.

"The last of the romantics. Fire up the microwave."

The bearded man released Mary and headed for the camper. Mary watched him leave but remained behind a few more minutes. When the sun was fully gone and the moon appeared in the eastern sky, Mary removed her hat and fanned her face. In another hour, the temperature would drop another twenty degrees. Soon enough, she would need a sweater or heavy jacket.

Mary turned from the moon and walked to an outcropping of stones between her and the van. She sighed. Their group spent most of the summer here, in this blazing heat, searching for anything worth salvaging. So far, they'd come up empty and the other temp workers were growing increasingly surly. If they didn't find anything worthwhile very soon, this whole summer would be a waste.

"That's life," Mary muttered. As a profession, there was nothing fair about scavenging. It tantalized with the possibility of fabulous rewards for those lucky enough and willing to do the intense work. More often than not, it offered a way to get by and make it through another day.

"It is what it is," she said. She continued forward and past several stones. Her left foot brushed a rock and Mary stumbled to the side. As she did, something under her right foot shifted. She heard a loud crack.

Mary immediately froze. Because of the poor light, she could not make out what she stepped on. She bent down to the ground and ran her hand through the sand. She felt a hard shape below her. It was enveloped in what felt like ragged fabric.

"By the Gods!" she gasped. She left her Geiger counter on the ground beside her discovery and ran to the camper.

When she entered the vehicle, she forced herself to calm down. It would not do to let the others see her this excited. They might try to share her claim or, worse, try to steal it outright. It happened innumerable times to scavengers who considered themselves far more clever than she.

Mary moved past the part timers and into the back cabin of the camper. There, she found the bearded man inside their private compartment. He was seated in his chair, studying a map.

"Edward," Mary said. Despite her best efforts, she couldn't entirely keep the excitement from her voice.

"What is it?"

Mary closed the door to the compartment.

"I found something," she whispered. "I'll show it to you when the others are sleeping."

At a little past midnight the duo silently exited the camper and made their way to where Mary left her Geiger counter.

"This better be good," Edward said. Though he loved his mate dearly, he didn't relish missing out on any sleep after such a brutally long day. Especially when the two of them had to be up early for another round.

"It is," Mary said.

They found the Geiger counter and Edward bent down close to the sand Mary pushed away a few hours before. He found the source of the loud snap immediately. It was a dark white bone, blasted by sun and sand.

"A femur?"

"Human," Mary said. She shone her flashlight at the ground and to the side of the bone. "See the clothing?"

Edward nodded. Below the spot where he lifted the femur were the remains of a pair of dark pants. Edward pushed away more sand. Parts of the skeleton and its tattered clothing were exposed.

"This might not be anything," Edward said. "A lost traveler, a desert rat."

"Then again," Mary countered. She bent down and helped Edward dig.

They kept their growing excitement in check as they exposed the rest of the skeleton. Mary found the dead man's skull. It smiled at her, as if thankful for the first taste of fresh air in many years.

"Look here," Edward said. He knelt next to the skeleton's legs. He found a dull black object underneath the left leg. He brushed away more sand and exposed a leather case. Unlike the skeleton's clothing, it was still intact.

Mary rushed to Edward's side. By then, Edward had the case in his hands and opened. From within he pulled a pair of faded road maps.

"They're at least ten years old," Edward said after a quick examination. He set them aside and again reached into the case. This time, he pulled out several loose sheets of faded paper. Whatever was written on them, if anything, had faded until it was illegible.

"Damn," Edward muttered.

For the third and final time Edward reached into the case. He produced a small black diary. The edges of the book were chewed up, but when he opened it, he found the writing within still legible.

"What is it?" Mary asked.

"Hold the flashlight steady."

Mary did as told. Edward read a few random passages from the book. His excitement grew to the point he was shivering with delight.

"We found it," Edward whispered. He closed the book and, along with the road maps and papers, returned them to the leather case. He held the case tight against his chest. "We have to bury the skeleton, make sure the others don't know."

"What is it?" Mary asked.

"It's what we've been looking for all these years."

With that answer, Mary suddenly found it hard to breath. Euphoria had her paralyzed.

"You mean?" she finally managed to say.

"Yes," Edward replied. The smile on his face was as bright as the sun.

Despite the chilly night air, Edward and Mary returned to the camper covered in sweat. When they awoke early in the morning, one of the temps discovered the water purification system had malfunctioned. Much was made of this very serious misfortune but, luckily for Edward and Mary, the temps didn't realize the failure was an act of sabotage. The camper had spare water containers, but only for six more days. That wasn't much of a margin for error and therefore it was urgent that the purification system be fixed immediately.

The temps unloaded their motorbikes from the side of the camper and, with the broken water purification parts tied to their machines, headed out to the nearest Octi Desertland base.

Edward and Mary stayed behind to watch the survey van. They didn't mind. They had two full days to do as they pleased. Their first act was to communicate with Octi Corp. about their previous night's find.

It took only four hours before an Octi helicopter arrived.

The helicopter landed in a cloud of dust barely thirty feet from the camper. Edward and Mary looked away until the dust fully settled. As the helicopter's blades slowed, a heavily armed soldier stepped out of the vehicle's cockpit. He approached the machine's side door and opened it. From within the passenger compartment exited a lean, well-dressed man in his mid-thirties.

"Is that?" Mary whispered.

"Yeah," Edward replied. "Robert Octi Jr. The boss' son."

Robert Octi Jr. walked to Edward and Mary's side.

"The diary?" he said.

Edward and Mary made no move.

"Our reward?"

The well-dressed man smiled. He reached into his suit, produced a wad of bills, and handed them to Edward. Edward began counting the money but stopped when he noted Robert's gaze.

"Sorry, Mister Octi," he said. "It's just that—"

"Count it," the well-dressed man insisted despite his obvious impatience. "If I were in your place I'd do the same.

But make it quick, I've got a full schedule and came here only on your say so."

"Yes sir," Edward replied. His fingers shook as he counted the bills. When he was done, he nodded and Mary walked to the camper. She was gone only a moment, and when she returned, she carried the leather case the two found the night before.

"It's all in there, Mr. Octi," she said.

Robert Octi Jr. opened the case and searched its contents. He pulled out the diary and carefully flipped through it.

"It belonged to Roger Martin," Edward said. "Do you recognize his name?"

"No," Robert said. "You told me he worked for the Demon?"

"That's what he wrote in the book."

"You read the whole thing?"

"Parts, just enough to make sure."

"And the others in your group? Do they know?"

"No sir. We made sure of that. They're off to Desertland Base 6, looking for some equipment we... we fixed."

Robert Octi Jr. frowned.

"Are you saying you sabotaged Octi Corp. equipment?"

The two survey crew members stiffened. They relaxed only moments later, when Robert winked and let out a cheerful laugh.

"I won't say anything if you don't."

Robert closed the book and tucked it back into the leather case.

"Whatever information we gather from this could lead to more finds," Robert said. "And that means more reward money for the both of you. I'd continue to keep your discovery a secret. Unless, of course, you want to share the rewards of your hard work with the rest of your crew."

"Hell no," Mary blurted out. Her face flushed red and Robert let out another laugh.

"So I trust we'll keep this our secret?"

Edward grabbed Mary by the shoulder and hugged her.

"You know you can trust us," Edward said.

"Good."

Robert shook both Mary and Edward's hands. "I've got to go, but we'll be in touch. Soon."

With that, Robert Octi Jr. returned to his helicopter. The armed soldier closed the door behind him and re-entered the cockpit. Seconds later the helicopter's blades became a blur of motion and she was up and off.

In spite of the flying sand, Edward and Mary waved until the helicopter was gone.

"He's so down to earth," Mary said. "Such a nice guy."

"I'm with you," Edward agreed. "He's my kind of leader. I'd rather have someone you can take out to a bar and share a beer with over those know it all intellectuals. We're so lucky to have him."

They laughed and hugged each other and kissed.

Robert Octi Jr. stared out the window at the monotonous view of the Desertlands. He pulled a handkerchief from his suit pocket and wiped the dust from his hands. Beside him lay the leather case. He didn't need to clean it. The scavengers –*what the hell were their names?*– already wiped the dust from its surface. A touching gesture.

Robert Octi Jr. turned away from the case and looked forward. Across from him sat a thin man with an intense stare. His gray eyes never wavered from Robert and he rarely blinked.

"I want them taken care of, Nagel," Robert said.

"What about the others, the ones they sent to the base?"

"They said there were three of them. Wait until they return, then take care of them all at once."

Nagel nodded. He sat back in his seat and closed his eyes.

"Oh, and one more thing," Robert said. "I gave those idiots one hell of a lot of money. I want that back, too."

2

"Snowflakes in August," the man with the thinning hair mumbled. He stared at the faded image of a news anchor emanating from the flat screen vid unit nailed to the corner wall. He followed this comment with a moist burp before pushing away from the bar's counter and stumbling to the restroom. Left behind was a half-finished glass of beer.

The two remaining men at the counter gave the glass a thirsty look.

"Flip for it?" the first man said to the other.

The second man rubbed his eyes.

"Thomas drinks *Selabro*," the second man replied. "That stuff tastes like goat piss."

"So it's mine?"

"Hell no."

They were quiet for a few seconds.

"That stuff *is* nasty," the first man said.

"Like you can afford anything better."

"You're the one that said it tasted like goat piss."

"Story of my life. Tell you what, it's yours, Roger, after you explain what that snowflakes in August shit was supposed to mean."

Roger nodded. He gave his friend a toothless smile and reached for the glass. Just before grabbing it, the prize was intercepted by the bartender.

"Sorry, guys," the bartender said. "Drinking clients pay for that privilege, even if it is *Selabro*."

"Come on Catherine," Roger moaned. "It's our last day here. Surely you can make an exception?"

"Last day? I'm not going anywhere. You're free to come back."

"But we like it quiet. The live band'll make too much damn noise."

"Then I'm sure you'll find a quieter hole to call home."

Roger and his friend watched in silence as Catherine Holland, the owner and, since the death of her husband five years before, sole bartender of the *Yoshiwara*, poured the dark liquid into the sink. "In the meantime, if you want a fresh cup, just holler, OK?"

"Yes ma'am," her two patrons replied in unison.

"I've got you trained like seals, don't I?"

"Yes ma'am," they repeated and laughed.

Catherine joined them, but only for a few seconds. There were always things to do, even in a nearly empty bar.

"I'll miss you guys, too," she admitted. "If you all just spent enough so I could pay my bills, there would be no need to change things around."

"No need to explain," Roger said.

Catherine nodded and walked away.

"Where were we?"

"Snowflakes in August?" Roger's friend said, returning to the previous topic of conversation. "Means something that don't happen. An impossibility."

Roger thought about that for a second.

"Makes sense," he said. "The president was on the news. Said he didn't have anything to do with that contract thing, the...uh..."

"The military contracts," Catherine chimed in.

"I remember. And he seemed like such a nice guy when he was elected."

"The fuck he was," a third man at the far end of the bar intruded. "He was always an asshole. There ain't no good people in this world. They're as rare as...as rare as..."

"Snowflakes in August?"

"Fuck yeah," the third man concluded. He shrugged as if to emphasize the point and placed a clear plastic mask snuggly over his mouth and nose. Once in place, he hit a switch on his belt. There came a low hiss and the face mask filled with a cloud of gray gas. The third man's eyes rolled up and his head gently dropped on to the counter.

Roger let out a low whistle.

"Ladies and gentlemen, Elvis has left the building."

"At least he pays for his drinks," Catherine said.

"Ouch," Roger replied.

His words were drowned out by the blare of street traffic. It reverberated through the quiet bar like a low level nuclear explosion. All eyes turned to the door leading out. It was wide open and standing before it was a tall woman dressed in a faded blue jean jacket and matching jean pants. She sported short, jet black hair and her eyes were hidden behind a pair of equally dark sunglasses. Her body was lean and athletic and there was an air of danger surrounding her.

Catherine tensed. There were plenty of poseurs in the big city, people who projected swagger but carried weapons because they could never handle themselves in a real tumble. The woman standing at the door, she sensed, was beyond such pretenses.

The stranger closed the door and silenced the outside roar. In the low lights of the bar, Catherine spotted a tattoo on the stranger's forehead, just above her right eyebrow. Three vertical blue lines. They were a simple design and somewhat faded with time.

To anyone who hadn't seen them before, they looked perfectly innocent, perhaps even stylish. For Catherine, however, seeing them sent a nervous charge through her body. She suppressed a gasp and tried, but failed, to also suppress some dark memories.

The three blue lines on the stranger's forehead were similar to the logo she saw way back in the Arabian Wars, when Catherine worked for Intel Division. Because of her expertise, she spent the war stationed far behind the main lines and at the staging grounds. One day she saw that logo on some very young boys that filtered into the base one particularly hot day not too long before the war's end. Once they arrived, rumors about them spread like wildfire throughout the camps. The young boys, it was said, were part of an elite fighting force known as the Desert Brigades.

The descriptions of their actions seemed more myth than reality. There was talk that these children were capable of cruelties both unheard of and unimaginable. Catherine didn't believe any of those rumors. That is, until the Desert Brigades' extreme actions proved the final solution to the Arab problem.

Catherine quivered.

It took those child-soldiers one bloody weekend to clean the Arabian deserts of their bothersome dwellers. What was left behind was a cursed and silent land. So very silent...

The woman at the door stepped deeper into the bar. Instinctively Catherine leaned closer to the twelve gauge shotgun she kept hidden below the counter. There was no way to tell if the stranger really was one of the Blue Brigade soldiers. After all, weren't they supposed to be dead?

Catherine kept her right hand close to her weapon. *Better safe than sorry.* With her left hand, she waved the stranger in. Even if the stranger was one of those murderous bastards, her money was as good as everyone else's.

"Welcome to the *Yoshiwara*," Catherine said. "There's plenty of space at the counter, or you can take one of the tables in the back."

The stranger noted the bar's emptiness. Her gaze returned to Catherine. For a second, Catherine thought she was in a daze, like she was...

God help me, Catherine thought. *She isn't Blue Brigade. She's a stoner looking for the live band.*

She forced herself to smile. *Is this what I've got to look forward to starting tomorrow?*

"You do know our format change is tomorrow, not today, right?"

The stranger's face remained blank.

"*Tomorrow* we bring in the live bands. Please tell me all that money I spent on advertising hasn't gone to waste."

"It's not too late to change your mind," Roger intruded. "Cancel the bands and give us our bar back."

Catherine ignored Roger's comments.

"Anyway, this is the last night of the old *Yoshiwara*. If you'd like, please sit back and enjoy."

The dark haired woman nodded and walked on. She passed a blond haired man sitting at one of the tables and found and sat behind another empty table at the far corner of the bar. From there, she silently eyed the vid screen.

Catherine bit her lower lip. It would have been much better if the stranger stayed by the counter. Now Catherine had to go to the woman and leave her weapon far behind.

Catherine stepped out from behind the counter area and approached her new customer. She carried a well-rehearsed smile. In the darkness of the bar's corner, it was difficult to get a read on the stranger. It was also hard not to stare at the tattoo. Despite her lingering unease, Catherine's business instinct kicked in. She judged the woman's worth and asked:

"What can I get you?"

Selabro, Catherine thought. *Just like what all the other cheap bastards around here drink.*

The dark haired woman reached into her pocket. She pulled out a couple of bills and counted them. They didn't amount to much.

"*Selabro*," the stranger said. Her voice was low and emotionless.

"Big spender," Catherine said.

"*Spend what you've got...*" the woman said, and paused.

"*...There might not be another day*," Catherine whispered, finishing the woman's statement.

Catherine suppressed a shiver. She heard those words spoken by so many of her fellow soldiers before shipping off to the front lines. There was no longer any doubt the stranger was a veteran of the Arabian Wars.

"A...ain't that the truth," Catherine added and let out a small, nervous laugh. "Some fellow said that the other day. Nice thought, isn't it?"

"I suppose."

Catherine walked away while the woman in the faded blue jean jacket checked out the other patrons in the bar. Their eyes were on the stranger but quickly turned away. She shrugged and leaned back in her chair. Her gaze returned to the flat screen TV.

Through a cloud of static a handsome -but not too handsome- reporter read from a teleprompter. The man's smile was pleasant but, like most reporters, not terribly genuine. His eyes were a strikingly blue, which reminded those old enough who could remember what the vast, unpolluted oceans once looked like.

"...and in business news, the stock markets continue their precipitous fall," the man said. "They closed at a ten-year low, with the ticker hovering at 56,091. Despite the depressed market, there remains one ray of light. Octi Corporation and its subsidiaries have so far weathered the storm and are one of the only companies immune to the current economic malaise. At the end of the day their shares were up 50 points. Our experts analyze just how high Octi could go..."

The woman in the faded jacket grinned.

"Miss?" she called out.

Catherine paused in mid-stride.

"Fuck the *Selabro*," the stranger said. "Get me a *Prestigio*."

3

A **silver limousine** pulled up to the *Yoshiwara's* microscopic parking space. It came to a stop next to an old and weathered motorcycle. The limousine's driver stepped out of the car and walked to the rear passenger door. He was dressed entirely in black and held his cap reverentially in his hand while opening the door.

"We're here, Mr. Donovan," the driver said and bowed.

Elliot Donovan exited from the passenger compartment. He was a man on the far side of sixty. His body was an oval, his head bare, and his face a wrinkled sponge. He was dressed in a dull blue suit and carried a beefy cigar in his right hand. He stepped up to the motorcycle and ran his hand over its beat up fuel tank.

"Slovak engine, a Malacky," Donovan said to no one in particular. "Frame's beat to shit, tires are bare. Figures."

"Sir?"

"It's her chopper," Donovan said. His voice was filled with irritation. "Engine's still warm. We're late."

"Yes sir," the driver said. "Sorry sir."

"Don't let it happen again," Donovan said. "There are plenty of other drivers."

"Yes sir."

Donovan straightened his tie and entered the bar.

Catherine watched with great interest as the elderly business man entered the bar. He couldn't have looked more out of place had he arrived dressed in a clown outfit and scuba gear.

"Can I help you?" Catherine said. The rest of the bar's patrons looked on. Roger and his friend had wide grins on their faces.

"The man looks lost," Roger said. His friend let out a soft chuckle. "Or maybe he was also expecting the live band."

Donovan frowned. He turned to the bartender and said:

"I'm looking for—"

"I thought this was a private club," the woman with the dark hair and vertical blue tattoos interrupted from the rear of the bar. "You lost?"

Donovan closed his mouth and shuffled past the counter. He approached the back of the bar.

"Nox?"

"Maybe you should ask a little louder," the woman replied. "I don't think the hooker spewing her guts out in the back alley heard you."

"That's quite an attitude you've got," Donovan sniffed. He pulled a chair out from the table, wiped it down thoroughly with a handkerchief, and sat down. His voice lowered to a whisper. "If you wanted privacy, you should have agreed to meet where I—"

"You pick the meet? Sorry, Mister Donovan, a Mechanic's life is short enough as it is."

"Mechanic? How delightfully old fashioned. I thought you people were billing yourselves as Independents nowadays."

"What do you want?"

"Two data disks," Donovan said. "Company property. Stolen from my office yesterday afternoon. Fortunately, I make it a habit to monitor my employees' activities both inside and outside the work facilities."

"Not well enough, apparently."

Donovan frowned.

"The one who took the disks kept a very regular routine after work. Yesterday, shortly before we discovered the disks' theft, he made a detour in that regular routine and stopped by a warehouse on the west side of town." Donovan reached into his suit and pulled out a piece of paper. "That's the address."

"They've had the disks since at least yesterday?"

"I know what you're thinking," Donovan said. "It's possible the data has already been compromised. My technical staff placed twelve layers of encryption on the disks and the information on them. They assure me that level of encryption requires at least a week to fully decode and copy."

"If I get my hands on the disks, how do I know they're the right ones?"

"They have holographic labels identifying them as Octi Corp. property. The disks also have a special non-stick surface. If the thieves painted or tried to tape something over the holographic label, it would peel off very easily."

Donovan closed his mouth and looked away.

"What else?" Nox asked.

Donovan's eyes returned to the woman before him.

"I'll be honest with you..." he began.

Nox leaned back in her chair. Though she tried, she couldn't help but clench her jaw.

"...you're not the first person we've hired since yesterday. There were two others before you, one last night and one early this morning."

"I'm not even your first bridesmaid?"

"Nox..."

"Don't tell me: You haven't heard from them since."

"They'll know you're coming. You must take precautions."

"Sure," Nox said. "What do you have for me?"

Donovan again reached into his suit. He pulled out an envelope and handed it to Nox.

"Thirty five thousand," Donovan said. "Small bills, just like you asked. The rest when I get the disks back. In a usable state."

Nox opened the envelope and counted the money.

"It's all there," Donovan said, a little testily.

After finishing her slow count of the money, Nox nodded.

"It sure is. Imagine that."

The Mechanic rose.

"I'll let you take care of the bar bill, too. If you ask politely, the bartender might even give you a receipt."

4

The warehouse lay in the city's old business district, some twenty blocks of low rent, heavily armed, and near identical metal buildings. At night time the hustlers, hookers, and addicts roamed the streets around the area like zombies from a low budget movie. They cruised around, linked up, and did their business, whatever it might be, all under cover of the deep shadows. They were kings of the night, at least most of the time.

The roar of the motorcycle was barely audible, buried by the sounds of traffic and other distant machines. Nox kept to the side streets, attracting as little attention as possible. Despite its worn-down condition, her chopper was a meaty target for the streets roamers. This was why Nox found and parked her vehicle before a twenty four hour convenience store and right in front of its plate glass entrance. Should a thief pass by, he would either be dissuaded from stealing the chopper because of possible witnesses or, conversely, find the store itself a far more tempting target.

But leaving the chopper here meant Nox was a distance from her own target. Twelve blocks, to be exact. It there was trouble and she needed to make a quick exit, it would have to be on foot. As always, stealth was the key to a successful operation, so Nox dressed entirely in a dull black body suit. It made her invisible in the thicker shadows of the night.

Nox removed the thin black backpack from her shoulders and checked the items within. Satisfied all was in order, she replaced the backpack and entered the convenience store. She did this to allay any suspicions on the part of the store's owner. They had a bad habit of keeping track of the vehicles parked in their lot. Anyone who parked and walked away without entering the store risked having their vehicle towed. By entering the store, the people behind the counter would connect Nox with her chopper and, given how busy the place was even at this hour, they'd think she was still around, shopping somewhere, even if she was gone. Nox figured she bought herself between forty minutes and an hour of free parking time.

The Mechanic would be back by then, or not at all.

Nox served herself a cup of fancy coffee and glanced at the fresh air pads, stain removers, electrical cables, and prophylactics. She kept her head down, purposely avoiding the surveillance cameras the stores mounted in all the usual places. Nox put money for the coffee on the counter and headed for the exit. Once outside, she dumped the virgin drink in the nearest trash can and set off for the business district.

It took her only a few minutes to reach the chain link fence that roped off the warehouses within. Nox climbed the fence and headed to the warehouse Donovan suspected held the stolen disks. It was almost identical to all the other warehouses except in one curious respect: There were no visible guards outside. Indeed, the only outdoor security feature Nox spotted was a camera positioned over the rear entry door.

Nox hid within a bush and its deep shadows. She watched the camera oscillate back and forth, memorizing its movement pattern. She then reached into her backpack and removed a pair of red hued glasses. She placed them over her eyes and hit a switch. The night's darkness was lit up in frosty infrared. Nox again reached into the backpack and this time pulled out a compact gun belt. She strapped it to her waist and, when she again looked up at the warehouse camera, it was in the exact position she expected it to be.

"Good," she muttered. She had memorized the security camera's movements well. Her next step was to disable it. Nox adjusted her glasses until she had a magnified view of the camera. She frowned.

Equinox 5300, she thought. *That's some shoddy shit.*

For a third time Nox reached into her backpack. She pulled out a thin rectangular hard drive. Nox then searched the bush and found a sturdy but small wooden box. It was good enough for her purposes. She picked it up and silently ran to the side of the warehouse and just out of the camera's view. Nox flattened her body against the warehouse wall and timed her movements. When the camera pointed away, she ran under it, laid down the wooden box, and climbed up. She was now close enough to the camera to begin her work.

Nox unscrewed the panel on the camera's side and stripped a pair of wires from its internal mechanism. With well-practiced efficiency, she connected these wires to the slim rectangular hard drive and screwed the entire apparatus into the camera's side. She waited a few seconds while the camera completed a couple of oscillations. When she was satisfied her hard drive recorded enough footage, she pressed a button on the device's side. The smell of burnt wires and fused machinery filled the air and the camera abruptly stopped. Its internal mechanism was fried and Nox's hard drive now feed its looped recorded images to the security guards, wherever they might be.

Nox stepped off the wooden box and hurriedly returned to her hiding place in the bushes. Although her work on the camera appeared perfect, there was always the possibility she somehow screwed up. If that was the case, someone would be on their way to check the camera. The next few minutes passed very slowly and Nox rocked impatiently in place. After ten minutes passed without any sign of guards, she was once again on the move.

Nox sprinted back to the door. In her hand was a thin set of lock picks. She had the warehouse door unlocked in seconds, but didn't open it. Instead, she put away the picks and removed another rectangular device from her backpack. She ran it along the edge of the door. The digital readout on the sensor did not change.

Nox replaced the device into the backpack. There were no other security devices present and it was safe to open the door.

Nox, however, remained in place. Her jaw tightened and loosened. She was in deep thought.

So little security. Why?

Nox carefully pushed the door open and stepped into the darkness within. Thanks to her infrared glasses, she was able to see a series of crates stacked one on top of the other in rows that seemed to extend for miles. At the end of the crates and on the other side of the warehouse came a dim light.

Nox approached that light. As she did, she heard voices. She froze in place and listened for a while. She detected five distinct voices, all male, engaged in casual conversation. Nox eased forward, until she stood beside the last of the distant crates. She peered around the corner.

Before her was the warehouse's large front door. In front of it was a small table and sitting around the table were five security guards. They were dressed in white shirts and black pants and carried automatic handguns in their waist holsters. They laughed, drank, and smoked while playing a round of poker. From the sloppy way they carried on it was obvious their game was well into its third or fourth hour.

Nox frowned.

What the hell is this?

Her body tensed and she reached for her gun. Despite Donovan's warnings, the break-in proved far, *far* too easy. If these poker playing security guards and a cheap security camera were the sum total of what the two other less fortunate Independents faced...

No. Something wasn't right.

Nox stepped back and looked around. Apart from the card players, everything was quiet. A sense of dull anger spread through the Mechanic. Donovan hadn't told her everything. There *had* to be some other danger present...

Either that or the Independents Donovan hired before coming to Nox happened to be the Big City's two *worst* Independents of all time.

Nox spotted wooden stairs on the east end of the warehouse. They led up to a glass encased office that overlooked the entire place. It was as good a location as any, Nox thought, to hide stolen disks.

The second floor office was small and square in shape. A plain wooden desk lay against the far wall and a door in the back of the office, Nox guessed, led to a private bathroom. The Mechanic would check on that later, if needed. The desk was positioned to allow its occupant a clear view of the warehouse below.

Nox eased into the room and kept away from the glass walls. When she first opened the office door, she scanned for motion detectors or laser lights but found none. The tension within her grew even more, but Nox moved on. She kept to the thick shadows and searched the desk. There were plenty of papers within, but no disks or false bottoms.

Nox focused her attention on the back wall. She searched for any sign of a wall safe but again came up empty. She then entered the office's back door and searched what indeed turned out to be a bathroom. There was nothing there but filth. The topless woman on a wall calendar pinned to the bathroom door winked at her, as if laughing at this so far futile search.

At least someone's enjoying themselves.

Nox exited the bathroom and, from the opposite side of the room, gave the place a long look. All seemed in order. All seemed so perfectly ordinary.

Nox smiled.

From this angle Nox spotted scuff marks on the floor directly beneath the desk. It was as if someone moved this very heavy piece of furniture back and forth, over and over again. Nox approached the desk and crouched down. She slowly, and very carefully, pushed it away, revealing the wood panel floor. Nox pressed down on the paneling. One piece was loose. Nox lifted it, revealing a small floor safe.

The Mechanic spent no time celebrating her discovery. She reached into her backpack and removed yet another thin black box from within. It was magnetized and clamped itself upon the safe door. A digital display lit up and a series of numbers circulated on the box's screen. One by one the numbers locked into place until a faint click was heard.

Nox removed the electronic decoder and stored it. She then opened the safe door. Tucked within were several documents, some cash, and, most importantly, two slim computer disks.

Nox grabbed the disks and ignored the rest. She opened the jewel case box of each and verified they had the Octi Corp. logo and proper serial numbers etched on their surface.

Nox placed them in her backpack and closed the safe door. She then pulled the desk back into place and made sure the office looked just as she found it. Satisfied all was in order, Nox headed for the office exit.

Nox quietly walked down the stairs leading to the ground floor of the warehouse. Once there, she listened for the sound of the guards. They were still engrossed in their card game and oblivious to anything else. Nox shook her head and turned to her right. She kept to the shadows while making a beeline to the rear exit door.

As she moved, she felt more and more tense. By all rights, she should be feeling elation. She broke in, picked up the merchandise, and was only a few feet away from the exit. But Donovan's warnings and the fate of the two other Independents weighed on her.

Anyone could have made their way into this place and gotten these disks. Anyone.

Theories and conjecture revolved around Nox's mind. She tried to rationalize the situation but couldn't.

"It's a trap," she whispered.

There was no other logical explanation. The best traps were the ones easy to get into but impossible to leave.

Nox looked around. She expected to see something, anything, coming after her. She was not disappointed.

The shadowy figure was at least six feet tall and shaped like a thick utility pole. It moved smoothly along the floor and directly toward the Mechanic.

Nox ran in the opposite direction as fast as she could, but the robot was already within firing range. A pair of guns mounted on its side released a deadly barrage of rounds. The bullets hit Nox squarely on her back. The Mechanic yelled as the impact slammed her forward several feet. The wooden crates at her sides were simultaneously ripped to pieces.

Nox fell to the floor but immediately sprang back to her feet. She ran down the hallway as fast as she could.

Gunfire from the robot dogged her movements and shattered everything in its wake. Wood splinters shot up and several jagged pieces lodged themselves into the side of Nox's face. The Mechanic felt warm blood flow down her cheek but ignored it.

Nox turned into an aisle and the gunfire momentarily stopped. She looked back and spotted the robot moving relentlessly toward her. The Mechanic reached for her handgun but didn't pull it out. On this mission she chose to carry a light weight, low caliber weapon. There was no way a bullet from her gun could penetrate the robot's thick skin.

Nox continued running.

If it wasn't for the maze of crates, the robot would have been on top of the Mechanic in seconds. As it was, it remained locked on its target and followed relentlessly. It gained ground while Nox's breathing grew labored and her movements slowed.

She didn't have much time.

As she ran, Nox scanned the floor before her. She spotted a small cardboard box lying in her path. According to its label, it carried copy paper. Nox picked it up and tossed half the sheets away. She then crumpled several individual papers and placed every single cartridge she had from her handgun along with the crumpled papers inside the box.

Nox stopped behind a corner and waited. In moments, the robot was just a few feet away. Its internal machinery clicked and hummed louder and louder. Behind it came the sounds of the security guards. Their poker game was finished, and they cautiously followed the robot's movements.

They aren't security guards, Nox thought. *These men are janitors. They're here to clean up my remains.*

Another burst of shots shattered the crates Nox was hiding behind.

Now or never.

Nox used her lighter to set the top sheet of paper on fire and hurled the box before the robot. Its internal sensors picked up the object's motion and weaponry locked on the new target. The robot unleashed a furious barrage of bullets which incinerated the box. That, in turn, set off the bullets Nox hid within.

Sparks flew all around, igniting the papers within the small box. Flames leaped out and fell along both sides of the corridor. Flaming sheets landed on packing material which, in turn, set off other fires. Within seconds heavy smoke and glowing fire filled the corridor.

The robot paused, confused by the conflicting thermal images. It circled around and fired a series of short bursts. The motion of the security guards behind the machine further confused it.

More targets.

More bullets fired.

From a safe distance, Nox watched it all. A grim smile settled on her face. The fire spread rapidly and was soon out of control. The robot, meanwhile, spun around in tighter and tighter circles and shot at *everything* around it.

Nox dashed out of the warehouse's rear door and back to her original hiding place in the bushes. The sound of the robot's relentless gunfire echoed throughout the night while thick clouds of smoke rose from the warehouse roof. The sound of gunfire was joined by the screams of the security guards.

"Technology," Nox muttered.

She examined her right arm. Blood flowed from a deep cut near her elbow, the result of one of the Robot's bullets. Nox removed her backpack and shirt, revealing a Kevlar-SimTech vest strapped to her upper body. When she took the Kevlar vest off and turned it, she wasn't surprised to find at least a dozen bullets plastered in close proximity against the heavy fabric.

Nox shook her head. She was lucky the damn thing held in place. As it was, this expensive piece of gear was all but worthless now and damaged beyond any possible use.

You served me well, Nox thought. If not for the vest, the Mechanic would surely have been cut in two.

Nox folded the destroyed material and inserted it into her backpack. She pulled out gauze and disinfectant. The wound on her arm was minor and required minimal care.

Nox laughed.

You just about became the third *stupidest private contractor in the Big City.*

In the distance, she heard the sounds of approaching sirens.

5

Donovan's office rested in a niche on the fortieth floor of the Octi Plaza. As with all the offices of Octi Corp's senior personnel, it was spacious and elegantly furnished. At its center was a large mahogany desk. Sitting behind it and talking on his telephone was Donovan. Apart from a small desk light, the place was immersed in darkness.

Donovan welcomed this darkness. At this point, he feared any light. He also shivered as he talked.

"How many died?" Donovan whispered into the phone. His face grew even paler when he heard the answer. Thin beads of sweat formed on his forehead. "Clean up the fucking mess. Hide the SR unit, hide everything you can. As far as we're concerned, we were victims of industrial sabotage, nothing more. If anyone suspects any different, it'll be your ass."

Donovan slammed the phone into its cradle and leaned back in his chair. He shook his head and closed his eyes.

"What a day," he muttered.

When he opened his eyes once again, he let out a gasp. Nox stood before him.

"Nox?" Donovan rasped. "How the hell?"

Nox reached into her pouch and pulled out a pair of disks. She tossed them on the desk.

"There they are," she said.

Donovan eyed the disks. Bullet holes pierced the body of both disks. Donovan took a few seconds to calm himself down before picking them up. He made a show of examining them, eyeing each and every hole before loudly cleared his throat and shaking his head.

"They're damaged," Donovan said. "Useless."

Nox offered no reply. After a few more seconds, the silence within the office was overwhelming. Donovan again cleared his throat and tossed the disks into the trash can. Ignoring Nox's presence, he reached for a folder on his desk and opened it. He shuffled through a series of papers and, as he did, his right foot pressed down on the panic button next to his desk's inner leg.

"You obviously had some trouble with the job and I regret any inconvenience," Donovan said. *Keep her talking, security is on the way.* "However, our agreement was for the disks to be recovered in a *usable* state. You broke the terms of our agreement and I cannot pay for incomplete work."

Nox smirked and shook her head.

"You hired me to give your robot a test drive, not recover some bullshit blank disks."

Donovan closed the folder.

"That's a vile insinuation. I can have you sued—"

"You're lucky you're still able to talk."

Donovan took a deep breath. *Any second now, security will break through that door and...*

"Don't threaten me. We had an agreement and you broke the terms of that agreement."

A buzzing sound came from Nox's jacket. The Mechanic removed a small cell phone from the jacket's inner pocket and laid it down on the desk.

"Not until after you did," Nox said. "Your guards aren't coming. I reset the panic button. The signal was rerouted."

Donovan laid the folder on the desk and grabbed Nox's cell phone. On its digital display was the originating number. His office.

Nox took the phone from Donovan and pocketed it.

"You know," Nox continued. "For a while there, I actually thought your job was legitimate."

"More insinuations?"

"I'd lay off the act, Mr. Donovan. It's gotten quite old."

Donovan frowned.

"What...what was my mistake?"

"Back at the *Yoshiwara*, when you said you were going to be 'honest' with me. That's usually the very moment a person is about to lie. How many Independents did you send before me?"

Donovan shifted in the chair.

"Come on, *Mister* Donovan. Are we going to settle this situation amicably or do you want this to get messy?"

"Five," Donovan whispered. He wiped sweat from his forehead. It glowed red with rage.

"I was lucky number six."

"Don't be so smug. This company invested millions of credits in the development of that fucking Security Robot Unit. They spent another boatload of cash testing it."

"My heart bleeds for your problems."

"I've busted my ass for thirty years for this company, and all that hard work is on the line because of that piece of shit..."

Donovan let out a breath and relaxed. After a few seconds, he laughed.

"Every year, we conservatively estimate losses of over fifty to one hundred billion credits thanks to people like you, people engaged in all types of industrial espionage. Security is big business, both for us and our competitors. That robot represents a breakthrough in security technology—"

"*If* you got it to work properly. Seems to me it has a problem distinguishing the good guys from the bad."

"It'll work, in time," Donovan insisted. "But we're under a very tight schedule and my rivals at Octi Corp. are circling this office like vultures. It doesn't help that the boys upstairs are also demanding results. So we had to test the prototype any way we could before sanctioning its production. Once in production, we're liable for any malfunctions."

"Like if the machine kills someone?"

"Someone? You mean those security guards? Fuck no. Those clowns are a dime a dozen. No, what worries me is the destruction of company property."

"More importantly, a warehouse full."

"In a real world scenario, a warehouse that size could be filled with up to a billion credits worth of product."

"Now reduced to a billion credits worth of ash."

"If that should happen, and the SR unit was found to be responsible for the destruction, company lawyers would descend on Octi Corp. like flies on shit. And who takes the blame? *Me.* The boss'd throw me to the wolves."

Nox took a step forward. Donovan's hands came up in a protective gesture.

"Don't try anything," he yelled. "Or I'll...or I'll..."

"It's been a long night. Mind if I sit?"

Before Donovan could answer, Nox slid one of the two chairs before the industrialist's desk to her side and sat down. She stared directly at Donovan.

"Now, about the rest of the money you owed me."

Donovan bit his upper lip.

"You failed—"

Nox leaned forward in the chair, revealing a shoulder holster and a large black handgun.

"You still want to play that game, *Mister* Donovan?"

Donovan let out a nervous laugh. *Business 101: Never give anyone the upper hand in a negotiation.*

"I'll get it for you."

Business 102: Live to fight another day.

Donovan reached down and pulled one of the desk drawers open. As he did, he noted the large handgun in Nox's shoulder holster appear like magic in the Mechanic's right hand. It was aimed directly at Donovan's head.

"It's been a long enough night," Nox said. "No tricks."

"No tricks," Donovan repeated.

Very, very slowly the Octi Corp. businessman laid a wad of bills on the desk before Nox.

"It's all there."

Nox put the gun away and grabbed the bills. As before, she took her time counting them. And as she did that, she pressed the heels of her shoes into the carpeted floor. Both heels silently detached. Nox pushed them deeper under Donovan's desk.

"I had you figured all wrong," Donovan said. He voice was high, almost giddy. "When I heard you got out of the warehouse, I thought you might take our...exercise...the wrong way. I assure you, Miss Nox, it was nothing personal."

"It never is."

"Anyway, I'm glad you could see beyond any pettiness. You're a good businessman...uh... business*woman*."

Nox folded the bills and stuffed them into a pouch. She gave Donovan one more contemptuous look before exiting the office.

When she was gone, Donovan sighed in relief. He reached for the phone and dialed "0"

"Security," he said. "Quickly."

Nox stepped into the hallway outside Donovan's office and moved toward the elevator at the corridor's end. Before reaching it, she felt a buzz in her jacket pocket. It was her cell phone.

Nox took the cell phone out of her pocket and stared at the digital display.

"Donovan," Nox muttered. The Octi Corp. businessman was making a call and, as with the panic button, its signal was forwarded directly to Nox's cell phone.

You couldn't leave well enough alone, could you?

The Mechanic pressed a button and the digital display on the cell phone read "Camouflage voice." She pressed another button and answered the call.

"Front desk," Nox said.

In his office, Donovan perked up.

"This is Donovan, office 4021. There's an intruder on the fortieth floor. Female, approximately six foot tall, black hair, black clothing, dark sunglasses. She's armed and very dangerous. She's headed for the lobby at this very moment."

"Forget all that... is she good looking?" replied a gruff male voice.

Donovan's eyes practically popped out of his head.

"What the fuck?" Donovan yelled over the phone. "Who cares what she looks like? She's a fucking Independent and dangerous as shit. Dispose of her. Use maximum force."

"Yes sir," Nox said. "I recommend you lock your door and remain in your office until the intruder is dealt with."

"If I wanted your advice, I would have fucking asked for it, you asshole," Donovan shouted and hung up.

"No need to get testy," Nox muttered. She clicked the cell phone off and put it away.

Nox calmly finished her walk to the end of the corridor. The elevator was open and waiting for her. A cylindrical ash can was propped against the door. Nox set the can aside and, once inside the elevator, pressed the "L" button. She then turned and stared out the rear glass paneling. It exposed the side of Octi Plaza and the lights of the city.

The elevator doors closed. Nox looked up at the camera and spotted the small box she had affixed to its side a little earlier. Security below would see an empty elevator on their monitors. Nox's only concern would be keeping her face away from the cameras in the lobby.

The Mechanic reached for her belt. She pulled a strip of leather off its side, revealing a compartment housing a small digital recorder. Nox pressed one of the buttons on the recorder, then another. Donovan's voice came over the recorder's tiny speaker.

"...You're a good businessman," Donovan said.

Nox turned the recorder off and replaced the leather strip. She then reached into another pocket and pulled out an equally small box. Unlike the digital recorder, it contained only a single dull red button.

"At least I don't take things personally," Nox muttered.

Do unto others before they do unto you. Business 103.

Nox pressed the button.

Within Donovan's office, Nox's discarded heels came alive with flashing green lights.

Within the elevator, Nox watched Donovan's office, now several floors above her, erupt in flames. Glass and heavy debris rained down the side of Octi Plaza and rushed past the elevator.

Though she couldn't be entirely sure, Nox thought one of those bits of debris looked an awful lot like a human hand.

The security guards in the lobby were in a panic. Fire alarms blared and several guards rushed past Nox, completely ignoring her when she exited the elevator. Nox returned the favor and made sure not to get in anyone's way. She walked past the lobby and out the building. Her chopper was waiting in the parking lot.

When she mounted the bike, she took one last look at Octi Plaza. Smoke billowed from the hole in the office of the fortieth floor. In the distance a series of sirens blared.

"Twice in one night," Nox muttered. She felt bad for burdening the city's firefighters. "Sorry to screw up your sleep."

Nox didn't need to see any more. After a couple of false starts, her chopper's engine roared to life. She shifted her into gear and drove off into the city.

6

In a dark and silent room, a phone rang.

It rang again and again, as phones tend to do when ignored.

Between the fourth and fifth ring came the sound of bed springs tensing. Something stirred in the darkness, very human and very irritated. A night light came on, revealing a large and luxurious bedroom. The man who turned on the light rubbed his eyes. Like Donovan, he was in his late sixties. Unlike Donovan, he was lean and, despite just wakening, projected an air of total control. His hair was silver; his eyes were alive with annoyance.

The young blonde sharing his bed groaned. Crystal clear blue eyes cracked open and focused on the elderly man beside her. If it wasn't for the fact that they shared a bed and were both naked, one might be forgiven for thinking she was his daughter. Or granddaughter.

"Who is it?" the pretty woman asked.

The elderly man rubbed his eyes and stared at the caller ID information displayed on the phone's cradle.

"Octi Plaza," the elderly man said. "Business. Go back to sleep, Julie."

The blonde shrugged and turned away. She appeared to drift back to sleep but, unseen by the elderly man, her eyes remained half-open.

The elderly man grabbed the phone.

"Hello?"

"Dad, it's me."

"This better be good, Robert."

"We've got some problems."

"The Desertlands Project?"

There was a pause.

"Not this time, Dad," Robert said. "Our immediate problem is Donovan."

Robert Octi Sr. sighed. He rose from the bed and stared at Julie's naked backside.

"I'm on my way," he said.

Octi hung the phone and leaned down to kiss Julie on the cheek. By this time, her eyes were shut tight.

"I have to go," he said.

Julie mumbled something unintelligible and drew the bed sheets closer to her neck. Octi smiled. He walked to the bathroom.

As soon as the door closed, Julie was up. She reached for the black purse beside her night stand, opened it, and pulled out a freshly packed memory disk. She removed the plastic wrapping from its case, removed the disk, and reached for the phone Robert Octi Sr. had just used. She unscrewed a metal plate from the phone's base, revealing a slim recorder. With quick, well-rehearsed movements, she removed the disk currently in the recorder and replaced it with the new one. Afterwards, she screwed the metal plate back and put the phone in its place.

She dropped the freshly recorded disk into her purse and lay back down just as Octi stepped out of the bathroom. Her face away from him, she smiled. By now she knew his routine very well.

As she expected, the elderly man walked to his closet and grabbed a dark suit. His face was neutral. He was neither annoyed nor surprised to be called out of bed at such an early hour. It was part and parcel of running a multi-billion dollar business. Octi hurriedly dressed and, when done, walked to the door leading out of the bedroom.

"I'll be back later, honey," he said.

Julie turned around. Her blue eyes burned with an icy heat.

"Take your time, sweetie," Julie muttered. "I'll be waiting."

Exactly forty five minutes later, Robert Octi Sr.'s limousine arrived at the Octi Plaza parking lot. At this very early morning hour, the lot was usually empty. Now, however, it was filled with private fire trucks and ambulances.

Octi eyed the spectacle with great distaste. He looked up, at the face of his building, and spotted smoke coming from a window near the top floor.

"What the hell?" Octi muttered.

Whatever happened up there, it would take a good deal of money to keep the story off the media radar. With the exception of Octi Corp., the stock market was tanking and investors were very skittish. The last thing they needed was an excuse to also sell off Octi's stock.

The rescue personnel made ample room for Octi's vehicle.

"Would you like to go to the private garage?" Octi's driver inquired.

"Fuck no," Octi said. "In trying times, it's good for company morale to see the boss take a first-hand interest in whatever disaster the company's gotten into."

"If you say so, sir."

Octi leaned forward.

"Companies pay me hundreds of thousands of credits for *any* advice I give them. I've just given you some for free, and you could give a shit. That's why I'm the boss and you're a minimum wage driver."

"Yes sir," the man replied. His face turned a deep red.

"Leave me by the lobby door."

The driver did as told. Octi exited the limousine and, as he walked toward the entry door, maintained a serious, commanding look. Reporters yelled questions from afar, but he simply shook his head.

When he reached the lobby door and his back was to the reporters, his expression changed. He gritted his teeth and tried to control his fury as he entered the building's lobby. Various technicians and fire fighters hung around the area. Based on their casual manner, it was clear whatever happened upstairs was contained. It was at least one bit of potentially good news.

Octi walked to the elevator. One of his security staff stood beside it, cradling a cup of coffee.

"Is it safe to use?" Octi asked the man.

"Yes sir," the man replied. His voice was overly chipper, another brown-noser in a company too damn full of them.

"I assume we had a fire?"

The security guard nodded.

"Yes sir. I could give you more details, but your son—"

"What was the extent of the damage?"

"A single office was incinerated. The fire was minimal and didn't spread beyond the explosion."

"*Explosion?*"

"Yes sir," the security guard said. He leaned in close and whispered: "We suspect foul play."

Octi's face turned to stone.

"Let me get this straight: There was an explosion in my building and you merely *suspect* foul play?"

The security guard swallowed.

"That's a fucking brilliant deduction, son," Octi continued. "I'm so damn glad I'm surrounded by such perceptive minds. Keep up the good work. At this rate you'll make mail room aid in no time at all."

Like his driver, the security guard's face turned bright red. Octi offered the man a cold smile.

"Anything else?"

"Your son called in structural engineers to assess any damage to the support columns. The city's code inspectors are on their way."

"Just what I need, more bureaucrats," Octi muttered.

Without saying another word, he stepped into the elevator.

The faint rays of the early morning sun penetrated the enormous windows surrounding the penthouse office. They fell upon a collection of precious rocks sealed in a heavy acrylic case. As the morning light drifted up, it revealed a collection of equally precious paintings hanging on the office wall opposite the window.

Otherwise, the room was sparsely furnished. The floor was covered in a dull gray carpet and, sitting before the windows, was a wide but functional desk. Before the desk stood Robert Octi Jr. He carried a small black laptop computer. Standing just behind him was Nagel.

Beside the doors leading to the private elevator were two bulky men in suits. They straightened up when the elevator doors opened and snapped to attention when Robert Octi Sr. stepped in. The elderly man wasted little time getting down to business.

"What the hell's going on here?"

"You better take a seat," his son replied.

Octi stepped around his desk and sat down. He closed his eyes.

"How bad is the damage?"

"Here?"

Octi's eyebrows rose.

"You mean there's *other* damage elsewhere?"

"I...I thought someone told you by now."

"They told me *you* wanted to brief me personally. What say we finally get on with it?"

"Yes sir," Robert said. "West Warehouse 74 is on fire."

Octi leaned back in his chair and sighed.

"I'm assuming the swath of destruction between here and there is somehow related," he said. "Tell me everything. From the start."

"Donovan's Security Robot went berserk," Robert said. "Five of our guards were killed before that thing finally ran out of ammunition."

"God damn him!" Octi yelled. "Was he testing that fucking robot *again?*"

"Yes," Robert said. "Worse, we found out he was once again using live subjects without getting the proper consent forms filled out."

"That does it! He's fired. Get him on the—"

"He's dead."

"Damn right he is," Octi hissed. He reached for the phone and dialed a three digit number. "Dammit, why isn't he answering?"

"Dad, his office was the one that got torched. With him in it. We think the last Independent Donovan hired survived his robot and got to him."

Octi replaced the phone and straightened his tie.

"Makes sense," he said. "Any employee that doesn't answer *my* call within a ring had better have a damn good reason. The police?"

"They came around and checked his office. I had a few of our people inform them Mr. Donovan and his wife weren't getting along. We told them they had threatened each other several times over the past couple of months and suspected their animosity grew to the point of physical contact. Wouldn't you know it, the police marched right over to the Donovan home and took his old lady out in handcuffs. She's their prime suspect in his murder."

"Thank the gods!" Octi said with a loud sigh. "As long as they don't connect this to his work, we won't have to explain anything to the stockholders. What about the warehouse?"

"I've already notified the insurance company. I don't see any problem with them covering our losses. Our only concern is the deductible, but I think we can get that reimbursed as well. We bought the property using the company's credit card, and they cover deductibles."

"Excellent."

Robert pulled a piece of paper from within his suit.

"As for any PR issues, we've released the following statement: From Octi Corp. ...etcetera... We are the victims of a break-in. The intruders gained control of an experimental Security Robot which, in turn, caused the deaths of five of our security staff. Octi Corp. prides itself in working with the Police, and will help in any way possible... etcetera..."

"And the security guards' families?"

"I calculate payment of no more than a million at a maximum for their grief, also covered by insurance."

"Good," Octi said. "But don't let the insurance company be so damn generous. They'll use any excuse to raise our premiums. See if they can knock that figure down a couple of thousand."

"Yes sir."

"So everything's taken care of but the Independent Donovan hired. Have you figured out his identity?"

"*Her* identity," Robert correct. "And, no. The bastard was real slick. She cracked Donovan's computer and wiped out all his private records. We'd be completely in the dark about this Independent, but we got real lucky. Donovan kept a log of his personal internet activity on a separate cloud drive. Either our Independent didn't know that, or she didn't have the time to crack it."

"What did Donovan do on the net?"

"He visited plenty of porn sites."

"On our time?" Octi said.

"Yes sir."

"God dammit," Octi spat. "Institute a check on all web based searches and clamp down on that tomfoolery. I'll not lose a second of productivity to any of these fucking sex addicts. *My* only mistresses are portfolios and oil."

Robert and Nagel stared at each other. *So much for free time fun.* Robert then looked away and cleared his throat.

"Anyway, Donovan contacted this Independent through the net."

Robert opened his laptop computer and placed it before his father. He pressed a few keys. "Take a look."

The laptop's screen went black. After a few seconds a dark, partially obscured figure appeared on it.

"What is this?" Octi asked.

"Web chat. We're seeing what Donovan saw when he contacted this Independent. For all we know, it might well be their first meeting. The Independent was smart enough to stay in the shadows, so there wasn't any way to positively identify her. Listen."

Robert pressed a button and the frozen figure came to life.

"Let's get on with this," Donovan said through the computer's speaker.

The obscured figure did not reply.

"Ok," Donovan continued. "I have need of your services. But I want to be sure of your credentials."

"You want a resume?" the figure said.

"That would be helpful."

"How about references? Would that help too?"

"Sure."

"All right, give me a couple of minutes to get it together. I'll send it by courier pigeon."

Donovan let out a sigh.

"Will you at least answer some questions?"

"Ask and we'll see."

"How many years of experience in this...uh... field do you have?"

"Enough."

"How illuminating. Can you be discrete?"

"Depends on the job. If you want me to entertain kids at a party..."

"Height?"

"Come on."

"Weight?"

"Goodbye."

"Hold on," Donovan said. "This is important. The job may require stealth and physical effort. You may be forced to enter tight spots, quite literally."

The dark figure leaned back in her chair.

"So, silly as these questions sound, they are important," Donovan continued. "Now, are there any issues I should know about? Color blindness? Phobias? Any problems with the authorities?"

"The authorities absolutely *love* people like me."

"What about liquor? Do you use it, or any drugs?"

"Seriously?"

"I must make sure—"

"My favorite movie is Mary Fucking Poppins."

"The Disney Corp. movie?"

"No, Mary *Fucking* Poppins, the porno. Stars Dick Van—"

"Very funny," Donovan said. He let out a far more melodramatic sigh. "I suppose these questions are borderline ridiculous. That's what you get for following standard business guidelines. Where can we meet?"

"I'll get in touch."

The image on the laptop went blank. Robert Octi Sr. faced his son.

"That's it?"

"Yeah. Nothing incriminating, and nothing at all that could identify."

"Not much at all, in fact," Octi said.

"Agreed." Robert again reached into his suit pocket and retrieved another piece of paper. "It took some effort, but we discovered the woman in the shadows sent Donovan an e-mail. Like that interview, there wasn't much on it, just a meeting time and place. But we were able to trace a name."

"What?"

"Nox."

"Nox? Is that a first or last name?"

"We don't know and it's all we've got. Anyway, she told Donovan to meet her at the *Yoshiwara* bar. This was not much more than nine hours ago."

Octi smiled.

"Now we're talking," he said. He read the time on his wristwatch. It was a little past seven in the morning.

Octi turned his attention to the two bulky men by the elevator.

"If this *Yoshiwara* is like the other bars in the city, it'll be closed by now," the elderly man said. "Regardless, I want you two to head over there. On the off chance the place is still open, ask around and see if you can locate this Independent. If the place is closed, initiate a surveillance routine. Maybe our Independent is a regular, so see who shows up when the place opens later tonight. If we're really lucky, and you get her, I want her brought here."

"Yes sir," the two bulky men said.

"Oh, and boys, you don't have to be polite. Understood?"

The two bulky men nodded and exited the office. When the doors closed behind them, Octi again focused on his son.

"That wasn't so bad," he said. "Now, tell me about the Desertlands Project."

Robert shifted in the seat. He scratched his neck and cleared his throat.

"We still haven't found anything."

"Nothing at all? How much are we in the red?"

"We... We're projecting a cost overrun of fifteen percent."

Octi's face turned red.

"Fifteen percent?!? By Jesu! Who else knows?"

"I'm keeping it off the books," Robert replied. "*No* one else knows."

"Make damn sure that's the case," Octi hissed. "If any of the stockholders get wind of that kind of overrun, we're fucked. How much more time do you need?"

"I can't say. But finding the Demon's base is important enough—"

"No, it's not. Both time and money are running out, son. You find something soon or we'll shut this operation down. Do you understand?"

Robert nodded.

"Yes sir," he said.

7

As Catherine promised the night before, the new day meant a new *Yoshiwara*. The change in format and the live band drew a big and very noisy crowd.

The sad lot of old regulars was nowhere to be seen. The fact that the group was no longer around proved bittersweet to the bar's proprietor. They didn't have to go, nonetheless they did. As expected.

"Out with the old, in with the new," Catherine muttered. She had earplugs ready and slid them in just as the band started up at a little past nine that evening.

"Hello night crawlers, we're *Virgin Slayer*," the lead singer yelled into his mike. His body was way too skinny and carried a head that was way too big. He shot the crowd a crazy grin. "Hide the children!"

With that, the band leapt into action. A wall of sound pressed hard against Catherine's chest as the singer wailed.

We moan into the mike...
We give you such a fright...
We'll be at your home all night.

Catherine shook her head.

Was our music that shitty to adults back then, too? She thought. But as the band's set progressed, she realized that, while the music sounded like it came from a hostile galaxy far, far away, the music's themes weren't all that different from what she heard while growing up.

Back in the Stone Age, she thought and smiled.

Rebellion, anger, love, frustration, and sex. Lots and *lots* of talk about sex. Every generation, she realized, worked through similar feelings but expressed themselves in their own way. The mix of hormones and the need to distinguish themselves, either by producing original works or putting down the older generation, fueled their lifestyle. The irony was that in a few years, when the next generation of kids asserted themselves, this group would likely say the same thing Catherine was thinking:

They don't make music like they used to.

Catherine couldn't help but giggle. *You're getting old.*

The door to the bar opened and the tall, muscular stranger with the vertical blue tattoos on her forehead entered. She moved between and through the young crowd, eventually finding a table for herself in the rear corner. Catherine walked to her side.

"My favorite new client," she yelled over the music. "Another *Prestigio*?"

"Make it two," Nox replied.

"Good times?"

"The best."

Catherine returned shortly with the drinks.

"What do you think of the band?" she asked.

Nox shrugged.

"Loud, quiet, it's all the same to me."

"For me, it'll take some getting used to," Catherine admitted. "But I need the traffic to pay the bills."

"Money isn't everything."

"Who you trying to kid?" Catherine said and winked. "Holler –holler *real* loud– if you need anything else."

Nox took down the first bottle quickly. She lingered on the second.

Virgin Slayer played for one hour straight before their first break. By that time the bar was uncomfortably full of young people. Catherine worked hard filling their orders and only looked Nox's way once or twice, which was fine by her.

For Nox's attention was on the door leading into the bar.

Two bulky, well-dressed men entered the *Yoshiwara*. They separated and filtered the floor, looking carefully at each person they encountered. One of them stopped Catherine as she was in the process of serving drinks. They asked her several questions. She shook her head and blew the man off.

"Good girl," Nox said.

She finished her second beer.

An hour and a half later *Virgin Slayer* was well into the second song of their second set. The noise proved too much for the two well-dressed men. After questioning most of the people within the bar and finding little information of any worth, they exited the place and were visibly relieved to hear the considerably lower level blares of heavy traffic. Compared to *Virgin Slayer*, the sounds of the Big City's congestion were like something one heard in a deserted monastery.

"Can you believe anyone would listen to that shit?" one of the men said.

"As if we needed any more proof the world's going to hell," the other replied.

They walked to their car, got in, and drove off. They didn't notice the beat up motorcycle following them from a discrete distance.

Larry, one of the two well-dressed men, lit a cigarette and leaned back in the passenger chair. Monty, his partner, rubbed his eyes and let out a yawn. After a few blocks of travel, their car stopped before a red light.

"Octi expects us to find a goddamned ghost," Larry said between puffs of smoke. "He gives us no full name, no family, no friends. Just that this Independent met Donovan at the *Yoshiwara*. Yesterday. Big fucking help."

"It's weak man," his partner agreed.

"We spend the whole fucking day watching this place and when they finally opened up, no one inside knows this lady from Adam."

"How the hell do you think Donovan first got a hold of her? You know, before that online chat?"

"Someone might have recommended her."

"If it was an Octi Corp. employee, we'd have heard about that."

"Then he got the information from the outside. Maybe from some other crappy bar."

"*That's* why we need to broaden our search," Larry said. "Start hitting *all* the bars on this end of town."

Monty shivered.

"We'll be deaf before the night is through."

"What other choice we got?"

"We can blow it off. *Say* we hit all the bars and take it easy."

"You're forgetting the trackers in the car. Old man Octi will check on our movements for sure."

Monty swore. All Octi Corp. company cars within the Big City were equipped with trackers. It was the only way to ensure the employees were using them for company, and not personal, business.

"I'll bet this Nox is hiding out. Yeah, she's probably scared shitless that the police or one of us will find her."

"What, you think we'll never see or hear from her again?"

"Exactly."

"But still, we've got to look around."

"Ok, we look around. Only, we pick and choose which bars we visit from here on out. Come tomorrow, we tell the old man we couldn't find her and that's that."

"Sounds like a plan," Larry said and chuckled. "Then, if he still wants to, the old bastard can find Nox himself."

"Excellent," Monty said. "Now, which bar you want to hit next?"

"Any of them," Larry said and winked. "So long as they've got lap dancers."

The first rays of the sun filtered through a haze of smog that enveloped the city. The two well-dressed men's car turned into the Octi Plaza parking lot. It came to a stop before one of the many empty parking spaces. The occupants of the vehicle, fresh from a very full night's worth of hard liquor and flashy dancers, staggered out of their car and stumbled toward the building's entrance. The fire trucks and ambulances were long gone, and the Plaza once again had the look of a deserted fortress.

Nox's chopper stopped across the street from the Plaza. She dismounted the bike and watched her pursuers enter the building. Though Nox prided herself on an awareness of her surroundings, she was so intent on the well-dressed men's movements that she didn't notice another car parked on the street a couple of blocks away.

The two occupants of that car silently watched Nox cross the street and head to the Plaza building.

Nox produced a shiny thin card from her weathered wallet. She inserted it into a slot beside the Plaza's entry doors and heard a faint buzz indicating the locks were disabled. She pushed the glass door open. The two well-dressed men that searched for her through the night waited in the lobby by the elevator doors.

Nox surveyed the rest of the area. She was in luck. The security guard's station in the middle of the lobby floor was currently empty. The guard was probably making his rounds.

Nox quietly walked up behind the two well-dressed men.

The elevator door opened and the two men stumbled inside. They entered a code into the elevator's control panel and pressed the penthouse key button. When they turned around, they were surprised to see Nox standing before them.

Elevator etiquette normally called for occupants to turn and face the door instead of each other. Nox didn't turn. The doors closed behind her and she continued facing the two well-dressed men. After a while, they found her sunglass-covered stare more than a little uncomfortable.

"Do we know you?" Monty asked.

Nox smiled.

"Candy gram."

The penthouse hallway was lined with plush carpeting and priceless original paintings. The elevator door opened and Nox entered this hallway. She looked as out of place here as Donovan did in the *Yoshiwara*. Appearances, however, were of little concern to the Mechanic.

As she moved forward, the unconscious bodies of the two well-dressed men spilled out of the elevator and onto the hallway floor.

Within his office, Robert Octi Sr. and Jr. sat on opposite sides of the room, lost in thought. The long, tense day gave way to a long, equally tense night and each of the Industrialists was eager for any early morning updates. Octi rubbed his eyes and stared out the window at the rising sun. Robert Jr. absently leafed through a magazine, his eyes focused on a point just before the magazine's surface.

All was quiet. All was calm.

Until a loud crash shattered it all. The door leading into Octi's office burst open. Nox walked into the room. In her hand was a large caliber gun. She aimed it at the elderly Octi and adjusted her dark sunglasses with her free hand. Robert reached for the gun in his vest.

"Wait," Octi yelled. He rose to his feet and approached his son, laying his right hand on the junior executive's shoulder before addressing Nox. "You were very busy last night. We all were. Perhaps we could relax and talk a little?"

Nox's face betrayed no emotions. After several tense seconds, the burly Mechanic took a seat near the door. She laid the gun on her lap.

"Let's talk," she said.

The tension within the room eased just a little. Octi straightened out his tie while his son's hands fell limp to his side.

"I know what you did to Donovan," Octi said. "And I know it was you who broke into our warehouse the night before last. I could have the police—"

Mr. Octi did not finish his statement. He was silenced by Nox, who pulled a diskette from her jacket pocket and flung it on the table before him.

"In case you're interested, that's a recording of all my conversations with Donovan," Nox said. "If something happens to me, these conversations will be released to the net. If I go down, so will your organization. From where I sit, you've got much more to lose than I do."

Mr. Octi eyed the disk, then Nox. A crooked smile crossed his face.

"That's it?" he said. The smile broadened. "That's all you've got? I thought you were smarter than that, *Miss* Nox. My PR boys'll tear the veracity of this so-called recording to shreds. And even if we were unable to prove it illegitimate, we live in a culture of apathy. What makes you think anyone, anyone at all, would give a shit about a conversation between you and Donovan?"

Robert looked up at his father. He had the same smile on his face. Nox shrugged.

"I've done a little investigating, *Mister* Octi, and it appears your grip on Octi Corp. is slipping," Nox said. "Up until last year, the board approved every one of your proposals and business schemes by unanimous consent. In this past year, things haven't gone quite so smoothly. You've had a string of six to five votes in your favor and –surprise surprise- some of your proposals were even shot down. If the five naysayers on your board should get a consistent sixth vote in *their* favor, you're effectively out as head of your own company."

The smile on Octi and Robert's faces faded. It was Nox's turn to grin.

"I'll admit, this recording may not be much," Nox continued. "Then again, it might be just enough incentive for one of those boardroom boys to permanently switch sides."

Octi again adjusted his tie. There was a scowl on his face.

"Anyway, that's your call," Nox concluded. "As I said before, let's talk. It's better than sitting around making mean faces."

Mr. Octi released his tie. His hand trembled slightly as he tried to hold down the fury building within. He made it this far in the business world through stealth and guile. He also made it a habit to stay several steps ahead of his competition. The humiliation of a lowly Independent getting the upper hand on him did not still well. Not well at all.

"OK, Nox," Octi said. "Let's cut all the bullshit and get down to business. What do you want for these recordings?"

"Nothing," Nox replied. "They're not for sale."

"They're not..." Octi began. He shook his head. "Then what *do* you want?"

"A trade. I won't release these disks to this apathetic world, and your big bad company won't bother me anymore."

"How do I know you won't change your mind? What guarantee do I have that you don't come back at a later date and we do this dance all over again?"

"I won't. My business with you is finished, Octopus."

"Octi."

Robert shifted in the chair.

"Why should we trust you?" he said.

"It's a standoff," Nox replied. "Because I sure as hell don't trust the two of you."

A deep silence settled in the room. After a while, Octi nodded.

"OK," he said. "It's a deal."

He walked to Nox's side as the Mechanic rose to her feet. Octi extended his hand to her, but Nox ignored it.

"It's a deal," Nox agreed. "Until you fuck up."

8

Nox strolled through the lobby of the Octi Plaza with her hands pressed deep in her jacket pockets. The hands gripped separate guns. Her muscles were knotted like steel; her senses were tense with anticipation.

The guards in the lobby stared hard at her but allowed Nox to pass. Nox counted six of them. She was sure another dozen were hidden in strategic places, waiting for the order to attack. Though she couldn't anticipate Octi's next move, she didn't think the corporate industrialist would try anything.

At least not here.

Given the events of the past days, the last thing Octi needed was more bad publicity at their headquarters. If Octi decided to act, it would be later, when there were no witnesses or obvious links to his company.

The visible guards watched each and every step Nox made as she walked past them and to the exit.

Once outside, Nox relaxed. Though her muscles still remained coiled, facing Octi personally worked and she was still very much alive. Nox walked to her chopper and turned on its ignition. She stomped on the kick-starter and the engine turned over but didn't fire up.

Nox swore.

She tried the procedure again, with the same results. She looked over the parking lot and at the entry to the Octi Plaza. Several of the security guards stood by the door, watching her.

"Any of you care to give a lady a boost?" Nox yelled.

One of the guards gave her the finger, the rest stared in silence.

Nox shook her head and tried again. This time the chopper roared to life. Nox smiled. As she drove off, she returned the guard's gesture.

It took Nox only a few seconds to notice the tail. Two women, muscular and dark, riding in an equally dark and very beat up vehicle mirrored her moves.

At first Nox thought it was Octi personnel, but that thought died quickly. Her pursuers drove such an old, loud, and noticeably shitty car that it was unlikely *any* Octi professionals would be caught dead in such a crate. No, this was the type of car kids on the east side of town could afford. Kids or low rent Independents. Given Nox's shadows were grown women, she guessed they were members of the Amazon clique. Tough gals, one and all, and low rent Independents to boot.

Nox sped up and slowed down. She took right turns and left turns and tempted very ripe yellow lights. And still the women behind her followed. After a while, they weren't even trying to hide their actions.

"Amateurs," Nox said with a sigh.

The neon lights over the *Yoshiwara* bar reflected in Nox's sunglasses.

She drove into the bar's parking lot and pretended not to see the black car as it came to a stop across the street. Though it was very early in the morning, Nox was surprised to hear the sounds of *Virgin Slayer* coming from within the bar.

They may not know how to play worth a shit, Nox thought. *But they sure are dedicated to their craft.*

She stepped into the bar and felt the wave of noise slam her body. Catherine spotted her and waved with her free hand while wiping the bar's counter with her other.

"Welcome back," Catherine said before turning her full attention to her chores.

Nox waved back. Business was excellent this first night of the new *Yoshiwara*. Several partiers remained on the bar's floor. They continued to dance, though with far less energy than a few hours before. Things were winding down, as they always did.

Nox made her way to an empty table in the middle of the crush. Almost immediately a handsome young red headed man spotted her and approached. He was a college boy, young and earnest and so very sweet.

He couldn't have looked hornier had he worn a bright neon sign around his neck proclaiming that fact.

"Weren't you here a couple of hours ago?" he yelled above the roar of music. He didn't wait for Nox to answer and took the seat beside her. "Care for some company, gorgeous?"

"Already got some," Nox replied.

"Who's the lucky guy?"

Nox pointed to the door. The two Amazon women from the black car entered the bar. The boy beside Nox let out a whistle.

"Please, *please* let me tag along,"

"You wouldn't like us."

"The hell I wouldn't."

"Sorry kid, our kind plays rough."

"Kid?" the college boy repeated. There was a look of disappointment on his face. Nevertheless, he was mature enough to accept the fact that he had no chance with Nox. The boy stood up and added: "Gotta give me credit for trying."

"If you want it."

The boy eyed the Amazons and frowned. "Hell, they're not even all that cute. You could do better."

"Probably," Nox replied.

The college boy disappeared back into the throng.

Nox slid out of her chair. She circled the bar's floor, hiding behind the dancers and the stoners and the crew-cut mob. She passed directly in front of Catherine, who noted her actions. Her face, weary from an already too-long night, grew wearier still. She too spotted the women in black that Nox was moving toward.

"No trouble," she said when Nox passed in front of her.

"None at all," Nox replied and moved on.

It didn't take long for her to make her way behind the two muscular Amazons. They looked around the floor, blissfully ignorant that their prey stood directly behind them. Nox removed her gun from her jacket pocket and stuck it into one of the women's back.

"Looking for me?" she yelled.

The women froze in place.

"I promised the owner of this place there wouldn't be any trouble," Nox said. "Don't make a liar out of me."

Nox nudged them forward. The trio worked their way to the dark back corner of the bar and sat behind a table. Catherine made her way to them.

"Would you like something to drink?" she asked.

"My friends are inviting," Nox said. "*Prestigio* for us all."

Catherine headed back to the counter.

"Wait," Nox yelled. Catherine returned to the table. Nox motioned to the Amazons, then to Catherine. "In this place, we pay in advance."

The women reached into their pockets.   They gave Catherine a couple of bills.

"Don't forget to tip," Nox said.

They again reached into their pockets and handed Catherine another couple of bills.

"Keep the change," one of the Amazons growled.

Catherine winked at Nox and disappeared into the crowd.

"For a while there I thought Octi sent you," Nox said.

The Amazons were surprised by the Mechanic's statement.

"Don't you work for them?"

"Once upon a time," Nox said. "Not anymore."

"Then why were you at their building just now?"

"I was negotiating a severance package," Nox said. "You know, it's been a long night, so let's get down to business. You were following me. Why?"

"We can't say," the second goon replied.

As the words left her mouth, Catherine reappeared with three bottles of *Prestigio* beer. She placed them in the center of the table. Nox reached for the one closest to her and, in a lightning fast move, smashed it against one of the Amazon's jaws. The woman was knocked out cold and fell heavily to the ground. Before the other Amazon could react, she found Nox's gun pressed hard under her chin.

Around them, the entire bar went silent. Everyone froze in place.

"You *can* tell me," Nox said, her voice cold and dead serious. She rose to her feet and motioned the woman before her to do the same. "And you will."

The Amazon leaned down and lifted her partner off the ground. The two, with Nox standing very close behind them, walked through the parting crowd and to the bar's exit.

"This your idea of no trouble?" Catherine asked.

"I'll try harder next time," Nox said.

The two Amazons and Nox made it past most of the crowd. Close to the bar's exit, Nox spotted the college boy who tried to pick her up. He looked like he was trying hard not to throw up.

"Still want to tag along?" she asked him.

The college boy shook his head.

"Maybe next time," Nox said.

The Mechanic led the Amazons to the bar's exit and quietly left the place.

Catherine managed a tiny grin. She eyed the lead singer of *Virgin Slayer*. Like all the other people in the bar, the man's face looked unnaturally pale.

Kids today, Catherine thought. The grin turned into a barely suppressed smile. *Their music is loud as shit but as weak as the fans.*

Catherine noted the broken glass and blood on the floor.

"Back in my day, that's how our evenings *began*," she said. She eyed *Virgin Slayer*. "Well? How about one last encore?"

"Right fucking on," the lead singer said and laughed.

He snapped his fingers and the drummer and guitarist laid into their instruments. Catherine grabbed a mop from behind the counter.

All things considering, not a bad first night.

9

The Salvation Brokers *Congregation* was one of countless religious organizations that, over the past two decades, sprung up in the inner city. In these tough times, religions flourished. Those who were inclined to wonder about these things theorized that the greater the economic despair, the greater the need for spiritual guidance.

The more cynical felt the already desperate crowds were much easier targets to those in the business of selling salvation. At least two dozen sects, the cream of the spiritual crop, grew to be big businesses. They gobbled up, Darwinian-style, those smaller sects unfortunate enough to pitch a tent anywhere near them.

Over time, these bigger organizations moved from the inner city to the business district and closer to their wealthier clients. Meanwhile, the smaller sects fought for whatever donation scraps they could find.

They were a bunch of small fish in a small pond.

The Salvation Brokers was a newcomer to the area, another small fish which served this part of the inner city and its poor. Their donations were anemic compared to the big boys and this was obvious to anyone standing before the single story shack that housed them.

Nox pushed the two Amazons forward and through the congregation's front door.

"Not that you're worth all that much, but where did a piece of shit place like this dig up the money to pay for you two?" Nox asked.

"Maybe we're doing this for a greater cause," one of the women replied.

Nox examined her two captives closely.

"Come to think of it, you two look exactly like the type of Independents a place like this *can* afford."

"Fuck you," the second woman spat.

The inside of the building was as weathered as it was on the outside, with one obvious exception: A gaudy neon altar. Nox eyed the altar wearily. If there was one thing you could count on in just about any house of worship was a fancy altar.

Facing it was a scrawny, forty-some year old man. He was dressed in a white robe and bent down in prayer.

"Thomas Rose?" Nox called out.

The man in the robe turned. His face was sharply angular and his expression way too sober, like he was in desperate need of a drink.

"What can I do for you?"

Nox waved her gun at her captives.

"Get out of here," she said.

The two Amazons hesitated. They eyed Thomas Rose and waited for his instruction.

"You may leave," Rose said.

The women reluctantly exited the chapel while Thomas Rose approached Nox.

"I am unarmed and far from dangerous," Rose said.

"Funny, that's what most religious folk say, just before they stick their claws in your back," Nox replied. Nevertheless, she put the gun away.

"That's a most cynical thought."

"It's a most cynical world."

"You have me at a great disadvantage, Ms...?"

"Nox."

"You work for Octi?" Rose asked.

"No, but your women followed me from Octi Plaza. They thought I worked for him. At first I thought *they* did."

"At first?"

"They're too low rent for a high roller like Octi. I was curious to see who they were working for."

"And now?"

"Now I know. Goodnight."

Nox turned to leave.

"You talk of Octi as if they're your enemy," Rose said.

"Have a good day, Father," Nox said and kept walking.

"Aren't you curious as to why a man of the cloth would hire Independents?" Rose called out.

Nox stopped for a moment and shrugged.

"Not really."

Thomas Rose ran after her.

"Please, Miss Nox," he said. "Stay for a few minutes. I have need of someone like you."

"What you need are wealthier patrons and a good contractor. Not necessarily in that order."

"I have money," Rose insisted. "I can pay your rates."

"You don't know my rates."

"This job will hurt Octi," Thomas Rose said. "*Bad.*"

Nox thought about that. She returned to Rose's side.

"Start talking."

Thomas Rose led Nox behind the Altar and into his private chambers. The room was decorated with the bare minimum: A twin bed, a table, a pair of chairs, a nightstand, and a heater. In the corner of the room was a small, rusted refrigerator and beside it was a door leading to a cramped bathroom.

Nox examined the chair's strength before sitting down. Thomas Rose sat in the remaining seat opposite Nox. He produced a small framed photograph and slid it on the table and to Nox. On it was a smiling young lady with dark hair.

"My sister," Rose said. "She was part of an Octi survey team. She worked in the Desertlands, searching for Uranium and the remnants of hundreds of small cities eaten up during the global meltdown."

Nox stifled a yawn and slid the framed photograph back to Rose.

"We were very close," Rose continued. He pointed to the weathered box on the center of the table. It was an old style wireless transmitter. "We'd communicate at least once a day without fail. A little over a month ago she stopped calling. Later that same week I received word from Octi Corp. that her party stumbled on the ruins of an old nuclear reactor." Rose paused and took a deep breath. "They said the entire crew was exposed to a massive dose of radiation. They told me they all died. My sister's discovery was sealed, and the survey crew's bodies were taken away in lead lined boxes."

"Tragic. So what?"

"Octi Corp. lied," Rose said. "The day they told me about the team –my sister's– death, I returned here to mourn my loss. Out of habit I turned on the wireless. Its frequency was still set to that of my sister's survey crew. I heard static and, after realizing just what I did, I reached over to turn the radio off. But just as my fingers brushed the knob, I heard it. Scrambled signals. The *same* signals the crew used to transmit their confidential reports to Octi Headquarters!"

A single tear ran down Rose's face.

"Don't you see?" he sobbed. "They were still alive *after* Octi said they were dead. They lied. Octi Corp. *lied.*"

Nox leaned back in her chair.

"Doesn't mean a thing. Maybe their onboard computer equipment sent out an automated update."

"A few hours later, there was another transmission. A *different* transmission. Several hours after that, yet another. All different. All unique. This was no automated call. Up to one full week after they were supposed to be dead, the survey crew, or at least one of them, was very much alive. I wanted to confront Octi Corp. with this information, but I knew they were hiding something big. Something that might prove dangerous to them if exposed. I kept quiet and made preparations to venture out to the Desertlands myself and retrieve my sister. In the end, I was too late. One week and one day after I discovered them, the signals abruptly stopped, never to be repeated again. Octi silenced them. Octi killed them."

"So you hired a couple of Amazon Independents to watch the Octi Plaza Building, hoping they'd find something?"

"What else could I do?"

"For one, you might consider not wasting your money," Nox said. "You won't find out anything about Octi's operations, especially those taking place in the Desertlands, by watching what goes on outside their main office building."

"I see," Rose said. "Yes, it was a stupid, desperate act. But what else could I -*can* I- do?"

Nox got to her feet.

"I'll give you a call tomorrow," she said.

Nox adjusted her sunglasses and turned to exit the room.

"Wait," Rose said.

Nox paused.

"You were right about the survey vans having automated signals. They're position markers. You send out a signal and the onboard computer automatically replies. Octi uses this to figure out where the vans are located in the event of catastrophe. My sister's survey group's primary signal is dead. But a long time ago she told me their van had another position marker, a spare, they kept hidden. That marker was, up until a couple of hours ago, still working. The frequency is 33412. Look it up. I know the crew is dead, but the van's been in one place for the past few weeks. Who knows where it'll be tomorrow."

Nox nodded and exited the room. After a few seconds, Rose heard the sound of the Congregation's outer door open and close. When it did, the door leading to his bathroom creaked opened.

A stunning blonde entered the room and walked to Rose's side. She laid her arms around him and they kissed passionately.

"I think she bought it, Julie," Thomas Rose said.

Julie's blue eyes burned with an icy heat. It was the exact same passion she showed Robert Octi Sr. in his bed.

"You're so persuasive," she said. She loosened the string around his waist and allowed his robe to slip down to the floor.

10

Izzy Greenfield sat in the driver's seat of his Impact, one of the last of the old time V-8's. As oil prices skyrocketed, the gas guzzlers faded into extinction, much like the dinosaurs before them. Izzy didn't care.

Izzy also didn't care when a group of kids threw small rocks at an apartment window and nearly shattered it. Izzy didn't care when the mailman arrived at the apartment building and, thinking he was unobserved, leafed through one of the girly mags he was tasked with delivering. Izzy didn't even care about any of the cars, new and old and in between, that filtered in and out of the building's parking garage.

But Izzy did sit up and take notice when he heard the rumbling of a chopper's motor. Realizing he was exposed, Izzy bent down in the car seat and peeked over the steering wheel. The motor's sound increased until he saw a woman with short, jet black hair, dark sunglasses, and three blue vertical stripes along the right side of her forehead ride her beat up chopper into the apartment complex's covered parking lot.

"Subject has arrived," Izzy whispered into a microphone. "I repeat, the subject has arrived."

Nox eased the chopper into one of a dozen parking spaces available within the covered garage. The chopper gasped and wheezed as her engine died out. Nox lingered next to the chopper, rubbing dirt from the side of her gas tank. It was then she noticed the man in the Impact parked just outside the covered lot.

Nox eyed him for a few seconds, but the man didn't move or look her way. If anything, he seemed to be taking a nap. Nox frowned but let it go. She walked to the elevator within the covered garage, got in, and pressed the fifth floor button.

The elevator rose from the garage and stopped in the building's lobby. A squat old lady carrying shopping bags on either arm stood waiting for her ride. When she saw Nox within the elevator, she hesitated.

"Good morning, Miss Abbott," Nox said. She held the door open for the elderly lady.

Miss Abbott closed her mouth tight and stepped inside. The elevator doors closed.

"How are you doing today?"

"Go fuck yourself," the old lady replied.

To that, Nox couldn't help but smile.

The elevator doors opened on the fifth floor. The old lady faced Nox. There was a bloody rage in her eyes.

"And I warn you," Ms. Abbott yelled. "You blast that Gods damned heavy metal music again and I *will* call the cops! Why don't you get some culture? Why don't you get yourself some headphones? Better yet, why don't you just find yourself another home?"

Nox was aghast.

"You want me to move? If I did, I'd miss you something fierce, Ms. Abbott."

They walked together to the end of the hallway. At that point, the corridor split off to the left and right.

"Oh, fuck off," the old lady spat.

"I'll take that into consideration," Nox said. She walked down the left hallway while the old lady moved to the right.

The smile remained on Nox's face as she passed a door labeled "Trash". She didn't notice it was ajar. She didn't notice it silently open when she walked past it.

A gleaming silver object that looked like an upright torpedo exited the room. It made no sounds as it moved on a pair of oversized treads fixed to either side of its body. Its arms were a pair of fearsome Gatling guns. Its body surface, for the most part, was shiny new. However, the robot had several burn scars on its back, the result of the warehouse fire it started two nights before.

Donovan's robot slid into the hallway a few feet behind Nox.

The Mechanic stepped up to her door and was about to put the key into the lock.

As she did, Donovan's robot locked on its target. The Gatling guns rose into place. They rotated slowly at first, then, with a barely audible click, the firing mechanism was engaged.

Nox spun around when she heard that soft sound. It took a fraction of a second to realize the danger she was in. Her reaction was instantaneous. Nox flattened herself against her recessed door just as a searing barrage of bullets tore down the hallway.

Hundreds of rounds chewed the wall and door frame around her.

Nox kept her body in the recess as flat as possible. Though she didn't get a good look at the robot in the warehouse, she knew this was the same creature because it fired the same type of high caliber bullets.

This time, however, Nox's Kevlar vest was gone. Her handgun, she was more certain than ever, was useless against its thick metal skin. And because she was pressed up so tightly against her apartment door, Nox didn't have the leverage to tear through the lock and burst into her home.

Horror filled Nox's face. The robot moved in closer and closer, and Nox was trapped and there was nothing, nothing at all, that she could do.

11

Nox squeezed her body closer to the door frame's edge.

The door's metal frame, standard in all the building's apartment units, for the moment protected her from the relentless barrage of bullets but it was giving way. Worse, Nox spotted the edge of the robot's slick body. The machine crawled closer and closer to Nox's shallow hiding place. It kept the Mechanic trapped in place while positioning itself for a kill shot.

Nox bit her lower lip and swore. She pushed against her apartment door but still didn't have enough leverage to force it open. Worse, just this past month she bought a stronger lock to prevent any break-ins.

Why did you have to get such a good lock?

Nox eased her handgun out of her jacket pocket and tried to point it at the lock but it was impossible to do this for the same reason she couldn't force the door open: Nox was pressed too tight against the door's edge and her body covered the lock. To shoot it off, she needed to take a step back. But to step back, whether it was to break the door in or shoot off the lock, meant exposing herself to the robot.

It meant certain death.

Once again Nox swore. There was no alternative. She had to chance it and take that step away from the lock. She was certain to take a bullet or fifty in the process, but if she was lucky, the bullets would only graze her.

Yeah, right.

Nox swore once again. There was no more time to think. There was no more time to worry. She'd either make it or not. Nox let the air out of her lungs and braced herself. She was about to move from her tiny sanctuary when she heard an angry voice rise above the barrage of gunfire.

"That's it you Gods damned—"

It was Miss Abbott. The elderly lady heard the commotion coming from Nox's hallway and, apparently, mistook it for Nox's music. So eager was she to confront the Mechanic that she still carried the grocery bags in either hand. Her face abruptly changed from fury to horror when she saw Donovan's security robot only a few feet away from her.

The robot, responding to her voice and movement, spun around to face her. It's still smoking Gatling guns aimed directly at the woman. Internal mechanisms targeted her frail body.

Miss Abbott froze. She gasped and, as she did, dropped her shopping bags on the floor and to either side of her body.

Donovan's robot sensed the movement and its Gatling guns locked on to the woman's groceries. The robot fired a punishing barrage of bullets which ripped the shopping bags and their contents apart. In seconds they were shredded into tiny little pieces.

Despite the fury happening around to her sides, the stunned old lady remained completely still. As a result, the robot ignored her and focused on annihilating everything that still moved.

The old lady was completely untouched!

Taking advantage of the distraction, Nox emerged from her hiding place and jumped on to the metal beast. Bare hands grabbed the white hot barrels of the Gatling guns and pulled them up and away from Miss Abbott.

The old lady snapped out of her paralysis and ran down the corridor. The robot fired wildly, ripping the corridor walls to pieces. Nox kept the guns up and away from the retreating tenant. The smell of Nox's burnt flesh mixed with cordite. Despite the searing pain in her hands, Nox did not let go.

The robot continued spinning around, like a metallic Bronco trying to buck its rider. Still Nox held on. Bullets tore the plaster from the walls and blew out the lone window at the hallway's end.

And, just as abruptly as the furious barrage began, it ended. Donovan's security robot was out of bullets. The robot spun around one last time before coming to a complete stop. Its offensive weaponry finally exhausted, it quietly shut itself down.

Nox slowly stepped off the robot and onto the floor. She took a moment to examine her hands and, seeing the horribly burnt flesh, looked away.

"Son of a bitch," she muttered.

Around her, the other apartment dwellers cautiously opened their doors. They looked out into the hallway to see what just happened. A couple of brave and, for the moment, unsupervised children walked up to Donovan's machine and marveled at it. Their parents hastily pulled them away.

No one noticed Nox.

She leaned against the wall and slid down until she sat on the debris strewed floor. She kept her hands in front of her while catching her breath. When she looked up again, Miss Abbott stood before her.

The elderly woman carried a can of lotion and gauze and leaned down to apply the soothing cream to Nox's burns. When she was done, she wrapped the gauze around the Mechanic's wounds.

"Thank you," Nox said.

"Thank *you*," Miss Abbott replied and smiled.

Nox smiled back.

"Doesn't mean I forgive you for all that shitty music you've been torturing me with this past year," she added.

"I'll keep it down from now on," Nox said.

"Much appreciated."

Nox nodded and painfully lifted herself to her feet. She walked past the apartment dwellers and made her way to the elevator. When it arrived, she entered and pressed the garage button.

There were people she needed to see.

Izzy Greenfield remained in his Impact even though the sound of gunfire had long since passed. He knew the cops and ambulances would arrive at any moment, yet still he waited. His orders were to verify the target's death, and he was certain to do so in the next few minutes. Afterwards, he was to meet with the police as a representative of Octi Corp.

The story he was to give them was a thing of beauty:

Rogue Independent Nox, contracted to perform a mission for Elliot Donovan, the prototype security robot's late designer, got greedy (as some of the more untrustworthy Independents are want to do) and stole this valuable Octi's property. Said prototype security robot turned on the Independent and killed her (and however many innocent bystanders got in the way). Though Octi Corp. adamantly denies any responsibility for the actions of their stolen prototype, they regret the damages incurred and are willing to cover any repair costs to the building over and above those not already covered by the building's insurance company.

Octi Corp. also insists their stolen merchandise, Donovan's prototype security robot, be returned right away.

Mission accomplished, just in time for happy hour.

So focused was Izzy on the entrance to the building that he didn't see Nox walk out of the covered parking lot and approach his car from the other side. Izzy didn't even notice her when she stood next to his prized V-8 and reached in through his open window. He did, however, notice when she grabbed him by his neck.

Izzy gasped. Nox's grip was strong enough to choke off his air. He desperately tried to free himself from the Mechanic's hand but quickly realized he wasn't strong enough. The bandaged hand turned ever so slightly. It pulled Izzy up and out of his seat and toward the open window. His eyes grew wide when he saw Nox standing next to his car.

Nox examined the small man as if she were considering an ant on a kitchen floor. Instead of trampling him, Nox leaned in close to Izzy and said:

"Tell your boss he fucked up."

12

Thomas Rose sat behind his desk reading snippets from several documents spread before him.   The morning light barely made it to his cramped room and, because he couldn't afford to waste electricity, the pastor used the muted light of a single candle for his readings. He pushed several papers aside until he had the Desertlands map front and center. His fingers traced lines from notation to notation.   Pen marks indicated the routes his sister's survey group followed and he tried to make some sense of where they were before…

He shuddered.

His finger ran across a bright red X.

"…marks the spot," Rose muttered.   It was where the survey van supposedly encountered the abandoned nuclear plant. It was where his sister supposedly died. Rose rubbed his eyes. He spent far too many hours on this. He closed the map just as his phone rang.

"Hello?"

Beside one of the nameless streets of the Big City stood a well-worn metal booth covered in faded graffiti.

It was one of the last of its kind and, more importantly, the comm-tele within it still worked. Nox's chopper was parked next to the booth and Nox was within, talking. She stared at her left hand, her free hand, through dark sunglasses. Like her right hand, it was hidden behind thick black gloves.

"I'm taking your case," Nox told Thomas Rose.

She offered no other words and, with a clumsy effort, hung the tele up. The anger within her built to the point where it was ready to explode.

Not here. Save it for the ones who deserve it.

Nox exited the booth and closed its door. She looked up, at the heart of the Big City. It lay before her like a cancerous tumor, ugly and massive and hopeless. Despite the filth and the greed and the betrayals, it was her home, and there was nowhere else she'd ever want to live. It pained her to leave, but she had to. She'd be back. Soon.

Nox approached her chopper. To the west lay a vast flat plain. Almost directly over the chopper was a large sign which read: *"DESERTLANDS: NEXT 1200 Miles".* Below that sign was another: *"No Restaurants, Few Gas Stations. Please Make Sure You Have PLANNED YOUR TRIP and KNOW YOUR DESTINATION and Are WELL SUPPLIED Before Exiting the City."*

As if to emphasize that final point, a leering skull and crossbones and the word *DANGER!* was offered as a final warning to those considering exiting the relative safety of the Big City.

Nox mounted her cycle. She switched on a radio transmitter that sat at the side its fuel tank and adjusted the frequency to 33412. A steady beep was heard over the chopper's speaker. On the transmitter's LED monitor appeared a single steady dot. It remained in place.

"X marks the spot," Nox muttered. She leaned into the chopper and, after a few tries, managed to start her up. She drove under the sign that marked the border between home and a sandy hell.

The exhaustion evident in Thomas Rose's eyes was gone. He smiled when he replaced the phone in its cradle.

"Thank you," he said. He put his hands together and whispered a brief prayer. *You have not forsaken me.* When he was done, he let out a triumphant laugh and pulled a cigar from his vest pocket. He lit it up and took a deep drag.

"Julie?" he said.

The door to the bathroom opened. Julie, cleaned up and elegantly dressed, stepped into the room and closed the door. She noted the disheveled bed as she walked to Rose's side. Her eyes turned from the bed to Rose. She found it hard not to grimace at the memory of what she had just done with the pastor.

"Was it Nox?" she asked.

Thomas Rose nodded excitedly.

"Yes! She's taking the job! We won't need to fumble in the dark anymore! She will do the work for us!"

Rose got to his feet and lustily hugged Julie. In the face of such triumph, his desire was back in force. He kissed Julie hard on her mouth while his right hand reached down and felt the curves of her ass. He grabbed her skirt and roughly hiked it up. Julie allowed him, even thought there was no passion in her response.

"We're all set, we're all set," Rose mumbled incoherently.

Rose was a man of the cloth, and somewhere deep in the back of his mind he remembered his original vows. He promised to avoid all earthly temptation and lead a humble life. How quaint those foolish ideals seemed now!

Through his experiences with Julie, Rose realized passion was a human experience and there was no need to fight it. He was with the woman of his –of any man's– dreams and there was no shame in that.

So focused was the pastor on her body that he did not notice the woman's continued cool response. He did not notice the shadow of a frown that lurked just below her porcelain skin. Most regrettably for him, he did not notice the shiny knife that slipped out of Julie's sleeve and into her right hand.

She thrust the knife forward and the blissful joy on Rose's face was abruptly replaced with an expression of unimaginable pain. Julie drove the knife deep into the strayed Pastor. It slid out easily, and she thrust it forward once again. Rose's body went limp in her arms, but Julie wasn't done yet. She slid the knife in a third and fourth time.

By then she knew Rose was dead, his heart sliced to pieces. She stepped to his side and allowed the pastor's body to fall to the floor.

"*I* won't have to fumble in the dark anymore," Julie said.

She spat on Rose. Her only regret was that Nox didn't make that call when she first arrived. She again noted the disheveled bed.

It would have saved Julie some extreme unpleasantness.

The call came in an hour later. An hour after that, Robert Octi Senior's limousine glided into its parking space at Octi Plaza. When the elderly CEO exited his vehicle, his son was there, waiting for him. He held the elevator door open for his father.

"What's this about?" the elderly Octi muttered. "Why is the board calling the meeting?"

His son allowed the elevator doors to close before speaking.

"They know about Donovan and the robot."

"They authorized and funded his venture. They're not going to turn around and pin this shit on me—"

"They also found out about Nox."

Octi's mouth closed tight. The anger within him grew to a boiling point. It took all his will power to not reach out and slap the stupid out of his son's face.

Relax. As satisfying as that would be, it won't solve a damn thing right now.

"How much do they know?"

"Just about all of it. Our cleanup effort didn't pay off. They've...they've got Izzy in the boardroom."

"That's just great," the elderly Octi muttered. "What about the recording Nox made of her conversation with Donovan?"

"They don't know about that."

"Thank the gods for small favors."

It would be another painfully long day.

The room temperature was downright chilly, par for the course while attending a hastily arranged emergency session. The members of the Octi Corp. board, those that still sided with Robert Octi Senior, were clearly nervous and it was up to Octi himself to convince them that all wasn't as bleak as it seemed. Standing before the board's table was Izzy Greenfield. He carried his hat in his hand. It was crumpled to the point of being unrecognizable.

"After the gunfire died down, I waited," Izzy told the board members. "I figured the cops and ambulance would arrive and I'd just have to make sure Donovan's Independent was in one of the body bags. But this gal Nox...she came out of nowhere after the shootings. She grabbed me by the neck."

Izzy showed the members of the board the bruise marks on his neck.

"Go on," Octi growled. He was thoroughly unimpressed with the man's injuries.

"She told me to tell you something."

"What?"

"Uh...she said...she said..."

"Spit it out."

Izzy nodded.

"Sorry sir. She said that you fucked up."

The room grew silent.

"That's all?"

"Yes sir."

The members of the board fidgeted in their seats. One of them leaned forward. He was Robert's age but carried himself far more coolly than Octi's son ever had.   Despite the grim news, he smiled.

"This Independent has a way with words," the man said and let out a soft chuckle.

Octi bit his lip. It was Carl Lambert who had just spoken.

Of course.

Of the eleven members of the board, Lambert was the lead malcontent in the minority group of five. He was a self-stylized intellectual know-it-all whose charisma and forceful arguments swayed enough of the other members to make himself a genuine threat to Octi's power. At first he hid his desire to take over the old man's position, but in the last few months his calls for change grew louder and louder.

Though it pained Octi to admit it, Nox's analysis of his position within his own company was spot on. At this point, all Lambert needed was one more consistent vote against Octi and he and his son were done.

"This cluster fuck is all Donovan's fault," Robert said, far too defensively.

"We know he didn't have Nox sign the proper consent forms," Lambert said. "But I understand this Independent came to see you personally. Why didn't you just pay her off?"

"We tried to reason with her, but she's a most unreasonable woman."

"Then why not have her arrested for trespassing? It's not like she's got anything on us," Lambert said, and paused just long enough to let the thought sink into the other board member's minds before adding: "Right?"

Octi managed a thin smile. Lambert was clever enough to know something wasn't quite right.

"You've seen our rivals' performance in the stock market these past few days," Octi replied. "We bring in the police to arrest an Independent on our premises and we're opening up a can of worms that might prove difficult to sort. Besides, it's my experience people like that are better dealt with head on. Forcefully."

"We saw the photographs of the Independent's apartment building," Lambert said and grinned. "You can't deal with anyone much more forcefully than that."

Octi's face turned to stone. Lambert looked away from him and eyed Izzy.

"Where is this Independent now?"

"I don't know. She got on her bike and drove off."

"You didn't follow?"

"No sir. I was told to stay there and retrieve the SR unit."

"And there wasn't other Octi staff around to—"

"We heard she fled town," Octi said.

"Oh? How certain are you of this Intel?"

"Seventy five percent," Octi replied. In his mind the number was closer to twenty or thirty percent. *Never trust the coked out bums on the edge of town, however good their news is.*

"You're certain she didn't go to the police?"

Robert angrily slapped his right hand against the table.

"You're making it a habit of questioning my father's every statement, Lambert," Robert said. He shot the man a poisonous glare. "The bottom line is that Nox is gone. As far as we know, we might never see her again. And even if we do, why don't you enlighten us all on what you would have done better."

"Well, junior, this lonesome cowboy act has made spectators of the rest of us," Lambert purred. "At least for the time being."

Octi's gaze drifted from Lambert to his son. The boy was ready to lash out. Octi reached forward and laid his hand on his son's shoulder. As he did, his son's cell phone, tucked in his jacket pocket, vibrated on. Robert leaned back in his chair and pulled the phone out. He read the message on its display and rose to his feet.

"Excuse me," Robert said before exiting the room.

"You should teach that boy some manners," Lambert said. "My sole interest lies in the success of this company. If my statements are somewhat harsh, it's only because the situation dictates it."

"Of course," Octi shot back. "Especially since you, Mister Lambert, were one of the earliest, and fiercest, proponents of Donovan's security robot project."

The smile on Lambert's face faded. *Gotcha, you bastard.*

"But I'm not in the business of pointing fingers," Octi continued, even though that was exactly what he had just done. "The fact is we *all* bear responsibility for the lost funds tied to a robot that isn't worth a shit."

"Exactly how much have we lost?" Lambert asked.

"We're estimating no more than sixty million," Octi muttered, well aware that the total was probably twenty million higher.

Upon hearing this figure, the board members faced each other and several conversations began at once. A cacophony of noise filled the room. Octi frowned. He didn't have time for this.

"Enough!" he roared.

The board members went silent. After a while, Izzy said:

"If it makes you feel better, the robot nearly got her. And you all saw the damage. The thing's a beast, sir."

"If we wanted a multi-million dollar wrecking ball, we would have had one made of gold," Octi replied. "Was there anything else you need to add to this discussion?"

"Uh...No sir."

"Then get the fuck out of here."

Octi swiveled his chair and stared out the window. Izzy Greenfield bowed and exited the room. After a few seconds of collecting his thoughts, Octi turned the chair around until he once again faced the dour crowd.

"The losses on the SR unit are both unacceptable *and* unavoidable," Octi admitted. "But the bottom line is that we can weather this storm, provided we keep a cool head."

Octi thought hard about what he had to say. Part of his continued success was his ability to anticipate trouble and keep several aces up his sleeve. It was a shame he'd have to use one of his best ones here and now.

"We have six separate profit statements we've held back for tax reasons. We were planning to release them in late summer, when, financially, things are usually soft. Because of these... difficulties... I have decided to release the profit statements now. They will easily trump any loses from Donovan's SR unit."

"What about late summer? What happens then?"

"We'll deal with that when the time comes."

The board members nodded. A few of them were noticeably happier. *Good,* Octi thought. *Just keep the peasants happy.*

"Now then, just so we're clear," Octi continued. His eyes settled on Lambert. "If I see an above average decline of Octi stock or panic selling within the next couple of weeks, I'll know one of you leaked our current problems to the press. Trust me, there *will* be repercussions."

"And Nox?" Lambert asked.

"She's our only loose end in this Donovan affair. I'm open to suggestions concerning what to do with her."

The board room was quiet for several long seconds. For a moment Octi considered adjourning the meeting, but one of the men raised his hand. He was a tall, medium built man with a way too pale white face. Octi tried to remember his name. Stedley?

"Go ahead," Octi said.

"Assuming Nox left town..." Stedley –or was it Steadman?– said.

"Yes?"

"We'll have to also assume she'll eventually come back. Maybe we should hire some more eyes on the streets, just in case."

"Agreed," Octi said while nodding gravely. *No shit, Sherlock.*

Another board member shifted in his seat.

"Yes?" Octi asked the man.

In response, the man stood up. *Brinkman,* Octi thought. He was one of Octi's most loyal board members and a true-blue ass kisser.

"We value your leadership," Brinkman began, proving the description fit. "You turned our investments into gold and, despite these difficult times, we have faith in you. I just wanted to say, we're with you all the way."

His chest puffed out and his face grew sober. He clapped once, then again. The other members of the board, minus Lambert, joined in. Soon, the chorus of applause was such that even Lambert reluctantly participated.

Octi smiled. *Fucking lemmings*, he thought. Sometimes it was good to have a brown-noser like Brinkman on the board.

After a few seconds, Octi raised his hands and the applause died down.

"We'll make it through these tough times," Octi swore. "We'll see our bonuses yet."

The members of the board roared in approval. As they did, Robert re-entered the board room. He walked to his father's side and whispered in his ear. Octi nodded once and again addressed his fellow board members.

"We'll discuss this again later," Octi said. "Gentlemen, if there's nothing else, I suggest we adjourn this meeting. I have some personal business to attend to."

The members of the board rose and exited the room. Lambert lingered by the door after the others were gone.

"Personal business?" Lambert wondered aloud. "What could be more important than the future of our company?"

"*My* company, Mister Lambert," Octi replied. "And she takes a backseat to nothing and nobody."

Lambert nodded.

"On this point we most definitely agree," he said and exited the room.

"Fucking bastard," Robert spat.

"He's nothing," Octi muttered. "Don't let him get under your skin."

"Sorry, Dad."

"Never mind. When did they find it?"

Robert's anger was quickly replaced with excitement.

"Just moments ago," Robert replied. "I can't believe we got this lucky!"

"Back in college my stoner friends called it Karma."

"I never knew you to be religious."

"Money is my only religion."

"If it's OK with you, I'll supervise the dig personally," Robert said.

Octi thought about that and nodded. It would be good to keep his son away from the pressures within the Big City.

"Do it," he said. "But you need to keep this information completely locked up. If anyone gets any idea of what's going on out there..."

"I know," Robert said. "Nagel is overseeing all security details."

"Good," Octi said. He eyed his son with something close to pride. "Don't come back without the secrets of the Demon's base."

Robert smiled.

"We'll get it, Dad. We'll get it all."

13

The daytime drive through the Desertlands proved almost unbearable.

Nox wiped the sweat from her forehead and reached to her side for the canteen. She took a deep swig of the warm water. Memories of her distant past flooded back. The air and heat felt the same. They *were* the same. All that was missing was the rubble. And the bodies.

Nox's chopper sputtered as she followed the desert road. Those who traveled it called her the path through hell. They were right. The Desertland road was a beat down stretch of hard sand that ran almost directly due west. It eventually led to the remains of the three very small central cities. If you wanted to keep traveling west, after another couple of thousand miles, give or take, you'd eventually reach the west coast and the other two major cities that hugged what was left of that coastline. Survey groups and suppliers used this route because it was the shortest and safest path across the country. The flat land could be reasonably well defended from the desert rats that lurked near the roads and were holed up in the hills.

Nox didn't worry about them, though. The desert rats tended to pick on slow moving, well stocked supply caravans. A lone rider on a beat up chopper was hardly worth their trouble. Or so she hoped

As evening approached, Nox reached the Devil's Boulders, a series of rock formations sculpted smooth by years of environmental wear and tear. It was there, among the rocks that looked like they were dipped in blood many millennia before, that Nox first spotted a group of desert rats. They were dressed in ragged clothing and hid among the crevasses and silently watched Nox drive by. They did nothing to impede her journey.

Nox soon exited the rocky terrain and once again hit a patch of smooth desert plain. The sun was setting and she was getting tired. She reached into her saddle bag and pulled out a well-worn disk labeled "Heavy Metal."

"My apologies, Miss Abbott," Nox muttered. She popped the disk into her chopper's stereo. The blare of heavy metal music filled the air. It was hardcore material, a wall of sonic mayhem that would send the members of *Virgin Slayer* running for cover. Nox hummed to the beat, until static and a high pitched squeal indicated the disk was fried.

"Shit," Nox muttered. She ejected the disk and tossed it. She again reached into her saddle bag and pulled out another disk. This one was marked "Heavy Metal-Replacement."

More heavy metal music blared, but after a few minutes it too died.

"Son of a bitch," Nox cursed. She threw that disk away and tried another. Then another.

Finally, Nox reached into the saddle bag and pulled out the entire box of disks. She tossed them over her shoulder and onto the Desertland road.

Miss Abbot would be pleased.

Nox awoke to the first rays of the rising sun. She got to her feet and stretched. The desert surrounded her as it had the day before, and the cool evening temperatures were rapidly dissipating. Nox folded her sleeping bag and approached the chopper. She eyed the odometer. She traveled a little more than four hundred miles before giving in to fatigue but her destination was very close.

Nox tied the folded sleeping bag to the back of the chopper and reached into her saddle bag. From within she pulled out a map of the Desertlands and spread it out over the chopper's seat. She ran her finger over a red line she drew on the map and then looked up at a large mesa in the distance. Nox's gaze once again returned to the map.

A mesa was indicated on the map, near where her finger lay. Nox gave a satisfied nod and folded the map. She replaced it in the saddle bag before mounting up.

It took a few tries before the chopper started.

Three hours later the sun was near its apex. The sky was bloody red and the eastern winds picked up. The heat was, once again, unbearable.

Nox's chopper stood parked against a boulder. A pair of footprints, Nox's, led away, past a weathered sign that warned: "DANGER: RADIOACTIVITY. DO NOT ENTER."

The footprints continued into a small valley. Nox, with her bulging backpack draped over her left shoulder, cautiously walked the shifting sands. In her right hand was a small Geiger counter. It gave no indication of any radioactive material present.

After close to an hour of searching the sands, Nox spotted a curiously sunken patch of loose dirt. She shut the Geiger counter off and replaced it in her backpack. She then grabbed a folded shovel and walked to the center of the disturbed sand. She laid her backpack down and started digging.

It took only a few minutes of hard work to hit a solid surface. Encouraged, Nox doubled her efforts. She soon had the entire roof of a large buried vehicle exposed.

Nox then dug down, until she exposed the vehicle's rear. When the van's rear door was half-uncovered, Nox was hit with the smell of rot. While it made her nauseous, it also proved encouraging.

Nox worked quickly and efficiently, digging down until she fully uncovered the rear door. She then dug outward. Soon, there was a wide enough space for her to open the door.

By this time, Nox was sweaty and full of sand. She replaced the shovel into the backpack and carried it to the rear of the vehicle. She turned the door's handle and tried to pull the door out, but it didn't budge.

Nox shook her head and sighed. Only a corporation would be stupid enough to make a car door that opens *inwardly*.

Nox leaned back and kicked the door in. A wave of nauseous air drifted from inside the vehicle. Nox allowed the desert wind a few seconds to dissipate the smell of rot before venturing inside.

Nox took a small flashlight from her back pocket and lit the interior of the van. She expected to find the rotting corpses of the survey crew but instead found a smooth, empty shell. All the seats, however many the van once held, were gone. The carpeting that covered the floor was ripped away, leaving only a few loose fibers swirling in the breeze. Compartments lining the walls were torn away. Left behind were shadows of darker paint and more emptiness. There were no papers, no notes, and no maps. Nothing.

Nox frowned. She followed the nauseous odor to the only item still left within the survey van, a small wall unit refrigerator. Within it were several packages of spoiled beef.

Nox closed the refrigerator door and walked the length of the vehicle. She leaned down to the floor and close to the walls in the hopes of finding something.

Anything.

After only a few minutes of searching she straightened up and rubbed her chin. Nox made her way to the rear of the van to exit. She abruptly stopped.

A small hole near the back door caught her attention. Nox examined it with her flashlight while pulling out a small jack knife. She unfolded the knife and pushed the blade into the hole. She then worked the blade until a black object, a bullet, emerged. Nox held the bullet between her fingers. Though grotesquely deformed from penetrating the van's wall, she calculated the bullet's weight and considered its source.

"357," she muttered.

More than enough to take care of a group of unwanted survey van employees.

Nox tossed the bullet aside. There was no way to link it to any particular gun. And, if by some miracle she did, so what? If she were to confront Octi Corp. with the bullet and gun, they could come up with any number of explanations for why someone shot a hole in this Octi van. The easiest explanation was that an employee cleaning his or her gun accidentally fired it. They could also say an over-excited employee took a shot at a snake or some other vermin that had somehow crawled into the van. Or they could say...

It didn't matter. There was no one alive who could contradict any explanation they chose to use.

But to Nox the bullet was a revelation. Its existence, coupled with her Geiger counters' non-readings and the continued radio transmissions after the survey crew was supposedly dead, proved beyond a shadow of doubt that they didn't run into any radioactive hot zone.

Thomas Rose was right. They were murdered.

Why?

Nox headed back to the van's exit. Her mind was so focused on these discoveries that it was only at the very last second she noticed the shadow flickering before her.

Nox's reaction was lighting quick. She shifted her weight and spun to the side, just as a bullet whizzed past where her head had just been and splattered into the van's metal door.

Nox kept away from the van's exit and swore. Her view of the outside was almost nonexistent. She could see a dune in the distance behind the wall of sand she dug up and nothing more. Nox looked at the van's interior. It was just as empty as before, only now it felt a lot emptier.

She was trapped.

There was no way to know how many people were out there, but even if she had to contend with a single attacker, Nox still had only the one way out. Her hidden enemy had a clear shot at Nox whenever she tried to leave. Unless, of course, she could hold out until night.

Nox shook her head. There were a good five or so hours left before the sun set. It was impossible to remain in this metal oven for that length of time. Her hidden enemy, on the other hand, had all the time in the world. And if they got impatient, there were plenty of ways to force her out.

Again the Mechanic swore.

Nox leaned closer to the van's exit. She still couldn't see anyone outside. However, the absolute silence was broken by a low hum. The hum grew louder, until Nox identified the sounds of a group of engines, from V-12's to four-cylinder compacts. They all roared in the near distance.

"Desert rats," Nox thought.

Her situation had gone from very bad to much, much worse.

The desert rats kept their distance. They circled the buried van with their patchwork machines. Most of their vehicles were rehabs from the corporation bases' scrap heaps while others were literally dug up out of the sand, much like this Octi Corp. survey van could be. The vehicles were shut off and the desert rats dismounted.

There were thirty of them. They converged on an emaciated fifty year old man who had a feral look on his face. His eyes were pale blue, like a faded memory. He examined the small opening Nox had dug, then scratched his bearded jaw and addressed one of his female disciples. She was his woman and sported closely cropped hair and a very skinny frame. She carried an ancient rifle and gave her man a toothless smile.

"She's in there?" the man asked.

"Trapped," the woman said.

"What of her vehicle?"

"A motorcycle. She left it a ways back there, by a boulder. The boys took a look. They say it's junk. Can't even get her started."

"Then forget the motorcycle," the man said. His face contorted into a wicked smile. "Let's smoke our unwanted visitor out of her hole."

The feral man faced his people. He was the alpha male, the leader of this pack. As his disciples converged, he felt his power grow. They would do anything for him, and he would do anything for *them*. The smile on his face widened.

"We eat well tonight," he roared.

His pack roared right back.

14

The desert rats wandered in and out of Nox's limited field of view. She counted twenty separate people but couldn't be sure exactly how many more, if any, there were. Based on the noises they made, Nox was inclined to think there were more. Plenty more. Nox kept her handgun aimed at the van's rear door. If they rushed her, Nox could take down a few before being overwhelmed.

Of course, they had no reason to do anything that rash. So what were they up to?

After a few minutes, Nox had her answer. The desert rats threw pieces of wood and other debris near the dug exit. When a large enough pile of flammable material was in place, they'd set it on fire to smoke her out.

Nox wouldn't stand a chance.

The Mechanic backed further from the van's exit and desperately searched its interior for anything she could use to defend herself. Other than the rot in the refrigerator, there was nothing. She turned her attention to the van's controls, but realized that not only was the interior of the van stripped but so too was its console. She doubted the van still had a motor.

The harsh truth, Nox knew, was that she was in a metal casket that had only one exit, and beyond that exit waited certain death.

Nox sat on the floor and faced the only way out. Since the desert rats had every advantage, there was only one thing left to do.

"Hello out there," Nox yelled.

There was no answer.

"You can have the van," she continued. "I don't want it."

Still no answer.

"If you don't let me go, I'll blow the whole thing up."

To this Nox heard a few excited voices. She bit her upper lip. The only thing left for her to do was try to bluff her way free.

"You're willing to kill yourself?" a high, shrill voice replied.

"You'll be left with nothing, and there's plenty of good stuff here in the van."

There was a pause, followed by a low laugh.

"Companies aren't in the habit of burying vans loaded with goods, my friend," the voice said. "If you're gonna blow yourself up, better hurry. You don't have much time."

The fire was lit, and smoke soon rose from the debris. The wind turned favorable for the desert rats and very unfavorable for Nox. It didn't take very long for the thick black smoke to filter inside.

"Son of a bitch," Nox muttered.

So much for bluffing her way out.

The smoke became a gloomy haze and Nox let out several loud coughs. One of the desert rats peered into the van.

Nox aimed and fired.

The figure dropped to the ground, wounded but still alive. He crawled away, leaving several droplets of blood behind. There followed a series of loud yells and a single shrill scream. The desert rats learned their lesson and, from that moment on, kept out of view. They were content to let the fire do its job.

Nox let out another cough. The smoke within the van was overwhelming and the Mechanic couldn't stay inside much longer. Nox stared at her handgun. It weighed heavy in her hands. A single bullet could end it all, painlessly.

Was there any other alternative?

Nox shook her head.

There were always alternatives.

Nox moved closer to the van's exit. The smoke was so thick that it actually offered limited cover. Perhaps she could...

What?

Run out under the smoke's cover and somehow shoot down twenty plus people with a handgun that carried nine rounds? Maybe the desert rats were that very rare breed of polite savage. Maybe they'd allow Nox time to reload her gun a few times before overwhelming her.

Despite the despair, Nox let out a laugh. It died quickly.

There was no way she could survive. None. All that was left was to make sure her death hurt them. Hurt them *bad*.

Nox crouched down low and took several deep breaths. She let out a cough and grimaced.

This is how it ends.

No regrets, Nox thought. It was fun while it lasted.

Nox rose to her feet and lurched toward the exit door. She stopped there. The desert rats spotted her. One of them fired, but his shot went wide. Nox raised her handgun and fired back. She couldn't see them, but they could see her. More shots followed. Several bulled chewed into the van, but Nox held her ground.

She fired her full clip and reloaded. As she did, she heard another, more distant shot. The desert rats ceased firing at the Mechanic. There came another distant shot. Hushed voices were heard. The desert rats scattered.

Nox spun away from the van's exit. A third distant shot filled the air.

"What in Hades?" Nox muttered.

Who was doing this shooting?

Outside, the desert rats were quiet no more. Their voices roared into a series of bloody screams. There was movement all around the buried van. An engine fired up, then another. One of the desert rat's vehicles drove off as yet another distant gunshot was heard.

Nox leaned in closer to the van's exit. She could tell several of the desert rats' vehicles were moving away. Cautiously, Nox exited the van and stepped past the fire.

Whoever was shooting did so with deadly accuracy. There were three desert rats lying dead still on the sand.

The last of their vehicles fired up and headed out. A final distant shot was followed by the sound of shattering glass. A desert rat that held on to the door of his fleeing vehicle fell off. Blood flowed from where his right eye used to be.

Nox kept low. She was free of her coffin, but feared exposing herself to the sniper. At this distance, the Mechanic could easily be confused for a desert rat.

Nox moved slowly along the edge of the burning debris. She spotted her chopper lying on the ground beside the boulder she originally left it parked. Though the desert rats had kicked it down, her vehicle looked to be intact.

If only she could reach it.

Nox spotted the dusty trails of the fleeing desert rat vehicles. They were converging on a mesa far off in the distance. No doubt that was where the sniper was holed up. If the man -or woman- was smart, they'd be on the run. Otherwise, the sniper had little chance against that savage group.

Nox ran in a zigzag pattern to her chopper. There were no gunshots, distant or otherwise, fired her way. She pulled the chopper up and turned on the ignition. The Mechanic was completely focused on starting the vehicle and getting the hell out of there.

Unfortunately, she didn't notice the tall, gaunt man emerge from the shadows behind a nearby boulder. The man carried a knife in his hand and thrust it forward.

15

Nox fell to the ground clutching her right side.

The knife nicked her deep, just below her ribs. The pain shot through her body like an electrical jolt and a stream of blood fell on the already red sand.

The lean man with the dull blue eyes didn't pause. He jumped onto Nox. Though he was considerably older and his body was ravaged by the harsh desert life, there was an animalistic fury that exploded from within. He pressed forward with his right hand and brought the bloody blade within inches of Nox's face. Moving on instinct, the Mechanic grabbed the older man's wrist just before the knife found its mark.

The lean man snarled. His left hand came up and sharp, dirty fingernails clawed at Nox's face. Nox smacked the hand away and spun her body. With a grunt, the older man found their positions were reversed. He was on the sandy floor with Nox on top of him.

"Give up," Nox growled. "It's over. No one else has to die."

The lean man said nothing. His lips curled into a hideous leer, revealing rotted teeth and a foul breath.

"Give up," Nox repeated.

The older man's fury, overwhelming only moments before, was now rapidly fading. Nox was younger, stronger, and had the advantage of her position.

"Please," she muttered.

The older man let out an eerie, animalistic laugh. He pushed the blade forward with all his might, forcing Nox to push back. The blade nicked Nox's sunglasses. The older man's laugh died. He looked deep into Nox's face and, just as suddenly, released his grip. Nox wasn't expecting this.

The Mechanic stared incredulously as the blade shot back, moving on momentum, and slid noiselessly into the older man's chest. His pale blue eyes stared up at Nox and then the sky. A weary sigh exited his mouth and his body became still.

"No," Nox whispered. She released the blade and rolled away.

The gaunt man was dead.

"What a fucking waste," Nox said. Though the man and his group tried their best to kill her, there was no need for more deaths.

Despite everything, Nox felt pity for the desert rats. They were abandoned by civilization and lived off this brutal, barren land. As horrifying as their actions were, they killed to survive.

Nox got to her feet and brushed the sand from her body. Along with the gaunt man she had just killed, there were five other bodies surrounding the buried remains of the survey van. Five more corpses to add to the growing list.

Nox removed her backpack. From within, she retrieved a small white first aid case. She opened it and tended to the wound to her side, sealing it with antibiotic tape before packing everything back up. She returned to her chopper. It took a couple of tries before it sprang to life. When it did, Nox stared out into the distance. The desert rat vehicles were long gone. Even the plumes of smoke they left behind had settled.

There was no movement at all. Nox wondered if they had captured their unknown sniper.

She was determined to find out.

It took a half hour to reach the base of the mesa. Had Nox chosen to, she could have taken a more direct route and made it there in only a few minutes. Instead, she chose a longer, more circuitous path which, she hoped, would keep any remaining desert rats from seeing her approach. There was no sense in tangling with them again.

Nox approached a rocky outcrop. She shut her chopper down and pushed it into a shadowy crevasse and outside anyone's view. If the desert rats were up on the mesa, they would eventually see her approach. Hopefully, they hadn't seen her hide her chopper.

There was a worn path wide enough for vehicles that, Nox figured, likely lead to the mesa's top. In the old days, tourists probably used this route for sightseeing. Nox noted several fresh tire tracks along this path. All of them belonged to the desert rats' vehicles.

Nox ignored the path and followed a tougher rock surface climb. The way was almost vertical and proved physically grueling. On the other hand, there were plenty of places to hide, should the desert rats make an unwelcome reappearance.

It took Nox close to an hour to work her way up. By the time she got there, she was confident no one saw her ascent.

Her caution proved a waste of both time and effort.

There was no one at the top of the mesa. The desert rat vehicles' tire tracks converged there before turning and heading back down.

Nox rubbed her side and winced. She kneeled down on the sand and allowed a few minutes to pass while she caught her breath. When she recovered enough strength, she walked the area.

Eventually her gaze turned to the sandy plain below. In the distance she spotted the still smoldering fire the desert rats set before the buried Octi Corp. survey van. She looked there and back to the mesa top several times, until she found a particular patch of smooth rock at the mesa's edge. She leaned in closer and again looked over to the survey van's location.

"Here," she muttered.

In a crack in a large flat rock she spotted something shiny. Nox reached down and fished out the object. It was a spent rifle cartridge.

".30 caliber," Nox muttered. There was a glimmer of recognition in her face. Despite her exhaustion, Nox managed a smile. "Cavalry to the rescue."

Nox tossed the spent cartridge and began the long walk back down.

16

The Eseno Gas Station lay rotting next to a rare stretch of uncovered ancient asphalt smack dab in the middle of nowhere. The asphalt was the last visible remains of Route 96, one of the old highways that, once upon a time, connected all the old big cities together. Like everything else out here, the desert swallowed the rest of the route up but in this valley and shielded from the more violent nocturnal winds, the weathered remnants of the past lived at least one more day.

Nox's chopper coughed and sputtered as the engine died. The Mechanic parked her vehicle in front of one of the station's two pumps and dismounted. The chopper was running hot and was just about out of fuel. Nox removed the gas cap and examined the station's fuel pumps. They were all locked up. Though she could easily pick the locks, Nox instead replaced the chopper's gas cap.

A cool wind blew from the east, taking with it the overwhelming desert heat. Nox removed her sunglasses and massaged her tired eyes. Afterwards, she replaced the sunglasses and unstrapped her backpack from the chopper's side. She then hitched it over her left shoulder and walked up to and through the station's front door.

The interior of the Eseno Gas Station was rotted with age and wear. The only furnishings were three sets of shelves that a very long time ago were likely filled with candies, chips, or the latest glossy magazines. They were bare now, with the exception of a couple of weathered and outdated maps.

Nox dropped her backpack on the floor. At the rear of the station was a circular brick well. Nox walked to it and, after fishing herself some fresh water, noticed a hand scrawled sign posted on the back wall.

Gone for Dinner. Be back in twenty minutes. No money in till, no valuables in the store, so don't bother. Help yourself to the water but please don't piss in it.

Nox grabbed her backpack and exited the station. The last of the day's light was fading fast and the cool winds grew with each passing minute. Nox pulled a leather jacket from her backpack and put it on. She sat in one of the wooden rocking chairs to the side of the station's entrance and took out her Desertland map.

She tried to focus on the many notations on the map but instead struggled with the harsh grip of exhaustion.

After a while Nox gave up and folded and put the map away. She leaned back in the chair and crossed her arms in front of her chest and, after a fashion, drifted off to sleep.

The sun rose through the gas station's window. Nox's eyes, hidden behind her dark sunglasses, fluttered open. An unusual sound, a bird singing in the distance, caught her attention.

Nox got up and stretched. The bird's song was stilled, replaced by a low rumble. Curious now, Nox reached for her backpack and grabbed a pair of binoculars. She walked down the asphalt remnants of Route 96 until coming to a stop at the far side of the road. Wisps of sand swirled around her as she got her bearings. She listened carefully for a few moments before turning to the south east and raising the binoculars to her eyes.

She spotted a convoy of three old style big rig trucks in the distance. Each carried a long and heavy payload. The payload, like the trucks themselves, was painted a dull red, good camouflage designed to keep stray pirates and desert rats from easily spotting their prey. Nox focused on the lead truck, increasing the binoculars' magnification until she spotted a small logo painted on its door.

Tower Co. Survey.

Nox lowered the binoculars. She took a few seconds to think about her next move. Once decided, she ran back to the gas station's porch. She stowed the binoculars and pulled the backpack over her shoulder. She then ran to her chopper and strapped the backpack down before mounting.

Nox turned the fuel key and shut the throttle. She was about to kick start the engine when a voice from behind stopped her.

"You're not going to follow them, are you?"

Nox turned the fuel key to the off position and let down the kick stand.

Standing on the porch and cradling a half-eaten apple stood a thin old man wearing dusty clothing. His skin was wrinkled and sun beat and a dusty black patch covered his left eye. The man carried an M30 rifle on his shoulder.

"You're late, Ellis," Nox said.

The old man smiled and took another bite of his apple.

"Couldn't help it," he replied. "Had an important meeting with the stockholders. They'd be dead without me."

"I suppose they would," Nox said. "And the desert rats?"

"They're pretty good trackers, especially when they're good and mad," Ellis said. "Took a while to lose them."

Nox dismounted her chopper and walked past Ellis and to the station's entrance.

"When you told me you were coming, I figured you might need a hand," Ellis continued. "You city girls may have that scene all locked up, but things work a little differently out here."

"Not really. Survival is survival."

"But familiarity with the territory is worth its weight in gold," Ellis said. The smile on his face broadened. "Been a while since we saw each other."

Nox stopped and, for the first time since she arrived, looked Ellis over. She could still see the youthful *Betty Lou* Reconnaissance Tank's navigator hidden under the accumulated age and wear. Perhaps Ellis still saw the youthful Blue Brigade soldier beneath the grown woman that was Nox.

"Yeah, a while," Nox acknowledged.

"I missed you too."

Despite her best efforts, Nox couldn't hold back her own smile.

"What's got you so fired up?" Ellis asked.

Nox's smile faded.

"Come on," Ellis prodded. "First you nearly get yourself roasted by a particularly mean bunch of desert rats, and now you're thinking of going after Tower Co. trucks. I never knew you to be suicidal, so I'm guessing there's some kind of method behind your madness. Tell me. What's gotten into you?"

Nox didn't reply. After a few seconds, Ellis angrily shook his head and frowned.

"I don't have to tell you how it is out here. You don't leap into something without *a lot* of careful planning. The desert rats are one thing. They have to see you with their own two eyes to attack. They'll kill you, gently, because they need the meat. But Tower Co.'s trucks' sensors will pick you up from five miles out, and when they do, the people in those trucks will use anything from long range sniper shots to guided missiles to take you out. And they'll do so without *any* hesitation at all."

Nox leaned against the station's door and folded her arms. Ellis' anger, now spent, was gone.

"Come on, Nox. What's got you so steamed?"

Nox closed her hands into fists. The old man looked down at the Mechanic's hands and spotted her thick black gloves and the bandages protruding out from within. Ellis shook his head.

"Is that what this is about?" he said. "Someone hurt you and you have to hurt them right back?"

Nox relaxed her hands.

"First rule of being a Mechanic—," Ellis said.

"—don't let emotions cloud your judgment," Nox finished. "Do your job like a machine: cold, efficiently, and unemotionally."

"And don't take anything –*anything*– personally."

The old man headed to one of the chairs along the porch. He sat down and motioned for Nox to join him. Nox sighed and did so. Her chair groaned under the weight.

"You're after Tower Co.?"

"No. Octi."

"Then why in the world are you interested in the Tower trucks?"

"I was planning to follow them to their base camp."

"And then?"

"Break in. Get whatever Intel they have on Octi Corp's operations in the Desertlands. Those two are fierce competitors in these parts. I figure Tower Co.'s got plenty of useful information on Octi."

"Indirect data mining. Not a bad idea. You're right, the bulk of Tower Co.'s interests are in this part of the desert. I'll bet they know more about Octi's operations here than Octi Corp.'s own personnel do in the Big City." The old man nodded and smiled. "Not a bad plan at all. Except you forgot one little thing: Because Tower's assets are *all* tied in to the Desertlands, they've invested far more resources on security than any other company operating out here."

"What kind of security?"

"Guess."

"Proximity mine fields?"

"That's one."

"Motion detectors?"

"That's another. At least five different models and types."

"Redundancy."

"And how. I can't vouch for what's inside their main compound, but I've seen the detectors stationed outside and heard a word or two about them from others who have gone in."

"That's all?" Nox said. She smirked. "I could get past them—"

"Hell no that's not all. Now we move to the visual scanners."

Nox's smirk disappeared.

"Infrared?"

"And ultraviolet and the Gods themselves know what else. But there's more: I've heard of guards running to a corner of the Tower Co. lot and firing off a series of rounds at what turned out to be a single poor, unfortunate groundhog."

"Seismic scanners," Nox said. She sighed. "What else?"

"The obvious: The compound's perimeter is protected with a five-layered electrical fence, at least twenty watchmen on call twenty-four hours a day, and a final thirty-foot high-electrified steel wall that surrounds the inner base. I've seen drones, not unlike the type we had during the war, circling the area, too."

"...damn..."

"Uh huh. There is, however, some good news."

"What?"

"You're after Octi Corp., so you can forget all about Tower Co. and their magnificent security systems and focus your energies on your actual target. Now, tell me: Why Octi?

"I was hired to do a job for them. Didn't work out so well."

"So now you have to get them before they get you."

"Naturally."

"What's your hook? What brought you way out here instead of confronting them in the Big City?"

"A couple of months ago one of their survey vans was decommissioned. Permanently. All scavengers working for that van were said to have met a most unfortunate end."

"And?"

"One of their relatives in the Big City found out at least one of them was still alive."

"Interesting," Ellis said. "Are they still?"

"No." Nox said and shrugged. "Either way, the survey crew stumbled into something very, very big. Something so big Octi Corp. had to silence them and quickly. But Octi moved a little *too* quickly. They released an 'accidental death' cover story before their hit squad killed the crew off."

"Ah," Ellis said. He finished the apple and tossed its core aside. "What happens when you figure out what the survey crew found?"

"I'm hoping the reasons behind their elimination are juicy enough to hurt Octi." Nox paused. She shook her head. "No, not just hurt them. I'm hoping it'll take them down."

Ellis let out a low whistle.

"You always were an ambitious child," Ellis said. "If I'm not mistaken, Octi Corp. is one of the top ten worldwide corporations. They've got deep pockets and plenty of muscle. Couldn't you find yourself an easier target?"

"You *are* mistaken," Nox said.

"About?"

Nox stared into the distance and leaned back in her chair.

"They're one of the top *five* worldwide corporations."

17

Nox and Ellis stood over one of the rotted tables within the gas station. Laid out before them was Nox's Desertland map. Nox ran her fingers from the Big City's borders and traced her progress from there and along the dusty trails. She pointed to one location and tapped her finger.

"That's where Octi Corp. claimed the survey crew hit a radioactive zone," Nox said. She slid her finger across the map and to the south west, ultimately tapping a second spot. "And that is where I found the van."

"It was a nice place to stash them," Ellis said. "Nothing, and I mean nothing, is out there." He let out a chuckle. "Other than the desert rats, of course. But as witnesses to some corporate skullduggery, they hardly count. Just try to get a formal statement from any of them. Yeah, it's a perfect place to get rid of unwanted articles small and large."

"That's what I figured," Nox said. "I'm guessing the crew was killed here but the bodies and whatever was in the van was packed up and shipped out. Afterwards, the van itself was buried."

"Bodies are small and relatively light. Not much of a burden to load up into another truck and take elsewhere for disposal. The survey van, on the other hand, is big and bulky and recognizable. If even one person at any Octi Corp. Desertland Base realized the van was still in circulation, then the whole radioactive poisoning story would be proven a lie. So Octi Corp. strips the van of all worthwhile parts and buries the shell. In a few weeks the first of the summer winds would have piled another few feet of sand over her. You were lucky to come when you did, Nox."

"Yeah. Lucky me."

Ellis pointed to another spot on the map.

"Octi Corp.'s main Desertland base is here, more or less," he said. "About three hundred miles from where you found the van."

"Where have you noticed the greatest movement of their workforce?"

"A better question is where they *aren't*," Ellis replied. "Truth is, Tower Co. and Octi Corp. constantly move personnel and equipment all over the place. I could offer you a dozen or more sites, but it would take months to check them all out."

"No offense, but I'm not planning to stay a minute more 'round these parts than is necessary."

"So says the city girl."

"Bad as it is, I can stand living there better than hanging around here."

Ellis nodded. He turned away from the map and stared at Nox.

"Have you heard from Sara?"

Nox shook her head.

"Not in a while. Someone told me she went corporate." These last words exited her mouth like a curse. "Haridan and Lowel."

"Those names don't mean a thing to me."

"They sell shit."

"Just like every other corporation."

"Have you tried talking to her?"

"After the war? No, not really. We really put our asses on the line, smuggling you in country without customs or the military knowing. Our relationship was never all that great, and with you in the mix..."

Ellis' thoughts trailed. He looked away.

"Not that I blame you for anything," Ellis said. "I mean, it's not like Sara and I were soul mates or something. We had our share of arguments about what to do with you. She's the one that got you listed as KIA."

"She knew her way around military red tape."

"Better than anyone *I* knew. Lucky for you."

"Is it true," Nox began and paused. She shook her head. "Is it true she originally wanted to turn me over to the brass?"

Ellis laid a hand on Nox's shoulder.

"It was a different time, Nox. You gotta remember, she was a soldier first and foremost. A damn good soldier. And damn good soldiers are trained to follow orders. Yeah, she might have thought pretty hard about turning you in, but in the end, she did what was right."

"I suppose."

Nox rubbed her nose and focused her attention back to the map.

"We're back to square one," she said. "I've got to break into Octi's main base and hope to get my hands on the right Intel.

Please tell me their security measures aren't quite as robust as Tower's."

"They're not," Ellis replied. "Especially in their satellite stations."

"Satellite?"

"Smaller bases spread out and about. These bases report to the bigger bases. They're usually made up of temp structures and are often poorly manned and far easier to break into. More importantly, they carry a decent amount of Intel. There's one of these satellite stations just a little over fifty miles from here."

"Good. Let's go."

"Better to wait for nightfall," Ellis said. "You break in, I'll watch."

"You have any connections in there?"

To that question, Ellis offered Nox a weary smile.

The blistering sun was gone and the night time darkness fell over the desert like it was the end of the world. The only sound heard for miles around was the purr of the wind as it danced across the dunes. A rusted fence circled an area of desert and, in its center, was a rusted warehouse and a somewhat smaller two story building. Faded white letters above the warehouse's door labeled it the Octi Desertlands Base 6.

Well outside the rusted gates, Nox and Ellis moved closer, eventually lying flat just outside the base's perimeter. Both were dressed in black and blended in with the night. Nox reached into her backpack and pulled out her binoculars. She stared through them while simultaneously hitting a switch on the binoculars' side. A low level whine was heard as the binoculars' visual enhancement mechanisms sprung to life.

Displayed within the binoculars in garish green colors was the Octi Corp. base. Nox examined the warehouse and the two story building behind it. A sign over the more distant building identified it as the "Octi Corp. Cantina". To its side was a small gas station. South of that building was a parking lot and within it were three Octi Corp. survey trucks. The makes and models of the vehicles were almost identical to the one Nox unearthed the day before.

After a few minutes of quiet examination, Nox laid the binoculars down.

"I don't see any guards," she said.

"This place is one of Octi's smallest Desertland investments," Ellis replied. "I brought you here not just because it was close to home, but because it's also got the least amount of security."

"Even if it was the smallest satellite base in all the Desertlands, there should be *some* guards. Why don't I see even one?"

"Well, I heard some stories," Ellis said and paused.

Nox waited for him to continue. When he didn't, she said: "Stories?"

Ellis still said nothing.

"Come on Ellis, what kind of stories?"

"I heard Octi Corp. removed what little security detail they had and replaced it with... with something else."

"What?"

"If I told you, you won't believe it."

"Try me."

"Ok, but don't laugh."

"Never."

"I heard they brought in some kind of experimental security machine."

"Machine?"

"Yeah, like a robot."

Nox's jaw tightened and her mouth compressed. She gave Ellis a sour look.

"Told you you wouldn't believe me."

Nox stowed the binoculars in her backpack and rummaged through it. When her hand emerged from within, it held a very large handgun. Ellis' eyes went wide.

"What the hell kind of gun is that?"

"It's not so much a gun as it is a can-opener," Nox said. "I'll be back."

Nox rose to a crouch, but stopped when Ellis grabbed her shoulder.

"Wait a second," Ellis said. He pulled a shiny plastic ID card from his shirt pocket and handed it to the Mechanic.

"You'll need this to get into the bar."

Nox took the card and looked at the picture on it.

"She doesn't look anything like me," Nox said.

"So don't give anyone a chance to look too hard at the picture," Ellis said.

"Wonderful," Nox said. She eyed the complex. "If I'm not back in an hour..."

"I couldn't possibly get that lucky."

It took only seconds for Nox to reach the outer fence. She paused for a moment before the rusted mesh and examined it. From her backpack she produced a pair of black cables connected to two six inch long metal spikes. She pushed the spikes deep into the ground and four feet apart. She then connected the cables to the fence directly in front of the grounded spikes.

Satisfied with her work, Nox produced a small wire cutter from her backpack and cut a small hole in the fence between the two cables. She set the cut line aside and crawled through the hole.

Once on the other side of the fence, Nox again paused. She ran her fingers through the sand before her as she crawled forward, making sure there were no trip wires or buried scanners. Satisfied there were none, Nox made her way deeper and deeper into the compound. Once she crawled over fifty feet from the fence's border, she rose and hurried to the side of the Octi Corp. Cantina. She heard the muffled sounds of people and music coming from within.

Nox wiped the sand from her body and took a moment to consider her options. Infiltrating guarded facilities was one thing, but mingling with the enemy was easily the most dangerous form of industrial espionage. When engaged in such activity, the most important thing to do, wherever you were, was to look like you *belonged*. That meant you had to be calm, collected and, especially, at ease.

Nox exited the shadows at the side of the Cantina and walked to the bar's door. She pushed the door open and let her instincts take over.

The first thing Nox noticed was that the place was sparsely populated. Not the best of scenarios. It was always easier to blend into a crowd.

There were a few survey crewmembers spread about the tables and counter. A grizzled couple danced in the corner while the rest of the clients focused on their beer. Lazy clouds of smoke drifted from several cigarettes, making the air within feel dense and cramped.

Beside the entrance of the bar was a very large female bouncer. Very few men, and almost all females, were shorter or smaller than Nox. Not so with this bouncer. She dwarfed the Mechanic.

"Let's see some I.D., stranger," the bouncer said.

Nox produced the Octi ID card.

"Jennifer Taylor," the bouncer read out loud.

"My friends call me Jen."

The bouncer gave Nox a long look. She noted the short black hair and the blue tattoos over her right eye.

"Someone as ugly as you got friends?"

"A legion," Nox replied. The bouncer's face went blank. Nox grabbed her ID card. "L-e-g-i-o-n. Look it up in a dictionary. You know what a dictionary is, right?"

The bouncer's mouth clamped shut.

"You're real funny," she finally said. The bouncer flexed her muscles and balled her fists.

Nox raised her hands and managed a weak smile.

"Some say I should take the act on the road, see how it goes."

"Don't bother."

"That bad?"

"And getting worse by the second." The bouncer's face turned sour. She no longer wanted to waste time with this potential client. "Tell you what, 'friend', why don't you get your drink and stay the hell out of my way."

"Yes ma'am."

Nox walked away. Sometimes being at ease meant making a pest of yourself.

Nox passed the dancing couple and found a free table toward the rear of the bar. Once she sat down, she motioned to the bartender.

The bartender was a well built, very tanned blonde woman who looked vaguely out of place in these dingy surroundings. She stepped out from behind the bar's counter and walked to Nox's side.

"What can I get you?" she asked. Her voice was clear and strong and incredibly sexy.

"Would you believe a tall glass of water?"

"What else do you ask for in the middle of a fucking desert, city girl?" the bartender replied. There was no maliciousness in her tone of voice, rather a playful humor.

To it, Nox chuckled.

"What's so funny?"

"I was trying to lay low, blend in. I didn't think it was so obvious where I'm coming from."

"Obvious enough. What part of the city you from?"

"West side."

"You work at Octi Plaza?"

"I've been there once or twice."

The lady stared at Nox's sleek black hairdo, muscular build, and tattoo.

"The place is run by a bunch of stuffed shirts. You must have made quite an impression on those boys."

"I'm sure I did."

"So what do you do for Octi?"

"Freelance stuff."

The smile on Natalie's face faded a degree or two.

"You're an Independent?"

"A Mechanic. The name's Nox."

"Mechanic, Independent, what's the difference?"

"I'm not a mercenary."

"Whatever," the bartender said. She extended her hand. "I'm Natalie. Nice to meet you and all that other happy horseshit. If you don't mind my asking, what the hell are you doing way out here?"

"Checking up on some workers. A survey crew had an accident and I was hired to verify the details. Insurance claims, that sort of stuff. The last thing a healthy company needs is a liability lawsuit."

"And I thought Independents were hired to kill people."

"As I said, I'm not an Independent," Nox said and smiled. Her smile was as cold as the tone in her voice.

Natalie let out a laugh.

"Either you're telling the truth or you're so full of shit you're about to pop. From where I'm standing, you look like you're about to pop. What crew are you investigating?"

Nox leaned forward in her chair. She motioned Natalie closer and whispered:

"Group 4."

The casual expression on Natalie's face dramatically changed. Her smile disappeared and was replaced with the look of fear.

"Who are you working for?"

Though her voice was low, Nox's muscles contracted. She eyed the bouncer, who, until that moment, was oblivious to them. The bouncer noted Natalie's tense reaction and a look of concern crossed her face. She rose from her chair beside the bar's entrance and took a few steps toward the duo.

Natalie stared deep into Nox's sunglasses for a moment before facing the bouncer. By then she regained her composure and casually waved the woman off. When her eyes returned to Nox, she was once again dead serious.

"You better talk quick, lady. Who are you working for?"

"Myself," Nox said. "I'm with your father."

Natalie's head snapped back. She pulled off her apron and returned to the bar's counter. Nox rose from her chair and followed. Natalie laid the apron down and caught the bouncer's eye.

"I'm taking a break," she said. "Ten minutes."

The bouncer nodded. Natalie and Nox stepped up to an almost hidden door by the bar's counter and entered a small storage room. The place was cramped and filled with an array of stacked boxes. Most were labeled *Selabro*, though Nox spotted a lone case of *Prestigio* buried in the mass.

Natalie switched the light on and closed and locked the door leading out.

"Start talking."

"You need to tell me everything you know about that survey group," Nox said.

Natalie stifled a laugh.

"Oh, really? What else can I do for you? Get you some cash? How about merchandise? If you want, I could open the warehouse doors and disarm the security."

"Do whatever you like, as long as you tell me what happened to group 4."

"The information you want is confidential. You know every Octi Corp. employee's signs a non-disclosure form. To violate the contract means termination of employment and immediate prosecution. Why the fuck should I risk my neck for you?"

Nox showed Natalie the ID card Ellis gave her.

"I wasn't lying about coming with your father. You are familiar with his handiwork, I hope."

Natalie eyed the card and shrugged.

"It means nothing. For all I know, you stole it."

"Your father isn't the type that lets anyone steal from him."

"Maybe you're not anyone."

"He's outside the fence. If you'd like, we can take a short stroll and have ourselves a family reunion."

Natalie let out a deep sigh and leaned against one of the boxes.

"I don't think so. Dad and I haven't exactly been close."

"He didn't tell me that."

"Nor would he. What have you gotten him into?"

"Nothing," Nox said. "All he's doing is showing me around."

"Sure," Natalie said. "He's always messing with you city folk. A lot of good it's done him."

"He's a grown man. If he didn't want to help me, he would have turned me away."

"He could have. Only he likes the excitement. The Gods alone know why."

"If it makes you feel any better, he trusts me. He and I go back a very long ways."

"What are you, my long lost step mother or something? Define 'a long time'."

"Since the Arabian wars."

Upon hearing those words, Natalie's face turned white and her hands came up to her mouth.

"You're—" she said and stopped.

Nox nodded and allowed Natalie time to compose herself. When she did, Natalie re-examined the woman standing before her. It was as if she saw her for the very first time.

"No wonder your name sounded familiar," Natalie said. She pulled out a pack of cigarettes and offered Nox one. The Mechanic shook her head. "The way Dad described you, you were something like nine feet ten and breathed fire. You're much shorter than I thought."

"I try to give people a good first impression."

"He told me you hated the desert."

"Only with a passion."

Natalie drew on her cigarette. Wisps of smoke disappeared into the shadows of the ceiling.

"All right Nox, this is what I know: Octi Survey 4 was manned by a loose nit bunch of temps. Sometimes they'd work together but most times they were spread out, depending on where their work was. In February most of that group rode Tower Co. vehicles, bringing supplies from one outpost to another. In March they shuffled heavy machinery for Galaxy Inc."

"I'm only interested in what they did for Octi Corp."

"They were tasked to investigate pre-sorted sectors. Typical pitch and scan: Set up camp and shift through the sands. I'm sure you've heard there's plenty of treasure buried out here. When the cities out here were swallowed by the sand storms, the citizens fled real quickly. They left behind plenty of loot for those willing to get their hands dirty digging it out. Computers, machinery, you name it. Octi Corp.'s interest was old but still worthwhile technology. And they were always on the lookout for research stations. They've made a damn good penny retrofitting old technology."

"What did the survey group find?"

"That's the million credit question. Nobody here has any idea what they stumbled upon. The group breezed by a couple of months ago and bought enough supplies for a very long stay on the road. Then, shortly after that, most of the group comes back on motorcycles hauling a broken down water purifier for the garage boys to fix. The survey van folks hang around the bar while their equipment was repaired. I talked to a couple of them and they tell me that, other than the wrecked purifier and the fact that they hadn't found anything worth a damn, everything was going fine. A little later, the garage boys finish with the purifier and the survey crew load up and head out. Not too long after that, the entire group falls off the grid. We tried to communicate with them, but couldn't. Octi Corp. sent out a search and rescue detail." Natalie paused. Her jaw tensed. "A few days later we get word they were found. All of them were dead."

"You see the bodies?"

"Nobody here saw the bodies. They were flown directly to Red Sands, Octi Corp.'s largest base, some two hundred or so miles to the north. From what I understand, the corpses were sealed in lead lined caskets. Only later we heard they stumbled upon an old nuclear facility and were exposed to massive doses of radiation."

Nox removed the Desertland map from her backpack and spread it over one of the boxes of *Selabro*.

"Where exactly did they say they were found?"

Natalie took a few seconds to orient herself on the map. She ran her finger across the grid lines until finding what she was looking for. She tapped down.

"The remains of the Coax Nuclear Reservoir," Natalie said.

Nox pointed to another spot on the map.

"But this was their last reported location, right?"

Natalie stared at the spot Nox pointed to. She suppressed a shiver and nodded.

"Yeah. That's about where they were when the purification system crapped out."

"And a couple of hundred miles away from where they were found."

"Yeah," she repeated.

"So everything is normal. The survey crew calls in when they're supposed to and their position trackers are green. Suddenly, they go silent. Maybe they didn't realize their radio equipment failed and maybe they had no reason to call in. But it would take a few days to make the trek from here to here. At some point they *must* have realized their radio equipment was malfunctioning. Would they continue their survey work through potentially dangerous areas without a working radio?"

"No more than they would with a bad water purifier."

"Thought so. Here's where it gets even more interesting." Nox pointed to a third spot on the map. "This is where I found the survey van. Only twenty miles from their *last* verified location."

"How?"

"They carried a second position tracker and that one *was* working. When I found the van and checked her out, there was no trace of radiation on it. And with the exception of a refrigerator filled with rotted food, its interior was stripped clean."

"By the Gods."

"There's one other thing I found."

"What?"

"A single bullet lodged in the van's back door."

Natalie covered her eyes and leaned back.

"Pirates? Desert rats?"

"No," Nox replied. "Though I'm guessing the van was left behind either for them or the sands to dispose of."

"By who?"

"Who do you think?"

Though she tried to keep calm, Natalie couldn't. A single tear ran down her cheek.

"We knew something bad happened out there," she said. "Octi Corp.'s stories never made total sense, but what could we do? It's hard enough making a living out here without badmouthing your outfit. Out here, we're family. The only family we've got."

Natalie's face wrinkled up with emotion. There was despair and hopelessness in her face and Nox knew both only too well. The individual worker meant nothing to the corporation while the corporation, and the jobs it provided, meant everything to the individual worker. She let out a sob and turned away from the Mechanic. In time, the tears dried.

"I'm making a damn fool of myself."

"It'll be our secret. Why do you think they were killed?"

"I don't know. I wish I did."

"Help me," Nox said. "Help me get them for what they did."

"What can I...?" Natalie said and stopped. She dropped the spent cigarette to the floor and crushed it under the heel of her boot. "You hurt them, you hurt me."

Nox said nothing. She folded the map and put it away. Though she tried to hide her disappointment, it was difficult.

The corporation meant everything to the individual worker.

"Thanks anyway," Nox said. She walked past Natalie and to the door.

"Nox, wait." Natalie said. "Can you get them without hurting us?"

"I can try," Nox said. "It's all I can promise."

Natalie thought about that for a few seconds.

"Robert Octi Jr. flew in yesterday," she said.

"To the Desertlands?"

"No. Here. To *this* base."

"Here? Why not go to Red Sands?"

"I don't know."

"Where is he?"

"He's been making the rounds. He's usually holed up in the warehouse."

Nox reached for the door knob.

"Don't go there," Natalie said. "Since he came, the warehouse is the only part of the base they've kept well-guarded. At least on the inside."

"Leave that to me."

"Cut the tough guy act. There are easier ways of getting to him."

Nox released the door's handle.

"Such as?"

"He also spends plenty of time upstairs, in the far less guarded office."

18

Nox exited the bar and paused as its door slowly shut behind her. When it was fully closed, she turned to her right and walked to the stairs leading to the office above. She ignored the growing chill in the air and kept to the shadows as best she could, climbing the stairs two at a time while maintaining a cat-like silence.

When Nox reached the top platform, she again paused. She crouched low and examined the area. The top level of the building was a small porch that overlooked the south side of the base. There was a single door a few feet from the top of the stairs and a pair of windows at either side. The office was dark.

Satisfied no one spotted her, Nox eased close to the office door. She listened for any sounds coming from within. None came.

Nox examined the door's flimsy lock and smiled.

"Child's play."

Nox entered the office and closed the door behind her. After the door was shut, Nox froze in place. All around her was an impenetrable black. For several long seconds she remained perfectly still. There were no alarms or voices to be heard.

Nox reached into her shirt pocket and pulled out a small flashlight. She clicked it on and ran the light across the length of the room.

The office was sparse, furnished with an old metal desk and three rickety chairs. On opposite walls were several cork boards. Various papers and receipts were pinned to these boards. The papers were yellow and brittle with age while the receipts were likewise faded. Nox scanned them, verifying they were worthless, before approaching the desk.

None of the drawers had locks. Nox frowned and shook her head. The lack of any security meant it was unlikely there was anything worthwhile stored within. Nox searched through each of the drawers anyway. She found more yellowed sheets of paper, lists of inventories from the previous seasons, a half-empty bottle of whiskey, and, in the last drawer, a pile of old magazines.

Nox examined the topless women on the covers of these magazines.

"Collector's editions," she said before replacing them.

Nox turned back to the door leading out.

What a waste of time, she thought. Just as she was about to grab the door knob, she again froze.

The sound of voices came from just outside. Without any hesitation, Nox wheeled around and looked the office over.

"Shit," Nox muttered.

There was nowhere to hide.

The door to the office opened and Robert Octi Jr. and Nagel entered. Robert carried a folder overstuffed with documents.

"Dark in here," he muttered.

Nagel fumbled around the side of the door before finding the light switch. With a loud click the lights came on, revealing the entire office and its meager contents. Robert considered the cramped and dusty place and noted the open window on the west side of the room.

"This is some place," he said as he walked to the open window and suppressed a shiver. "During the day it's hot as shit. At night it's way too fucking cold."

Robert slid the window shut. He didn't notice the shadowy figure crouched just outside of the window and below its frame.

Robert walked back to the desk and sat down. He leafed through the documents he was carrying before closing and laying them on the desk.

"Nothing," he muttered. "Another day's waste of time and money."

Nagel offered no reply. He quietly sat across from Robert.

"I figured once we found it we'd find..." Robert began and stopped. He shook his head and reached into one of the desk drawers. He pulled out the bottle of whiskey and a pair of cups. He filled them both and let out an angry laugh. "It's always something, Nagel. Just when you think you've solved all your problems, a bunch of new ones pop up to make sure you're never completely out of the woods. The old man always warned me life was a series of obstacles with little bits of joy sprinkled between them."

Outside the closed window, Nox inched up. She had a clear view of Robert and his silent bodyguard.

Robert took down the shot of whiskey and slapped the cup on the desk. He noticed the other cup and pushed it toward Nagel. Nagel didn't move.

"Drink up," Robert said. "That's an order."

Nagel grabbed the cup and cradled it. Robert smiled. He stared at the office ceiling, as if seeking guidance from above. He then reached into his jacket and pulled out the worn diary the lost survey crew found among the skeletal remains. He opened it and scanned several pages.

"How tantalizing you are," Robert said. He closed the book and dropped it on the desk and on top of the folder. "If only you could talk."

Outside, Nox eyed the diary with great interest.

Robert closed and rubbed his eyes. His face, Nox noted, was pale with exhaustion. The young executive poured himself another shot of whiskey. He took this drink down slowly before pouring a third. He eyed his bodyguard.

"Another?"

Nagel shook his head. The cup in his hand was still full.

"You never were much of a drinker," Robert said. He sealed the bottle of whiskey and returned it to its drawer. He then picked up his shot glass and gulped down his last drink in one swallow. Robert laid the empty cup down and leaned back in his chair. He hummed a few bars of off-key chamber music. His eyes closed and, soon after, the humming stopped and Robert's breathing turned heavy. Nagel remained in his chair, watching. After a while, he placed his shot glass on the desk. Though he made no sound, the movements awoke Robert. The young executive's eyes were red with exhaustion.

"Oh," he said. He ran his fingers through his hair and stretched. After a long yawn, he managed a weak smile. "It's late. Let's get the hell out of here."

Robert and Nagel rose in unison and stepped to the door leading out the office. Nox watched intently as they left. Her eyes returned to the worn diary and the folder of documents still lying on the desk. With a flicker, the lights of the office turned off, leaving the place completely dark.

Nox smiled. She reached for the window and slid it open just as...

The office lights came back on.

Nox dropped away from the window as Robert re-entered the office. The young executive headed straight for the desk and, while muttering some unintelligible words, retrieved the diary and the folder of documents. When he turned to leave the office he noticed the now open window.

"What the hell?" Robert said. "Nagel?"

Nagel entered the office. Robert pointed to the window.

"I closed it when we first arrived. Did you open it again?"

Nagel's hand slid into his jacket. When it emerged, it held a sleek black handgun. He motioned for Robert to keep back. Nagel inched forward, until he stood next to the open window. He looked out, but found no one on the ledge below. He turned to Robert and shook his head.

"Whoever it was, he's still here, somewhere," Robert said. The young executive pressed one of the buttons on his wristwatch and spoke into it.

"This is Robert Octi Junior. We had an intruder at the office. Initiate security measures."

Nagel faced his boss and frowned.

"Oh, right," Robert said, realization dawning on him. "Well, the alert's up. It's too late to stop it now. We'll just stay right here and hope that tin can doesn't blow the whole fucking place up."

Nox slid among the shadows between the warehouse and the bar. Her eyes gazed forward, taking in the surroundings and expecting security guards to appear from anywhere.

None did.

She heard Robert and Nagel reenter the office. She knew they were aware of her presence. She knew they must have raised the alarm by now.

So where was everyone?

Nox ran to the end of the warehouse. Beyond it lay over a hundred feet of sand surrounded by wire fence. Just beyond that, freedom.

Nox stiffened until she became a statue. Everything was too damn still. She considered making a run for the fence but felt a growing tension in the air. Once again she wondered: Where was everyone?

As if to answer her unasked question, Nox heard the sounds of internal combustion machinery coming to life. She pressed her body against the edge of the warehouse wall.

The engine sounds grew as the machine approached. She heard other mechanisms within it whirl to life. And then, abruptly, everything went silent. It was as if the machine shut itself off. Nox knew better. The robot was running in stealth mode.

A shadow appeared beyond the south edge of the base. It grew in size as it moved from south to west. Nox could just make it out. Tall, cylindrical. In the moonlight she spotted the glare of metal.

And then it moved into one of the mercury spotlights that circled the base.

"Hello again," Nox muttered. Before her was Donovan's security robot.

It was the exact same model she encountered twice before. It had the same burn marks on its rear paneling and the same Gatling guns which burned her hands.

But on this sandy surface, its movements were far from smooth. It trembled and shimmied and started and stopped. For a second its treads got caught in the soft sand. The stealth engines whined until they were once again audible. The robot very nearly tipped over while freeing itself.

Once free, it moved forward, circling the compound and searching for its prey. It approached the corner of the warehouse and the area Nox was hiding in. It didn't notice a small garbage can and bumped into it.

The Gatling guns came to life and aimed at the can. Internal mechanisms worked furiously to determine whether the impediment before it was friend or foe.

Nox shook her head.

Technology.

She reached into her backpack and produced her very large handgun.

It was hard not to savor the moment.

19

Ellis lay on his stomach in the sand and fought off his growing boredom as best he could. He gently ran a finger along the sand and created a series of patterns. A distant memory, like a match struck in the pits of a coal mine, flared up. The last time he worked on a rock garden, he was trapped in the barracks of Fort Pigeon.

Considering what some of the other soldiers did in their spare time back then, his rock garden hobby was downright saintly. In the end, however, it offered little comfort, and the temptations to avoid the gruesome reality of war proved too great.

Ellis pushed a pebble in place. The pattern was pleasing to his eyes. Now, some twenty years later, he felt a calm he was unable to fully experience back then wash over him. He smiled. Change is inevitable, and though he was no longer a young man, he could achieve that elusive inner peace. He could—

A fierce explosion ripped through the quiet of night and lit up the Octi base.

The pebble so gently put in place rolled away and obliterated the sand patterns around it.

"What the hell?" Ellis yelled. He grabbed his binoculars and stared at the heart of the base.

He spotted a small group of security officials and Octi personnel run from the bar and warehouse. They circled a bizarre looking metal cylinder with black treads for feet and a pair of Gatling guns for arms. It lay on its side on the sandy surface. An enormous hole in the center of the thing bellowed flames and thick black smoke.

The view of the destroyed robot was momentarily blurred by an approaching figure. Ellis lowered the binoculars. Nox was thirty feet away and approaching fast.

"Was that you?" Ellis asked.

Nox jumped down beside Ellis. She had a large grin on her face.

"Why the hell did you do that?"

"Because I could. And because I really, *really* wanted to."

"What?"

"Relax. I just did everyone in that base a huge favor. If I hadn't blown that piece of shit up, there's no telling how many of them it would have killed."

"Come again?"

"I've had a couple of run-ins with that machine before. Octi Corp. sent it out here, to the middle of nowhere, because they knew the damn thing's defective. It can't tell the good guys from the bad, so when it senses danger it splits the difference and takes out *everyone* in its path."

"Everyone?"

"Yeah. Even your daughter. The only way Octi's getting their money's worth off that thing is if they remove its weapons and shave off every one of its sharp edges. They could use it as a paperweight or maybe box it up with every kid's unhappy meal."

Ellis sighed.

"Did you find anything?"

"Yes and no. Robert Octi Jr.'s here. He wouldn't leave the comfort of the Big City unless there was something big going on here."

"In that respect, he's a lot like you."

Nox glared at Ellis.

"Just a joke," Ellis said. He considered Nox's words for a few seconds. "Your theory about that survey van is looking good. First Octi Corp. silences them, and now the company's second in charge is personally nosing around. There's definitely something going on. What's the plan?"

"Whatever Robert's doing, I doubt it involves this particular base. Sooner or later he'll come out, and when he does, we follow."

"That's your whole plan?"

"It's a work in progress," Nox said. She rolled onto her back and eased her hands behind her head. Far above them, a half-moon bathed the blood red sands in a soft white glow.

The rising sun obliterated the night. In the base, warehouse doors opened with a loud groan. The sound awoke Nox. She stirred for a moment before retrieving her sunglasses and putting them on. Ellis, lying beside her, stirred as well.

They were both wide awake when a sleek blue helicopter was rolled out of the warehouse and towed some fifty feet from the warehouse doors. Nox stared hard through her binoculars, examining everyone involved in this early morning action. She spotted two people emerge from the warehouse and walk to the vehicle.

"It's Robert Octi Junior and his bodyguard," Nox said.

The two entered the helicopter while those that remained on the landing pad stepped back. After a few moments, the helicopter's blades began a slow spin. With time, they gained speed until the sand below the chopper was whipped into angry swirls. The helicopter took off and headed east, as if on a collision course with the rising sun.

"Damn," Nox muttered.

She hurriedly rose and rolled up her sleeping bag. Ellis did the same.

"We can't follow them," Ellis said. "They're too fast. Shit, even if they didn't see us their scanners would pick us up."

"What's the range of their scanners?"

"I don't know. It depends on the equipment they're using."

"You said the Tower Co. trucks could spot a pursuer at five miles."

"Yeah."

"Let's assume the helicopter uses similar scanning equipment. Unlike the trucks, we can follow a flying object from a far greater distance." Nox handed Ellis her binoculars. "You'll be my eyes. Guide me."

"That's some plan."

"Better than what I had last night."

The two mounted Nox's chopper. Ellis zeroed in on the helicopter's position.

"Let's go," he said.

Nox kicked the chopper's ignition, but nothing happened. She frowned and swore.

"They're getting away," Ellis said. "You might want to hurry."

Nox swore again. It took five tries before she had her chopper going.

They tore through the soft desert sands at reckless speeds. Ellis, seated behind Nox, kept his eyes on the Octi Corp. helicopter. At times he almost lost sight of it, but it was the only foreign object in an otherwise clear blue sky.

Nagel piloted the helicopter. Though his eyes seldom strayed from the view outside, he spent more and more time staring at the scanner beside the directional radar. After a while, a faint blip appeared at the corner of the scanner. It faded away, only to reappear again a few minutes later. Nagel pointed to the blip.

"Yes Nagel," Robert Octi Jr. said. He was in the passenger seat next to his bodyguard. "I noticed it, too. Do you think someone's following us?"

Nagel looked directly into Robert's eyes. He offered a cold smile. Robert laughed.

"Of course they are. Probably the same person that put Donovan's piece of shit robot out of its misery. Hmmm...I wonder if they're Tower Co. spies."

Nagel said nothing.

"Whoever they are, they made a big mistake," Robert said. He picked up the radio receiver. "This is Octi One. Please respond Octi Base 32."

Static filled the receiver for a few seconds before clearing.

"This is Octi Base 32. Come in Octi One."

"We're five miles from Mesa 12, heading north," Robert said. "We've got an unidentified ground vehicle following us. Our direction is 45 by 38. We request someone discourage the vehicle's driver from continuing his activity. Do you copy?"

"We copy. One of our trucks is in your area. ETA for interception is fifteen minutes."

"Excellent. Octi One out."

Robert put the receiver back in its place.

"Whoever it is —*was*— won't be bothering us much longer."

Nox's chopper kicked up clouds of dust as it roared past the uneven dunes. A desert road intersected their path and Nox turned on to it, thankful for a smoother way. Ellis cleaned the dust from the binoculars. When he was done, he put them back over his eyes. His jaw tightened. He lowered the binoculars and tapped Nox on her shoulder.

"I don't like this," he yelled above the choppers' engine. "The helicopter's slowing down."

"So?"

"They haven't changed altitude or direction, only speed. It's like they *want* us to follow."

"They know we're here?"

"That's my guess."

Nox stared out at the horizon. They were currently riding flat desert land but, in the distance, she spotted a group of three mesas. Almost directly over them, some five hundred or so feet in the air was the Octi Corp. helicopter. Until now, Nox needed Ellis and his powerful binoculars to tell her where they were.

Until now.

"Where are we?" Nox asked.

"Route twenty one," Ellis replied. "Some of the supply trucks use it now and again."

Nox considered this.

"Which means other Octi vehicles could be in the area."

"Yeah," Ellis said. "We should stop. Turn arou—"

The loud crack of a rifle shot interrupted Ellis' words.

Nox's chopper veered wildly to the side and Ellis was the first to fall off. He hit the ground hard and rolled around like a rag doll. Nox tried to keep the chopper up, but another bullet crashed into her vehicle's gas tank and sent a spray of volatile liquid all over the Mechanic. Nox released the handlebars and fell.

For her, the entire desert world turned upside down.

20

Nox tucked her body tight when she hit the ground. The sand was burning hot and scrapped the flesh from her elbows and ripped her pants.

While the world spun around her, another bullet whizzed past and shattered a rock. Nox could do nothing about it. The next shot could well be the last.

But luck was on Nox's side. She felt her body rise into the air and float for a second before crashing between the narrow walls of a small ditch. It lay beside the desert road and hid Nox's body from the sniper. The shooter was clearly furious that his target was no longer visible and fired a barrage of bullets into the ditch's opening. None ricocheted within.

Nox felt blood drip down the side of her face. She opened and closed her eyes and tried to get her bearings but was too dazed. Instead, she remained flat on her back, staring up at the blue sky. The gunfire eventually stopped. So too did the spinning in Nox's head.

Nox checked her body and found all bones were intact. Her only serious injuries were a deep cut on her forehead and a bad scrape on her right knee. Neither was life threatening. Nox next examined her surroundings. The bullets came from the west, from the direction of the mesas. The ditch was higher on the west side, so she was able to look up and over and at the road she was on.

The first thing she saw was Ellis lying beside a large boulder. The elderly man was unconscious and blood spilled from an ugly gash on his head. Had Ellis fallen a second later, he would have rolled into the boulder and smashed himself to pieces. Had he fallen a second before, he would have rolled to a stop in plain sight of the sniper. As it was, the boulder's mass provided a perfect shield.

Between Ellis and Nox was the chopper. Its frame was bent and its handlebars twisted from the crash.

"Damn," Nox muttered.

She checked her belt. Other than a small pocket knife, she was defenseless. The Mechanic let out a laugh.

"Would you be so kind as to come in a little closer," Nox told the hidden sniper. "You do and I'll give you a hell of a cut."

Nox again stared out of the ditch. Beside Nox's chopper lay her back pack and, next to that, her water canteen. It made for a beautiful lure.

"You didn't get us, but you must be smiling," Nox said.

She eased up a little and cautiously stared off into the distance. She spotted the three mesas to the west and replayed the events of the last few minutes in her mind. She tried to determine exactly where the shots came from. After a while, she gave up. The sniper was most certainly in one of the mesas but it was impossible to tell which.

And that was assuming there was only *one* sniper.

Nox thought about this for a few seconds but discarded the idea that there were more. The fact that both Ellis and she were still alive not only proved they were dealing with a single shooter but also that the person's skills with a rifle were, at best, mediocre.

The ambush was hastily drawn. Robert Octi Junior spotted Nox's tail and called in the nearest personnel. Though he failed to kill his targets, the sniper had pinned them down. It wouldn't be long before reinforcements arrived to finish the job.

Nox turned away. Her eyes once again settled on the canteen and backpack.

If Ellis and she had any chance, any chance at all of surviving...

Nox's body tensed. She had one chance, all right. Could she...?

This is fucking crazy, Nox thought.

Yeah, so what else are you going to do?

Nox let out a breath and closed her eyes. She suppressed a shiver. *There's nothing else you can do. It's all or nothing.*

"All or nothing," Nox whispered.

Here we go.

With all her remaining strength, Nox leaped out of the ditch and ran for the canteen.

She ran as fast as she could, zigzagging along the way.

The canteen lay thirty feet away, then fifteen...

She took a breath. She would make it.

Ten feet, then five.

The canteen was within reach. She just had to lean down, pluck it off the ground...

Nox abruptly changed directions. Just as she did, the roar of sniper fire echoed through the air and the canteen erupted. A second bullet hit the ground directly beside it and in the exact spot where Nox would have been had she actually reached for the canteen.

Instead, Nox's change in direction brought her to the backpack. In one smooth, fluid motion the Mechanic reached down and grabbed it just as a third bullet tore into the ground a few feet away. The sniper was tricked into thinking Nox was going for the water and wasted every one of his shots.

Nox zigzagged back to the ditch and hurled herself into it. One last bullet sought, but failed, to find its mark.

Nox hit the ditch walls hard. Darkness crept up on her and she let out a groan. After a few minutes, the pain faded. Nox wiped the sweat from her forehead.

I was right, she thought. *You are a piss poor shooter.*

Nox took her handgun out of the backpack and also removed a small black container. Within it was a barrel extension, a grip extension, and a small targeting sight. Nox screwed each piece into place on the handgun until it resembled a miniature rifle.

"Show yourself again," Nox muttered to the unseen sniper. She stared down the sight and adjusted it until she was satisfied. "Just one peek."

But Nox still had no idea which mesa the sniper occupied. It was likely, too, that he changed his position. Especially after his target got hold of a backpack containing who knows what within it. Still, the sniper had little to worry about. Nox and Ellis were locked down and the cavalry was that much closer to arriving.

Nox shook her head.

Despite the effort and risk, despite the comfort of carrying a weapon, Ellis and she were still hopelessly trapped.

The sun beat down relentlessly on Nox's hiding place. She felt the ferocious rays sap her strength but there wasn't a damn thing she could do about it. She thought about the Big City and she thought about all those shitty bars she hung out in.

At least they were air conditioned.

Nox smiled. At least there was that.

Nox's thoughts turned to the distant past. She remembered the heat of the Arabian deserts and just how much she despised the place. She swore she'd never again venture into the sands yet here she was. These sands just wouldn't let her go.

Nox's thoughts were interrupted by a loud groan. Ellis was stirring.

"...son... of a... bitch," Ellis moaned.

"Stay where you are!" Nox yelled.

Ellis rubbed his head and got to his knees. He noted the boulder lying in front of him and leaned against it. He let out a laugh.

"Sniper?"

"Yeah."

"Now I know how the desert rats felt," Ellis said. He coughed. "Fucking karma."

"Karma?"

"Heh. Something the stoners back in the military talked about. Spiritual crap. You know, the type of shit you don't believe in."

"Thank god I'm an atheist."

Ellis laughed.

"You... you got your gun?"

"Yeah."

Ellis continued rubbing his head.

"Back in the Arabian Wars, we had this bad-ass sergeant who told us *exactly* what to do when dealing with snipers."

"What did he say?"

"Call in a missile strike, flatten the whole town the sniper's in," Ellis said. He chuckled. "You wouldn't happen to have any missiles stored away in your back pack, would you?"

"Afraid not."

"Didn't think so. Anyway, he also trained us on how to deal with sexually transmitted diseases. You haven't lived until a seventy year old man tells you where *not* to stick your tongue."

"That's one class I'm glad I skipped."

Ellis was quiet for a few seconds.

"The sergeant said that if we were pinned down by a sniper and couldn't call in outside help, there was only one way left to flush the bastard out. You had to do it personally. Nox, *I* have to draw him out."

Alarm filled the Mechanic's face.

"Stay where you are!" she barked. "The sniper's green. He'll show himself."

Ellis let out a sigh.

"You know the sniper's got back-up on its way. As it is, we might be too late."

"You're a better shot, Ellis. I'll throw you the gun. I'll be the target."

"That's mighty noble of you, but I wouldn't trust me with any sort of long range shot right now. That fall did quite a number on me and I'm not seeing so well. Anyway, if you throw me the gun, it could get damaged. We're fucked as it is and we'd be truly fucked if the gun's barrel got bent."

Nox was silent.

"Besides, why let him know we're armed? At least we've got the element of surprise."

Nox remained silent. Ellis frowned.

"We haven't got all day, Nox. Are you ready to take the shot?"

"All right," Nox finally said. "*Fuck.*"

"I know the feeling."

"Look, I wasn't kidding. The shooter's skills are shit. If you move quickly enough, you can get through this."

"I can't move quick, Nox. I can barely move at all. That's why I'll make a good decoy. You just take your shot."

Nox thought hard.

"Look," she finally said. "Forget it. We don't know if *any* backup is coming. The sun'll set in a few more hours and we can—"

"No, Nox. The cavalry's coming, but it's coming for the other side. Are you ready to get him?"

Nox stared at the mesas. She drew her handgun and rested its stock on her shoulder. She stared through the telescopic sight.

"I'm...I'm ready."

The smile returned to Ellis' face.

"When you see my daughter, tell her... tell her..."

"Tell her yourself."

"I've done plenty of things to be ashamed of, Nox. Almost all of them happened during the war. But I never had any regrets about her. Nor about you."

Nox bit her upper lip so hard she drew blood.

"I'm glad we got to know each other. I'm glad you survived. Maybe one day, you can tell everyone who you are and what you did, as well as what they did to you."

"Why would anyone care?"

"The world needs to know.   It's...it's like we've been sleepwalking all this time, happy to hide in our comfortable homes and let others run our lives.   The ones in power get richer and more powerful while we're squeaking by and hoping for better days. Those days aren't coming."

Ellis rose to his feet.

"I'm babbling, Nox," Ellis said and let out a chuckle. "The fall must have done me more harm than I thought." He was silent for a few seconds. "Send every one of those bastards to hell."

Ellis stepped away from the boulder and was in plain view of the mesas.

21

Nox immediately spotted the puff of smoke. It came from the mesa on the far left. Nearly a full second later she heard the roar of the gunshot. By then, Nox was firing her own weapon, over and over and *over* again. She sent an entire clip of bullets at the exposed attacker.

Afterwards, she paused and waited. There was no return fire. The sniper managed only that one shot.

Nox laid the handgun down. It took a great deal of effort for her to turn and look at Ellis for Nox knew what she'd see.

The elderly man lay on the ground next to the boulder. Blood flowed freely from a stomach wound.

Nox rose to her feet and fully exposed herself. There was no more point in hiding. Either she eliminated the sniper or not. If she didn't, there was no use in delaying her fate. The sun beat down on Nox and a second, then two, passed. No more shots were fired her way.

Nox peered at the mesa.

Got you, you son of a bitch.

The Mechanic climbed out of the ditch and ran to Ellis' side. The old man was still alive, though his eyes were sunken in their sockets and his breathing was shallow. Nox cradled her old friend.

"You dumb bastard."

"D-did you get him?" Ellis muttered.

"Yeah."

The windshield of the Octi Corp. van parked on the top of the mesa was shattered to pieces. Lying in front of it and still cradling a sniper's rifle was a man in his late twenties. His shoulder and forehead were colored bright red. His left eye was shot out. The kill shot.

Beside him lay his spotter. The man looked away from the horror that lay there, but his breathing remained heavy and he couldn't stop shaking. It took several tense minutes for him to crawl away from his original spot and get behind the van. Once there, he opened the vehicle's back door and entered.

Within the van was a small bathroom. The spotter hurried inside and stared at his reflection in the mirror. His partner's blood was splattered on his face and hands.

"Fuck me," he mumbled.

The sniper's spotter cleaned the mess and exited the bathroom. He then cautiously walked to the front of the van and, while keeping all body parts away from the shattered window, reached for the radio receiver.

"This is Octi 45," he said into the microphone. "I have a man down."

There was a pause followed by a burst of static.

"Acknowledged, Octi 45," came his response. "What about your target?"

The spotter leaned forward enough to see past the remains of the windshield. His partner remained in place and somewhere far below was his killer. The spotter's jaw tightened. He again moved away from the window.

"John took one of them out before the other... the other took *him* out."

"Are all targets down?"

The spotter suppressed a shiver.

"Yes," he lied. "They're all dead."

"Backup is on its way. Eta—"

"It won't be necessary."

There was a pause.

"Please confirm, Octi 45. You no longer require backup?"

The suppressed shiver burst through and passed the spotter's body. He felt like he was going to faint. *My partner's dead and I've really stuck my foot in it now.*

"No. I don't need any backup."

Our targets have no means of transportation and no water, the spotter thought. *They might not be dead –yet– but they were as good as dead. Let the sands take care of whoever's left alive. For now.*

"I repeat, I don't need backup. I'm coming in."

"Hide the bodies," the voice on the radio said. "That includes your partner's. None of this happened. Understood?"

Only too well.

"Yes sir. Over and out."

The spotter shut off the radio. He shook his head and slid into the driver's seat.

The buzzards can take care of all the bodies, he thought.

No way in hell he'd stick around.

No way in hell.

On the road below, Nox and Ellis heard the distant sound of the Octi van starting up.

"They're leaving?" Ellis asked.

"Guess so."

"Fucking cowards. We gave them more of a fight than they could take."

Ellis let out a bloody cough.

"What kind of men sends kids into a war?" he muttered.

Nox held Ellis close.   Ellis' words were slurred and increasingly confused.

"Follow them. Get them..."

"I can't leave you here," Nox said.

"It's your only chance."

Nox lowered her head.

Despite his weakened state, Ellis was right. Nox *had* to follow the Octi van. It would head to a nearby base or, if Nox was lucky, it might even be on its way to wherever Robert Octi Jr. was going.

But to leave now meant...

"You'll die."

Ellis stared at Nox. His eyes were distant, unfocused.

"Forget...forget about me."

The old man's final breath drifted out of his mouth and dissipated into the desert air. The tension in his face was gone. His lips curled into something resembling a smile.

Nox gently propped the body against the rock that shielded Ellis only moments before. In the distance, she saw the faint trace of dust kicked up by the Octi Corp. van on the mesa. They were moving away.

Nox walked to her chopper. She hoped the damage she saw wasn't quite that bad.

It was.

The chopper's handlebars and frame were badly warped. The gas tank was pierced and all the fuel had drained into the sand.

Nox reached for the pouch hanging at the chopper's side. She removed the shovel she had previously used to uncover the Octi Corp. survey van. She then walked back to Ellis' side.

Nox stared at the freshly dug grave. It was the best the Mechanic could do for her old friend. When this affair was done, Nox swore, she would return and give Ellis a proper burial. One befitting a veteran.

"There are few words I can offer," Nox said. She slung the backpack over her shoulder. "You lived your life the way you wanted and you were a good soul. What else is there to say?"

Nox smiled at that thought.

"Everyone should be that lucky."

Nox then walked down the road. When she was far past the sniper's mesa, she spotted the Octi Corp. van's tracks. Nox leaned down and memorized the tread. She then stood and stared through her binoculars and into the distance.

She spotted a tiny puff of dust far off to the east. Nox put the binoculars in her backpack and continued her long walk.

It would be tough, but not impossible, to follow the sniper's van.

It took only a few more minutes before she could no longer see any sign of the van through her binoculars. But by then, Nox knew the van was moving off the main dirt road and maintaining an easterly course. The tracks proved easier to follow at that point, though she feared the evening winds might obliterate the path.

Nox moved on, a solitary black figure almost invisible against the stark rusty red sands.

Her movements slowed with the passage of time and as the oppressive heat inevitably sapped her of strength.

Much later, the sky grew dark. Nox had long since lost track of the time and didn't bother to look at her wrist watch.

She kept her head low and steadily moved on.

The arrival of night brought the first of the cool winds.

Nox sat on a stone overlooking a flat plain. She removed her boots and flexed her aching toes before laying her heavy backpack on the ground.

The Mechanic relished the change in temperature. She turned her chapped and blistered face into the wind and soaked up the cool air.

Though she desperately wanted to continue following the van's tracks, she had to stop for the night. There simply wasn't enough light left to see anything in the red sands.

As the hours passed and the evening winds rose, Nox grew more and more worried. If the wind grew too strong, there was the very real possibility that all the van's tracks would be gone by first light.

And even if the wind maintained its current strength, the tracks would be very faded by morning and all that much harder to follow.

Nox wondered how far she had come but worried even more about how much farther she still had to go.

Her life depended on it.

22

In the morning Nox awoke thirsty and feverish. She slipped her boots back on and got to her feet but her legs felt wobbly and her body screamed for her to stay down. To do so, Nox knew, meant she would never move again.

The desert sands had done plenty of damage to the Octi Corp van's tracks, but there remained enough of them here and there for Nox to follow. She did so robotically, passing one grueling mile after another. The vista around her was unchanged. There were no mesas, there were no hills, and there were no valleys.

Only the monotonously smooth sandy plain.

Nox kept her eyes from the blazing sun. There was still a very long way to go.

The hours passed...

Once in a while Nox tracked the sun's position by her shadow. It moved across the sands like a primitive hourglass. Nox's gaze inevitably shifted away from the shadow and to the sands themselves. The tracks of the van were at times very faint. For a while she lost them but kept moving forward anyway. Luckily for her, the van continued its monotonous straight path.

As she followed the increasingly faded tracks, a nagging worry gripped the Mechanic. If she didn't find the van's destination by this night, by morning what was left of the tracks would most certainly be gone and with them any hope of survival.

The first winds of late afternoon came as a surprise to the Mechanic. Nox looked up and was shocked to see the sun setting far off to the west. The sky was a bloody red rose and wisps of sand danced before it.

The terrain had changed. She was now in a section of the desert populated with smooth hills. Much farther in the distance were several mesas. When Nox squinted, she could just see the outlines of mountains still further off. She wondered if they were real or a hallucination.

Nox's breathing was labored, and the skin on her face peeled and blistered. She shuffled as she walked and found it almost impossible to swallow. Her hands felt so heavy and she had so little energy left.

Nox stopped and cocked her head to the side.

"What?" she mumbled. Her voice sounded like a leaking tire. She looked back from where she came and listened hard. Had she heard something?

After a few seconds, Nox shook her head.

Hallucinations.

She continued forward. But after a few steps, she once again stopped.

No. *Not* a hallucination.

Nox listened for several long seconds until she was sure. There was a rumbling coming from somewhere behind her. It was the sound of a mechanized caravan. Nox stared into the distance and kept perfectly still. After a while, she spotted a dust cloud.

Though it pained her burned lips, the Mechanic cracked a smile.

Nox hurried forward and climbed a small hill. She pulled her binoculars from her backpack and stared into the distance. There were five trucks moving in her general direction. A mark on the front of the lead truck identified it as belonging to Octi Corp.

The smile on Nox's face widened.

She hurried down the hill and found a place to hide between two sand mounds. She had a plan. The timing would be tight, but if she was quick and had just enough strength left, she could jump the last of the vans and stow herself away within.

The trucks closed in on her position as the last of the sun's rays winked out. The trucks' forward lights came on all at once as their massive engines roared ever closer.

Nox shook her head. They were moving fast. *Too* fast. She hoped they would slow down as they entered the hills but, if anything, they seemed to speed up. Nox had no hope, in her weakened state, of jumping them. Her only alternative was to force them to slow down.

Nox removed her assembled handgun from the backpack and aimed it at the second vehicle's rear tires. Her hands shook from the weight of something she held without any problem innumerable times before.

Can you make the shot?

Nox took a deep breath of the rapidly cooling air. She had only one chance to pull this off and, despite the loud noises coming from the trucks' engines, there was no guarantee the occupants of the vehicles wouldn't hear the gun shot. If they did, Nox was done.

Let the engine noises be loud enough, Nox hoped.

The Mechanic exhaled and stared through the gun's sight. The image within shook. Nox clamped down and held the weapon as steady as she could. She aimed carefully and, when she felt comfortable enough, Nox squeezed the trigger.

To Nox, the single shot exploded with the sound of an atomic bomb. The Mechanic leaned down and away. She quickly stored the gun into the backpack and dare not look up.

They heard it, she thought. *You screwed it up. There's no way they didn't hear that sound.*

Nox was certain despair had pushed her into making a fatal mistake. The drivers would arm themselves. They would come for her. They would...

The trucks' forward movement slowed. Nox took a chance and peeked over the mound she was hiding behind. The caravan was still quite far away, but they were indeed slowing.

Please let them think it's a flat tire. A flat tire and nothing more.

The caravan came to a stop and the crews dismounted. They walked around the stricken vehicle and the driver of that truck kicked his useless tire.

Nox tried hard to contain herself. The drivers moved around casually, joking and pointing to the flat, as if they suffered only a temporary misfortune. They didn't hide behind the van's metal body, they didn't arm themselves...

They didn't hear the shot!

Nox closed her eyes and forced herself to relax. This was only the first part. She still had a way to go.

Off in the distance, the driver of the disabled truck shook his head and scratched the back of his neck. He waved to several of the other drivers. Two of the younger members of the team headed to one of the lead trucks. When they returned, one of them rolled a spare tire while the other carried a heavy jack. The man with the spare tire let it drop on the sand and helped his partner set up the jack.

The others walked around, smoked, and stretched. A couple drank from a canteen mounted on the second to the last truck's side.

In the growing darkness, Nox silently worked her way toward the trucks until she was behind the last of them. She crawled under this truck and forward, until she was directly below the vehicle's engine. The effort left her winded and seeing stars. Nox feared she might pass out.

If she did, and they drove off...

Nox closed her eyes and rested for a few seconds.

The break proved beneficial. The caravan's occupants had their fill of the canteen water and left it beside the rear truck and only a couple of feet away from Nox's position. While the members of the crew leisurely roamed elsewhere, Nox crawled out and grabbed the canteen. She took a long, deep swig of the warm water and almost choked. Despite this, the water felt like the essence of life poured back into a cadaver. Nox took another long pull before spilling water over her face and upper body. She soaked her shirt and brushed away the damned sand. She felt like laughing out loud but forced herself to keep her mouth shut.

She was in heaven.

Though still quite weak, Nox felt strength return to her body. She took one last long sip of the warm liquid before putting it back in its place. The spare tire was almost mounted and Nox had little time. She crawled back and out from under the truck. She inspected the vehicle's cargo bay and found within it several large boxes of rations. Nox opened one of the containers and removed a couple of individual packets. Nox then took one last look at the caravan's occupants. The spare tire was mounted and the crew joked at the wasted time and inconvenience. All members headed to their respective vehicles.

Nox climbed the back of the truck and lay down on the roof of its cargo bay. She opened one of the stolen ration packs and was halfway done eating it by the time the trucks started moving.

A little later she was fast asleep.

The burning sunlight woke her.

Nox covered her eyes and noted the position of the sun. Morning was almost gone. To her surprise, she had slept some fifteen hours. Nox turned on her stomach and peered ahead.

The caravan proceeded east. It moved through and around a series of low lying hills. The terrain forced the drivers to cut their speed and move carefully. Nox involuntarily shook. It was sheer dumb luck she came across this caravan. Considering the distance they had traveled since she hitched this ride, it was also clear she would never have caught up with the sniper's van.

She was lucky to still be alive.

The vans continued their trek. The terrain smoothed out but Nox spotted deep valleys to the north. Eventually, the vans turned off into one of those valleys. Off in the distance Nox spotted a metallic reflection. She pulled her binoculars out and studied what lay ahead.

She saw a sand colored canvas port shielding a pair of Octi Corp. trucks. The entire contraption was set up next to a rocky hill. From the air, no one would see the parked vehicles and the port was large enough to fit the entire caravan.

Nox examined the two vehicles already parked under that canvas port. The front windshield of the first van was shattered by three bullet holes. Nox's jaw tightened. She caught up to the vehicle she was following.

The caravan slowed as they approached the rocky hill.

Nox didn't wait for them to park. She lowered herself off the top of her truck and jumped to the sandy ground. She hit it hard and rolled off to the side. Once hidden behind a couple of boulders, Nox watched the caravan enter the canvas covered port and park. The occupants of the caravan disembarked and, for the next few hours, unloaded their supplies.

The crew used hand trucks to move their cargo to its destination which was somewhere behind the rocky hill. When all the boxes and containers were unloaded, the drivers and crew returned to their vehicles, started them up, and drove off the way they came. The entire caravan passed within a few feet of Nox's hideout.

Once they were gone, Nox dashed forward. She made her way to the van with the shattered windshield and looked it over. A gun rack behind the driver's seat sported a sniper's rifle.   Seeing the weapon that had most likely killed Ellis brought a wave of fury within the Mechanic.

Nox let the anger dissipate.

Now isn't the time.

She followed the footprints and tracks the caravan occupants made when they moved their cargo.   She walked around the rocky hill and into a narrow crevasse.   Nox slowed down and searched for any security devices.

She warily inched forward, fearful she might walk into view of a camera or motion detector or find herself face to face with a guard or guards.

Her fears proved unfounded.   The crevasse continued for a few more feet before stopping at a rocky dead end.

Nox edged closer to the dead end.   She stared at the footprints in the sand and noted their makers traveled right up to the rocky surface *and beyond.*

Nox felt the smooth wall of rock before her.   She noted a minor discoloration from one rock surface to the other.   She ran her hands over this part and found a very small crack.   It was uniform and straight.   Way too straight for any natural occurrence.

It was a hidden doorway.

It took Nox another minute to find the latch.   Like everything else on the rock wall, it was camouflaged to look like another part of the surrounding area.   Nox pushed the latch down.   It moved smoothly, like a well-oiled hinge.

Before her, the dead end rock wall opened, revealing a dark corridor.   Beyond it she heard sinister whispers and the sounds of heavy machinery.

23

Nox cautiously entered the dark corridor. She stuck to its sides and allowed time for her eyes to adjust to the low light within.

Nox's muscles were rigid, her senses on high alert. She spotted a distant light some fifty feet away, at what looked to be the end of the corridor. The Mechanic knew she would have to go all the way to it. Doing so meant completely exposing herself. There were no side rooms or other corridors to hide in.

Anyone could spot her. Anyone could see her coming.

Let's do this before I get any older, Nox thought.

The Mechanic leaned in to the side of the wall and sprinted forward. It took several tense seconds which, to Nox, felt like a lifetime before she reached the end of the corridor. The voices and sounds of machinery grew as she approached the distant light.

Nox came to a stop at what proved to be an intersection. The light she saw came from a pair of corridors that stretched out in opposite directions. To Nox's right were the sound of machines. Tracks in the dirty floor indicated that this was where the supplies from the caravan were headed. Perhaps, the Mechanic reasoned, there was a storage room back there. To her left came the sound of distant voices.

Nox chose the left corridor.

She was exposed once again, but this corridor, unlike the first, was very well lit.

Here we go again.

The Mechanic hurried through, eventually reaching a solid steel security door. The door's safety machinery was familiar to her and very old. She recalled seeing similar security features back in Arabia, inside the bunkers of corrupt despots and madmen. Hidden computers monitored heavy latches and a dim panel to the side of the door recorded heat patterns and handprints.

These doors were always such a bitch to open.

But that was in the past. This heavy door and its computerized security were long dead. A camera above the door hung loose, its electronic eye focused on the opposite wall. There were scorch marks along the length of the door's latches. The marks were fresh.

Nox pressed up against the door and pushed. It quietly swung open, a three ton rectangular mass balanced so precisely that even a child could push her. The lights beyond the door were even stronger than those in the corridor. Nox eased her way inside. For a moment she considered pulling out her gun but decided against it. It was best, for now, to keep her hands free and look as innocent as possible.

Nox stepped into the light beyond the door and paused.

The Mechanic stood atop a heavy metal spiral staircase and balcony overlooking an enormous hollow cylinder carved into the desert rock. The staircase led down, with exits on each of the ten floors below. At the very bottom of the massive hole was a landing pad. The helicopter Ellis and she followed was parked down there.

Nox looked up and realized the top of the rocky hill, at least what she saw from outside, was in reality a movable panel. Nox's gaze returned to what lay below. People circulated on each of the ten floors. They worked on ancient electrical equipment scattered along the balconies or stepped in and out of rooms filled with even more ancient equipment.

They were engrossed in their work and none of them noticed Nox. Not willing to push her luck, the Mechanic stepped away from the balcony and returned to the shadows. She took several minutes to familiarize herself with the lay of the base and to form an opinion on what she was seeing.

The equipment the people were working on was, like the security door, quite old. The way they examined this equipment suggested they were performing a detailed inventory of items or, conversely, searching for something. Once a particular piece of equipment was fully examined, it was tagged with a bright red sticker and shuffled off. Each floor had a section loaded with such stacked and tagged equipment. Wooden boxes were piled next to this equipment. Some or perhaps all of the tagged equipment would eventually be packed up in the boxes and transferred elsewhere, most likely back to the Big City.

Nox scratched her chin.

So what are they up to?

The place was clearly an old research facility. But researching what? Considering the expense involved in hiding this base, it was obviously very well financed when it was operational. That meant, in turn, it had the backing of very powerful individuals in either the old government or the business class.

In time the research facility became another casualty to the radical changes in weather over the past two decades. And now, following its discovery by Octi Corp., it had proven to be a valuable asset.

How else to explain the murder of Octi Survey Group 4 and the fact that Robert Octi Junior had personally made a trip to this place to oversee...

What?

Nox needed to find out.

She headed for the stairs and cautiously descended a flight. Before her were several computers, all at least a couple of decades old.

Wonder if they play Pong? Nox thought.

She continued down the stairs, avoiding several Octi researchers who, thankfully, were so engrossed in their work they didn't notice her. When Nox made it to the lowest level of the desert base, she looked up. She felt like she was at the bottom of an enormous chimney. Here and there on the roof she spotted slivers of sunlight. For years the top paneling faced the brutal Desertland conditions and slowly failing.

Nox stared at the helicopter and the floor around it. Sand from the desert above penetrated the cracks and fell down. In another few years the roof panels would collapse and fall to the floor.

Right about here.

From a door behind Nox appeared two Octi researchers dressed in white. Nox could not avoid being seen by them, so she leaned down and examined a black metal box that lay at her feet. She opened the box and found several screwdrivers and wrenches. She fumbled through the gear. The researchers approached, and Nox let out a loud, frustrated sigh.

"No Phillips head," the Mechanic lamented.

"You never find what you really need," one of the researchers replied. The two walked away.

Look like you belong.

"Have a nice day," Nox called out.

She rose and, after allowing a generous amount of time to pass, followed them. The researchers entered a large door and headed down a dark passageway drilled into the solid stone hill. There were lights in the distance and the sounds of even more people talking.

The researchers turned a corner and disappeared.

Nox moved in, closing the gap between herself and her prey. When she reached the corner, she found another large room drilled from the rock. Its roof had collapsed, leaving rubble and sand in its center. Recovered equipment, some of it damaged well beyond repair, lay at the corners of the room. A group of people dug through the sand and stone with great care, as if archeologists uncovering electronic fossils.

Nox kept to the sides of the room and made her way to the recovered equipment. She found a set of file cabinets among the stacked items. She opened one of the cabinets and noted a pile of yellowed documents within. Nox picked up a random page and read it.

Attn. Red Clearance Personnel, Note following changes in procedure:

-All paperwork to be destroyed must first be cleared for said procedure. ABSOLUTELY NO COPIES are to be made without clearance. All information is company property and, as such, falls under company rules.

David Lemner

Nox frowned.

"David Lemner?" she muttered. The name sounded awfully familiar.

Nox retreated to the helicopter landing pad. Though she initially feared discovery, it was obvious that all the Octi Corp. personnel in the buried base were so preoccupied with their work and so secure in the belief that no one could infiltrate this place that they paid little attention to her. Nox hung around the corners and the shadows and, when someone did see her, picked up whatever equipment lay in a stack nearby and moved it to another stack a farther distance away.

And that's how she once again became a temporary employee of Octi Corp.

"Lady, that needs to stay where it is."

Nox stiffened. She laid the computer panel back in its place. The man who addressed her was in his late forties or early fifties and had a sickly complexion. His dress was casual, like most of the lowly workers.

"Sorry," Nox said and walked toward another pile of computer towers.

"Hey, you," the man called out.

Nox slowed her pace.

He knows I don't belong, she thought.

Nox considered her options, but there were few. She had a knife hidden in the side of her boot or could go for the gun in her backpack. It would be messy, but it seemed the only way to—

"Why don't you take care of these boxes instead," the man said and pointed to the other side of the room. "Move them out with the others."

Nox noted the boxes.

"Others?" Nox asked.

"Yes, the others," the man said. There was growing irritation in his voice.

Nox took a step forward and stopped. She looked around the room and spotted at least five other piles of boxes.

"Oh for Jeb's sakes," the man said. "The ones by the helicopter."

"Oh yeah! Yes sir."

Nox moved forward, but the man grabbed Nox's shoulder and stopped her.

"I've had just about enough of you temps," he said. "Shape up, do your job, or we'll cut you all loose. It's a long walk back home."

Nox nodded.

"Tell me about it," she said.

It took the Mechanic a half hour to move the boxes to where they were supposed to go.

In time Nox developed a clear idea of where the most important sections of the base lay. She also discovered through quick, casual friendships made with her fellow workers that Robert Octi Jr. tended to stay in and around the base's lowest level and not far from where his helicopter was parked.

With that knowledge, Nox decided she would keep to the edges of the third floor. She was far enough away from the bottom to minimize any risk of running into Robert Octi Jr. or his bodyguard yet close enough to spot and tail them when they finally did appear. As far as the Mechanic knew, Robert Octi Jr. and his bodyguard were the only people within the base who could recognize her.

At dinner time, a horn sounded and the workers Nox hung out with headed to the makeshift cafeteria. They were in a good mood, pleased with their progress and the obvious importance of their job.

Nox took in any stray bits of conversation she could. She had developed a good feel for the place, but not enough to discover what everyone was doing here. After waiting in line for over ten minutes, it was her turn to be served. Nox pushed her tray forward, but the old lady serving the dark colored hash didn't move.

"Let's see your ID badge," she asked her.

Nox made a show of searching her pockets and backpack before offering the old lady a sheepish grin.

"Must've left it at the station."

The old lady shook her head.

"No one's allowed any food unless I see an ID."

"Damn," Nox said. "And I really had my heart set for some of that...some of that...are those grits?"

"*Pansette de Gerzat*, asshole."

A worker standing next to Nox let out a laugh and said:

"Jesu, by all rights *we* should be asking *you* for ID."

"What?" the old lady asked.

"Yeah," the worker said. "How about showing us some proof that you're really a cook?"

The others in the line laughed. The old lady's face remained stony, but the ghost of a smile lurked below the surface.

"Come on," the man continued. "This lady's been working like a dog."

The old lady relented and gave Nox a sly smile.

"She'll eat like one, too," she said. She shoveled some of the dark confection onto a metal plate and slapped it on Nox's tray.

"Bon appetite, *darling*."

Nox retreated to one of the tables by the edge of the third floor balcony. She took a spoonful of the mush and tried it. She was surprised to find the processed crap tasted vaguely like chicken.

Nox was almost done with her meal when, for the first time since her arrival, she spotted Robert Octi Jr. exit one of the many rooms on the bottom floor. He was flanked by his ever present bodyguard. Nox took the tray to the trash and tossed the remains of her food. When she passed the old serving lady she said:

"Your *Pansette* could use a little more blue cheese."

"Take it up with management, smart ass."

"*Merci*, madam."

Nox hurried down the stairs and, from a safe distance, followed Robert and his bodyguard into what turned out to be a large, two-story tall room. The area was heavily guarded and Nox tried to keep her distance from the guards. The cafeteria lady might let the ID badge slide, but the guards around Robert Octi Jr. wouldn't.

Or so Nox thought.

"The boss wants that shit out of here," a guard who noticed the Mechanic said.

Nox nodded and, with a by now well practiced indifference, headed for the equipment. She lingered there and watched as five Octi researchers sorted through boxes of old documents. Dusty computer consoles lined the walls of the room. They were huge machines that didn't have the processing power of even one modern laptop. Noisy generators gave life to some of the old consoles and even noisier fans pushed the generators' hot and toxic exhaust out of the area.

Nox grabbed the specified equipment and headed to the opposite side of the room. She noted a group of three researchers huddled against one of the many monitors lining the walls. Their fingers glided gracefully over their keyboards, but their faces reflected a frustration shared by almost every researcher Nox had come across.

Whatever they were looking for, they weren't finding.

Beyond them and near the center of the room stood Robert and his bodyguard. Their backs were to Nox but she kept her distance on the off chance that they might take a look around. As with the other researchers present, Robert's face bore a thinly veiled disgust. He approached a researcher standing before one of the larger computer consoles. She was a pretty young brunette who frowned at the information displayed on the monitor before her.

"Did you get into the system?" Robert asked her.

The young woman shook her head.

"No."

"How long have you been on this?"

"Twelve hours, sir."

"What progress have you made?"

"I...I haven't seen anything like this, Mr. Octi. There are more locks and safeguards and redundancy systems—"

"When will you break the codes?"

"I'm not sure."

"That's not what I asked, Rebecca."

The young lady lowered her head. She suppressed a shiver and nervously eyed her boss.

"N... No sir," she said. "I think it will take—"

Robert held up his hand. The motion silenced the employee. The other two researchers by the consoles stiffened. Robert's hand drifted to his side. A growing darkness filled his face. Like lightning, his hand shot up and he savagely struck Rebecca on her cheek. The researcher fell back in her chair and slid to the floor, crying.

Robert let out a grunt and stared at all the other researchers and security guards around him. They were silent, one and all.

"I'm through waiting for you so-called experts to break these codes," Robert yelled. "It's here! *All* of it! And not one of you can find one fucking thing worth taking back? Do you know how over budget we've gone?"

No one moved, no one talked.

"You're making me look like an idiot!" Robert continued. "My father is not a patient man. Neither, I assure you, am I. If we don't show him something—"

Robert stopped talking. Nagel's hand grasped his shoulder. The silent bodyguard leaned in and whispered something into Robert's ear. Upon hearing Nagel's words, Robert's fury dissolved. His body became limp, spent.

"We don't have much more time," Robert said. He was no longer yelling. "The contents of this base are vast. They will take at least two more weeks to properly clean out. We don't have that time. Our spies in Tower Co. tell us our movements in this area have not gone unnoticed."

Robert paused to collect his thoughts. His anger gave way to something far more pathetic: hopelessness and despair.

"We have, at most, forty eight hours to figure out the Demon's computer system. If we don't make any breakthrough by then, we can expect Tower Co. interference. Do I make myself clear?"

The crowd around Robert Octi Jr. murmured agreement and returned to their stations. Robert looked down at Rebecca. She remained on the floor, holding her red cheek.

"I... I didn't mean to hit you, Rebecca. I..."

Rebecca rose to her feet. She was in no mood to listen to her boss' apologies.

"Can I take a few minutes break?" she asked. Without waiting for an answer, she walked away. Robert's shoulders slumped. He did not follow her.

"Come on, get back to work," Robert told the rest of the staff.

Rebecca came to a stop in one of the empty passageways leading away from the computer room. She leaned against the wall and fished a cigarette from her lab coat pocket. After lighting it up, she took a very deep pull. She felt the side of her face with her free hand and winced when she touched the welt on her cheek.

"Cigarettes aren't good for your health."

Rebecca turned. From farther down the corridor came Nox.

"Who are you?"

"A fellow employee."

Rebecca examined Nox for several long seconds. Finally, she shrugged.

"Nice suntan. You just arrive?"

"Just today."

"Bullshit," Rebecca growled. "We had a load of supplies brought in, but no new workers. They don't come until the end of the week, although it looks like we'll be long gone by then. Who the fuck are you?"

Nox gently grabbed Rebecca's cigarette and took a deep drag of her own. She then pulled out her handgun and held it loose at her side and in full view.

"Cigarettes may be bad," Nox said. She waved the gun. "But they've got nothing on this."

Rebecca smirked.

"Spare me the tough guy act. I've seen enough cowboys in this desert to last several lifetimes."

"At least I don't make it a habit of hitting defenseless women."

"Yeah. It's *so* much more polite to threaten them with guns."

Nox gave Rebecca her cigarette back.

"What can I do for you Ms...?"

"Nox."

"You from Tower Co.?"

"Nope."

"So why are you here? Is this a stick up? Because if it is, I left my purse at home."

Nox smiled.

"I'm impressed," she said and put her gun away. "You're like me. A city girl."

"I may be from the city, but I'm nothing like you," Rebecca said.

"You're right," Nox said. "I'd have broken that fucker's hand the second he touched me."

Rebecca frowned, annoyed, but the frown faded.

"I suppose you would."

"Why do you think I'm here?"

"You're looking for information on what Octi Corp. is doing in this place and you're hoping this poor, abused little lady is angry enough to spill her guts. Well, my friend, you're out of luck. I don't talk. Especially not on a first date."

"I'm sure there are exceptions."

"You want me to tell you everything, then *you* tell me who *you're* working for. And tell me it's a *really* big company, lady, because betrayal doesn't come cheap."

"I'm self-employed."

Rebecca let out a laugh.

"You're freelancing? How much are you worth?"

"Not a whole lot."

"Mom always said I knew how to pick 'em. Sorry Nox, honesty doesn't pay the bills." Rebecca finished her cigarette and tossed it aside. "So you're one lone Independent—"

"Mechanic."

"Mechanic?" she smiled. "How quaint. A knight in shining armor. You're one lone Mechanic up against the entire Octi Corporation. What do you have against them?"

"Their service. It's lousy."

"Then why don't you write a letter and stick it into one of their suggestion boxes? I hear they take constructive criticism very seriously."

"What is Octi looking for?"

Rebecca thrust her hands into her lab coat's pockets.

"I couldn't tell you. As disrespectful as Mr. Octi Junior is, he *is* my boss, and I have sworn allegiance to the all-mighty Octi enterprise. I'm five years away from tenure. I'd be a shame to screw that up by turning into a whistle blower. Especially to someone who doesn't have much cash to offer."

Rebecca's right hand slid out of the lab coat pocket. In it was a small black cylinder. A green light on its surface flashed.

"I'm really sorry about this," Rebecca continued. There was genuine regret in her voice. "You seem nice enough, but I called security anyway. They'll be here any second."

The corporation means everything to the individual worker.

Nox gritted her teeth and turned.

She took two steps before stopping. A group of security guards approached from the center of the desert base. Nox hastily turned back and ran down the hallway and past Rebecca.

The researcher watched Nox disappear down the corridor. The guards ran to her side.

"What happened?"

"Infiltrator," she said. "She went down that way."

"Dead end," the guard said. "Bad choice on her part. You did a good job. You're sure to get a commendation."

"Stick it with all the others."

The guards ran past the researcher. Immediately afterwards another group of four guards appeared and followed the first group into the darkness.

Rebecca watched them disappear. Her face betrayed neither joy nor sympathy.

Nox moved deeper down the dark corridor. She avoided fallen panels and burnt out cabinets but noted the walls surrounding her were heavily damaged and had partially collapsed from age and wear. Nox held her handgun close, but knew at this point it wouldn't save her.

She was trapped.

There were no lights down here and the high value equipment was long gone. After stumbling in the dark for several seconds, Nox reached the end of the corridor. Before her was a mass of solid rock that collapsed and completely chocked off the passage.

Nox shook her head. Should the guards choose to do so, they could fire blindly at her until she was dead. If they wanted to save bullets and time, they could lob a single grenade in her direction. Then again, they could hang back and starve her out.

Nox didn't think the last option would merit serious consideration.

The guards moved about in the darkness, positioning themselves some thirty or forty feet away. They held back, gathering strength, until there were at least a dozen strong.

Nox rubbed sweat from her forehead. She could go out in a blaze of glory, firing at them, but what good would that do? She had come to take down the Octi Corporation, not a few low paid guards.

"I'm coming out," Nox yelled. She received no answer. "I'm unarmed."

Nox laid her gun on the floor and raised her hands until they were over her head. She took a step forward. In the darkness she could barely make out what lay before her. She took another step, then another. She knew this was the end, and a feeling of calm enveloped her.

The Mechanic moved half a dozen feet and still had no clear idea of where the guards were yet felt their eyes on her. Hateful, vengeful. To them, Nox was their sworn enemy, a lowly spy come to steal food from their plates. In the business world, spies were dealt with very harshly.

A metallic sound came from her right side and Nox froze. She closed her eyes and let out a breath.

A black metal pipe came out of nowhere and viciously slammed against the Mechanic's jaw. Nox fell to her knees. She could barely see and her body felt like it was on fire.

The metal pipe hovered in front of her face. A heavily insulated glove held its grip. Nox drew back, but the blow she just received staggered her and she couldn't move quickly enough. The metal pipe touched her shoulder and sent a searing electrical jot throughout her body.

Nox's teeth slammed shut and all the muscles in her body locked. Nox collapsed onto the ground. She could no longer move, she could no longer think. And then her body convulsed and bile rose into her throat.

She saw her gun lying on the ground beside her. It was no more than three or four feet away. It might as well have been on the other side of the world.

Nox saw someone picked it up.

Then she saw nothing at all.

24

The room was bare and steaming hot. Nox sat in a metal chair bolted to the floor. Her hands and ankles were tied down with razor wire. The wire dug into her skin, ripping and tearing it and sending droplets of blood down her fingers and feet and onto the dirty concrete floor. Fresh blood mixed with a larger puddle of old, dry blood.

Nox's cheeks were slashed. Her lower lip was inflamed and raw. Her eyes were swollen. The Mechanic convulsed. A wheezy gasp caught in her throat and she heaved before spitting out a glob of coagulated blood. It splattered on the floor, providing more company for the other crimson stains.

When consciousness returned to her now and again, Nox found there wasn't any part of her body that didn't feel pain. They worked her over. Slowly, painstakingly. *Completely.*

Nox's head rose and she got a better look at the room. A single fluorescent light was her only company, at least for the moment.

I wore them out, Nox thought. *They must have bruised their knuckles something fierce.*

She let out a laugh, but it sounded strange in this bare, tiny room. Nox closed and opened her eyes. Her breathing remained heavy and she had a hard time maintaining consciousness beyond a few seconds.

In time, the dull aches receded and Nox felt some strength return. Soon, she was able to stay awake for a longer time. By then, the air in the room had grown terribly stagnant. The smell of perspiration and urine, most likely Nox's own, were overwhelming.

How long had it been since they captured her?

How long had it been since they last beat her?

It can't be all that long, Nox thought. Robert Octi Jr. said their group had forty eight hours before Tower Co. had a fix on this base. That was Octi Corp's deadline. How much more time could be left?

For the next hour or so, Nox tested the wire's strength. Each time she did, the rusty cord ate into her wrists and ankles and sent a fresh wave of pain through her body. Eventually, Nox gave up. She couldn't free herself. She simply couldn't.

Close to an hour after that the door to her cell opened and Robert Octi Jr. and his bodyguard entered the room. Robert came to a stop before Nox and stared at his prisoner, as if examining a new found treasure. A satisfied grin filled his face.

"I had a feeling we'd meet again," the young executive said. He gave his bodyguard a slight nod and Nagel delivered a crushing blow to Nox's right cheek.

Nox's head and body snapped back. If the chair hadn't been bolted to the ground, Nox would have fallen over. Doing so might have proven far less painful.

"Oh, how rude of me," Robert continued. "I forgot to introduce my bodyguard. Nox, this is Nagel. Nagel, this is Nox."

Nagel delivered another vicious blow to Nox's face. Fresh blood poured down the Mechanic's nose and chin.

"Nagel's a man of few words. You know how it is. Actions speak so much louder."

Nagel swung again. Stars filled Nox's eyes.

"You should have vanished, Nox. Disappeared. In time we would have forgotten all about you."

"I wouldn't... have."

Nagel punched the Mechanic in her stomach. More blood spilled from Nox's mouth and onto the floor. She tried to shake it off, but her breathing was labored and her vision blurry. Robert chuckled.

"You know, something just occurred to me," Robert said. "If things were just a little different, you might have made a really good employee of the company. You're motivated, you're persistent. Hell, you found this place, so you're obviously resourceful. I could see you collecting your annual seven percent salary increase and gaining tenure in five –no, make that three– years. Yes sir, we could have accommodated you very nicely."

"I'll send you my... my resume."

Robert let out a cruel laugh.

"It's far too late for that, Nox."

"Doesn't ma... matter. You... you run a shitty organization anyway."

Robert's laughter abruptly died. The same darkness Nox saw right before Robert hit Rebecca appeared once more on the young executive's face. Robert reached into his jacket pocket and pulled out a small pocket knife. He leaned down close to Nox's face and held the shiny blade before her eyes.

"You keep rubbing it in, Nox. You don't know when to stop."

Robert pressed the blade against Nox's right cheek and slid it up. As it moved along, Robert applied more and more pressure until the skin ripped and blood flowed from the fresh wound. The blade drew closer and closer to Nox's right eye.

"This is where it gets interesting," Robert whispered. "If I were you, I'd keep very still."

The young executive ran the blade up some more, stopping just below Nox's eye.

"No more quips? Nothing smart to add?"

Nox held still.

"I could make your last seconds on this planet so very messy."

Nox kept her eyes open. They stared deep into Robert's eyes. The Mechanic said nothing. She hardly breathed.

"You're a brave woman," Robert said.

The young executive's next movement was quick and deadly. He slid the blade *into* Nox's right eye. The Mechanic's head jerked back and she howled in pain.

Robert's smile disappeared. He wiped the bloody blade on Nox's stained shirt.

"Felt that, didn't you?" Robert yelled. "Fuck you Nox. Fuck you and *all* your fucking arrogance. You think a little nobody like you has any chance against *us*? You're a small time loser up against fucking royalty."

Once again Robert leaned in close to Nox. The blade shot forward, this time toward Nox's left eye.

"I'll take the other one with me, too."

Nagel stepped to his boss' side and grabbed the young executive's hand. Robert angrily tried to break free of the grip, but Nagel persisted.

"What the fuck?" Robert yelled.

"Let her see what's coming," Nagel whispered.

The words' effect on Robert was instant. The fury within him dissipated. The young executive smiled before letting out another cruel laugh.

"Of course," he said. Robert put the knife away. "Nox *should* see what's coming. Even if it's through one eye."

Robert adjusted his tie and faced the Mechanic once again.

"My father always told me not to delegate my work," Robert said. "But in this day and age, someone in my position can't afford to dirty his hands too much. You wouldn't believe all the liability issues. It was a pleasure seeing you again, Nox. Rot in hell."

Robert walked to the door leading out of Nox's cell. He signaled to someone outside the room. While he did, Nagel delivered a final kick to Nox's stomach. Nox wheezed and gasped for air. Her right eye was shut tight. A steady stream of blood flowed out from within.

Nagel spat upon the helpless Independent and joined Robert at the door. A burly, red-haired Octi Security Guard appeared following Robert's summons. The man wore a green jumpsuit and carried a large caliber handgun in a holster on his belt.

"This animal needs to be put out of its misery," Robert told the Security Guard.

The Security Guard nodded. His face reflected the blank neutrality of a worker going about his job. The Security Guard drew his gun.

"End of the line, partner," the man said. He pointed the gun at the Mechanic's head and cupped his left ear.

Nox's remaining eye looked up at the gun. Nox knew the make, the model, and year this deadly instrument was made. She knew the ammunition it used and she knew the exact speed of the bullet when it exploded out of its barrel. She knew the force of impact and, given the distance between the barrel and her head, the likelihood of survival.

None.

She thought of this as the Security Guard moved the barrel even closer to her forehead. She thought of all these things once more as the barrel touched her skull. With one last burst of energy, she pulled at the razor wire around her wrists.

This time, she thought. The world grew darker around the edges as every last bit of energy she had pulled at those wires. As before, they dug into her skin, deeper and deeper. Blood cascaded from the fresh cuts and Nox kept pulling and pulling. And pulling. Her energy waned. Her energy was gone.

The wire held.

Defeated, finally defeated, Nox eased back. She knew the odds of taking out Octi were slim. It was a valiant attempt but she could rest now. She could finally rest.

Nox's remaining eye closed and a deep, comfortable weariness overcame her.

Robert and Nagel exited the room. The corridor beyond them was bare except for patches of desert sand. Like a petulant child, Robert kicked at one of them.

"We lost," he said. "Our time is up."

Robert rubbed his chin. There was two day old stubble there and it made him feel so dirty. How could people live like this? Didn't they miss showering?

"If a lone wolf like Nox could figure this operation out, then Tower Co. can't be far behind. It pains me to say this, but Dad was right. It's time to cut our losses."

Nagel nodded.

"You've got one hour to pack up as much hardware as possible," Robert added.   "I want it all transported to warehouse 23, back in the Big City."

The two reached the end of the corridor and stood before the balcony rails. They were on the top floor of the desert base, staring down at the workers below. The workers looked like tiny insects moving about on their own, ants in a long forgotten electronic hive.

"It's a real shame about them," Robert said, referring to the people below. "We can't afford any leaks. Whatever's left needs to be sterilized. *Completely* sterilized. No loose ends. Understood?"

Nagel nodded once again just as a muffled roar filled the corridor. The two turned to see the burly Security Guard opening the door leading to Nox's cell. The man entered the corridor and put away his still smoking gun before approaching the duo. There were drops of blood and gore on his green jumpsuit. The Security Guard wiped the stains and said:

"It's done. Nox is dead."

25

A single weathered cargo truck tore along the desert road. A sandstorm flared up in its path, sending waves of sand into the vehicle's windshield. The truck sped on, cutting through the haze and uneven terrain. The storm grew stronger and the truck's driver reluctantly slowed down. They wanted desperately to move on, to finish this particular delivery. They had a feel for the land and the extreme weather conditions the desert threw at them. What they weren't used to was their grim cargo.

While the drivers moved their truck cautiously forward, they chatted, laughed, drank, and ate. Their laughter was nervous, their conversations stilted. It seemed their every action was forced.

They didn't talk once about cargo.

Instead, memories of it lingered in their minds. Just a couple of feet behind them and in the truck's cargo bay were at least three dozen male and female bodies. They were spread about one on top of the other. Many of the corpses were pristine. They looked like they were only sleeping, a sure sign of poisoning. At least half of them, however, sported ugly bullet wounds and blood. Plenty of blood.

Loading them was the worst.

When the drivers were first called in, they found the bodies lying at the base of a rock valley in the middle of nowhere, ready to be carted away. A single Octi Corp. pencil pusher waited for the drivers to arrive. The first thing he did was have them sign the standard non-disclosure forms.

"Load up," the pencil pusher said after the paperwork was properly dealt with.

"Where should we take—"

The pencil pusher stared deep into the drivers' eyes.

"Somewhere very far away and very, *very* deep. If your... cargo... should ever reappear, and inquiries are made, it's your asses."

One of the drivers pointed to the bodies and said:

"Are they contaminated? Should we wear some protection?"

"Do you see me wearing any protection?" the pencil pusher said.

"What happened to them?" the other driver asked.

The pencil pusher lowered his clipboard. Once again he stared at the drivers. As before, his eyes were ice cold.

"You're paid to do a job, not ask questions. If you don't want to do this, we can always find someone else."

It took them an hour to load the bodies. At first they counted them, one at a time, but after a while they lost track and decided it was best to hurry up and finish. By the time the bodies were in the truck, the drivers were tired and hungry and knew their work was only half-done.

The pencil pusher nodded in satisfaction.

"We never met and you never did this," he said. He gave the drivers their money and walked away, disappearing into the rocky hills.

"Goodbye to you too," one of the drivers called out as the other counted the cash.

"It's all here," the driver counting the cash said.

"Then let's go."

The trip to the pits normally took three hours. Their slow trek became a crawl, until the fierce storm forced them to stop. The drivers popped open their coolers and had some beer.

They still did not talk about what they were hauling.

In the cargo bay, the twisted corpses lay still. Most wore researcher uniforms or casual work clothes. At least three corpses wore Security Guard uniforms.

Nox lay next to one of them.

She was pale and deathly still, a minor element in a grisly plateau. There was a considerable amount of dried blood on the right side of her face.

The cargo bay lurched with the growing winds. One of the hands before Nox's face shifted. Cut razor wire was wrapped around the hand's wrist. It was her own.

Nox's left eye opened and she let out a low moan before closing it again. Her body was still for several long minutes. When she once again came to, the storm was dying. Faint slivers of light broke through the cargo bay's walls.

Nox looked around, surprised to be alive and confused by her new surroundings.

"What...the hell?"

It took her a while to fully comprehend what she was seeing. Her last memories involved staring into the barrel of a gun without any possible escape. She had slipped into unconsciousness and reluctantly welcomed her end. She was finished.

There was no way the Octi Security Guard missed that shot. There was no miraculous salvation. Nox examined her arms. The razor wire was cut to free her from the metal chair, but strands remained tied around her wrists. She unwound the wire and moved her body. The limbs of the other corpses shifted as she did. It took her a while before she was on top of them all. She felt her arms and legs and stomach and back.

She had taken a severe beating and lost her right eye, but sported no gunshot wounds.

What exactly happened back there?

There was only one possibility: The Security Guard rejected Robert Octi Jr.'s order and decided not to kill her.

Why?

Nox tried to find some reason, something that made some kind –*any*– kind of sense, but couldn't.

No use thinking about it. You're alive. That's all that matters.

With each passing minute, Nox felt more strength return. Despite the beatings, despite the torture, her conditioning was good and she knew in time she would recover.

But first she had to get out of here. Now more than ever she had to finish what she started.

The truck's engine once again came to life and the cargo bay lurched as she moved forward. A body flopped beside Nox. Familiar eyes stared up at the Mechanic. It was Rebecca, the woman who Robert Octi Junior hit and the very same woman who turned Nox in.

There was a single gunshot wound to the side of her head. A kill shot, the exact type of wound Nox should have received. The back of Rebecca's head was a hollowed out mess. Nox reached forward and gently closed the woman's still open eyes.

"I'm sorry," she said. Despite her actions, Nox could not fault Rebecca for what she did. She had become, like the members of the Octi survey van and the researchers in the hidden base, another victim of Octi Corp.'s Desertlands project.

Whatever the Corporation was involved in here, it was something they wanted kept secret at *all* costs.

Nox crawled to the back of the truck's cargo bay. She searched for a latch or handle, anything that would open the rear door, but found nothing. The door was securely bolted down and, without any tools, there was no way she could force it open.

Nox leaned back against the cargo bay wall and waited. Where ever they were going, they would reach that destination soon enough. By then, Nox hoped, enough of her strength would be back.

She'd need every ounce of it.

For over an hour the sound of clashing gears intruded on Nox's sleep. Finally, brakes engaged and the enormous truck shivered and stopped. Moments later, its engine died. Nox heard laughter and the sound of casual conversation coming from the driver's cabin. She heard only two distinct voices.

The drivers stepped out of the truck and, for a very long time, those voices were muffled by distance. Nox then heard the sound of shovels biting into dirt. After a while, one of the drivers said:

"That's deep enough."

They approached the back of their truck and opened the cargo bay. Brilliant sunlight bathed the interior of the cargo bay and the full scope of slaughter to the Octi staff was clear. Nox kept perfectly still, yet found it hard to believe the amount of carnage surrounding her. The last time she saw something like this, she was in a small village in Arabia. The memories screamed at her and Nox fought hard not to shake.

One of the truck's drivers grabbed the legs of the nearest victim and pulled him down.

"I think you did the right thing," he told his partner. "The Delta medical insurance is far better than that shit the boss was peddling, even if it costs a few more bucks each month."

"Tell me about it," his partner responded. He grabbed a lady's arms and pulled hard.

"If it were up to them, we'd be performing surgery on each other to save them a credit or two."

"You gotta ask questions. If you don't, they'll stick you where they want to. Did I tell you how many forms I had to fill to get some fuckin' aspirin last time I got sick?"

"Shit."

"Yeah. I can't wait to tell them about the loose cap. I— Man, it's starting to smell real bad."

The two pulled the corpses across the desert floor and to the freshly dug hole. A pair of shovels stood to the side, thrust in the sand in front of the pit.

"If you hold your breath and shut your mouth, we get this done a lot quicker," the first man said. He rolled a body into the hole.

"Wish they were paying by the hour."

"In that case, we'd make the job last all day. Smelly corpses? I don't smell nothing. Far as I'm concerned, we're working in a fucking rose garden!"

They laughed and turned back to the truck to retrieve another pair of corpses. Neither of them noticed the two shovels they left behind was now a single shovel.

"When we get this done, we should head to the Cross-Town bar," the first man said. He was a few feet ahead of his companion. "I've developed a powerful thirst. How 'bout you, Bobby?" He took a few steps. "Bobby?"

When his partner didn't answer, the man spun around. His face turned deathly pale. His partner lay face down on the sand, the back of his head crushed and bloody.

Standing over his corpse was a vision from a nightmare: A bloody and bruised dark haired woman holding a bloody shovel. The woman's right eye was sealed shut. Her left stared forward, directly at the truck's remaining driver.

There was no pity in her one eyed glare.

No pity at all.

Nox wiped the sweat from her face. Behind her were thirty five individual graves. Only one of them was marked, for Nox knew the name of only one of the victims. She used a loose wooden board she found in the truck's cargo bay and a tire iron to write that name out.

Rebecca.

When she was done with the burials, Nox disconnected the cables that held the truck to its now empty cargo container. She was exhausted and her body was racked with pain. Fortunately, the truck drivers had plenty of rations and a canteen. She drank and ate and searched some more before finding a first aid kit.

It was filled with salve, gauze, and a bottle of *Go!* pills. Their label stated they were "the anti-biotic/anesthetic of choice for the man on the *Go!*" Nox was familiar with the drug. During the Arabian Wars, soldiers used experimental medication similar to this to fend off disease or injury. Not only did they heal your body, but they were good stimulants. The last thing any army needs in time of war is a tired, injured soldier.

"Just what the doctor ordered," Nox muttered.

She wrapped the gauze around her injured eye and used another roll to patch up the most significant cuts on her body. She then took four *Go!* pills and, after some fifteen minutes, felt the old, familiar rush of adrenaline. She rooted around the truck's cabin some more and found a map in a compartment behind the driver's seat.

Nox was pleased to find the drivers marked the areas they traveled. This gave Nox an excellent idea of the direction she needed to take from here. When she had her bearings, she examined the compass mounted to the dashboard.

Ready or not...

Nox felt the blood pounding in her temples. She turned the ignition and the truck's engine roared to life. Nox shifted the truck into gear and tapped on the accelerator. The truck lurched forward and Nox curled her lips into a fierce snarl.

...here I come.

26

The ride back to the Demon's base was bumpy and taxing but Nox made good time.

Now and again the Mechanic stared at the map or the compass or both, but by and large her route across the monotonously flat desert was straight and due south.

After a few hours, Nox spotted familiar rocks and small valleys. She also saw, in the very far distance, an inky black smoke rising into the sky.

She knew what it meant.

Nox arrived at the entrance to the buried base by late afternoon. The rock formations that formed the outer walls of the base were gone, replaced by an enormous black hole. The sliding roof was collapsed and heavy black smoke billowed into the air. Overhead came a buzzing, and Nox spotted a single helicopter approach the area.

Nox ignored it and walked to the edge of the enormous pit. Dying sunlight illuminated the ruins below. The remains of each of the ten floors were ripped apart and the smell of spent explosives was heavy in the air.

There was nothing left to see. Robert Octi Junior made sure of that. Nox returned to the truck. The helicopter was much closer now, and Nox recognized the blue and white colors of Tower Corporation. The rival company's aerial surveyors were there to check out what happened.

Nox waved to them as she drove away.

"It's all yours," she said.

Night time fell slowly, and Nox fought off waves of fever induced chills. Her temperature spiked, so she took another four *Go!* pills. They cleared her head and reduced her fever while waking her right up. But the beatings and injuries had taken their toll, and even with the stimulants, she knew she couldn't drive much longer.

Nox searched for a place to hide the truck and found it in a rocky cleft. She hadn't seen any other helicopters in the sky but worried Tower Co. personnel pursued her.

Either that, Nox thought, *or the stimulants are making me paranoid.*

Nox fought back a smile.

That's why the army discontinued the drug's use. Worse than a tired, injured soldier is a wired, paranoid soldier looking to frag anyone near them, friend or foe.

Nox's hands trembled when she parked and wild thoughts filled her head. She didn't want to face Tower Co. She had enough problems with Octi.

The thoughts lingered even while Nox drifted off to sleep.

In the morning, Nox was ravenous.

The fever, for the moment, was gone. Her injuries, wet and oozing yesterday, were almost all dry and healing today. Nox removed the wrapping around her right eye and examined it in the rear view mirror. Her eyelid was sealed with dried blood and horrifically inflamed. She felt along the eyelid's edges and a spurt of yellow puss drizzled out from within.

Nox gnashed her teeth as a fresh wave of pain flooded her body.

In time things calmed down. Nox used canteen water to rinse the dried blood but was very careful to not touch the most sensitive wounds. She laid some salve around the eye and re-wrapped it before eating breakfast.

She then took another four *Go!* pills and drove off.

After several hours of driving, Nox spotted the three mesas she was looking for. She recognized their shapes and in particular the one that held the Octi Corp. sniper a few days earlier. Nox corrected course and aimed the truck at that mesa. She rode around it and eventually found the dirt road she traveled a few days before. She also spotted her wrecked chopper.

It lay exactly where she left it, untouched except for a fresh layer of sand over her body. She also spotted the boulder behind which Ellis had fallen and died. Nox walked to the boulder. Ellis' blood was long gone, covered by the blowing sands. She looked past it, along the side of the road.

Ellis' grave was there, but its shape was different than how Nox left it.

Nox frowned. She stumbled forward. A look of horror filled her face. Someone found Ellis' grave and dug it up.

Nox jumped into the shallow grave. Her bare hands furiously pushed away the accumulated sand and her breath grew ragged with the effort. Despite that, she continued on, digging several feet before giving up.

Ellis' body was gone.

Nox got out of the hole and brushed the sand from her clothes. For several long seconds she stared down. A sudden realization hit her like a bolt of lightning.

"Natalie."

The words escaped her mouth as a silent whisper. If Octi Corp. found Ellis' body and identified it, they must surely know about his daughter.

Nox ran to her chopper and, with great effort, lifted it out of the freshly accumulated sand and onto the rear of the truck. She tied the motorcycle down hastily before running to the truck's cabin.

Within seconds the truck's engine roared to life and the rear tires skidded in place before gaining traction. Dust and sand flew in all directions as she pulled away.

She rode for an hour straight without once easing on the accelerator. After a while the engine whined in protest. It was not used to such constant strain and would not be able to take it much longer.

Nox didn't care.

By the second hour she was closing in on Octi Desertlands Base 6. There was no way she could enter the base with this stolen vehicle, nor did Nox try. She found a hill to the southeast of the base that was sufficiently high enough to hide the truck from any guards' eyes.

Nox made the rest of the trek by foot.

She retraced her steps from days before and found the entry point she cut in the electrified fence. The metal rods secured to the ground were still in place. In all this time, no one noticed or cared to find out how their intruder from days past entered the base.

Nox pushed the cut wire aside and crawled into the base's perimeter. She hugged the warehouse wall and listened for any sounds.

The base was eerily quiet. Too quiet.

Nox moved along the warehouse wall, working her way to its entry. This was where Robert Octi Junior's helicopter was kept. Nox found a window and peeked through it. Perhaps

Robert and his bodyguard were back. How she hoped this was the case.

The warehouse, however, was empty.

Nox moved on. She made her way to the two story structure that lay beside the warehouse. The bar's lights were off and the office on the second floor was dark.

Nox stepped up the bar's door and tried the door knob. It was unlocked. Nox cautiously opened the door and stepped inside.

The bar was also empty.

Shelves that housed drinks were bare. The cash register and the interior furniture were all gone. The place was abandoned.

Nox stepped into the middle of the bar and slowly spun around. Along with the secret Desertland base, Octi Corp. had cleared this place, too. In time and unless some other company claimed it, the wind and sand would swallow Octi Desertland Base 6 and it would become another of the desert's many, many lost landmarks.

Nox walked to the window and stared out. Exhaustion and hopelessness washed over and threatened to overwhelm her. Her hands pressed against the window sill and she lowered her head. Darkness intruded at the corner of her remaining eye. She shut it and, for a moment, drifted off. She wondered where Natalie was and worried she had joined her father.

A sharp squeak intruded upon the deathly silence. Nox spun around and saw the bar's door open. A burly, red-haired man entered. He held a gun in his right hand and pointed it at Nox.

"Hello again," the man said and smiled.

Nox fell back against the window. She was facing the same Octi Corp. Security Guard who was ordered to execute her back at the buried base.

"What...?" Nox managed before shutting her mouth.

An elegant blonde stepped into the bar behind the burly Security Guard. She was one of the most beautiful women Nox had ever seen. Her face was like classic porcelain; her body rigid and trim. She walked on severe high heels and carried a small black purse.

"We finally meet," she said. The blonde walked to the bar's counter and leaned against it. "Too bad they took away the chairs. My feet are killing me."

The Security Guard smirked. He remained in place with his handgun pointed at Nox. Nox shook her head and stepped away from the window. She approached the blonde's side.

"Stay where you are!" the Security Guard yelled. His grip on the handgun tightened and his eyes narrowed.

Nox shook her head.

"If you wanted me dead, you would have killed me when you had your first chance," she said.

The red-headed man growled, but made no effort to stop Nox. The blonde let out a chuckle.

"She's got you there," the blonde said.

The Security Guard lowered the gun. He approached Nox and the blonde.

"Try anything and I'll finish the job."

"At this point, just about anyone could," Nox said. "Including your boss."

"She's two for two," the blonde said.

The Security Guard's lips pressed together until they were tiny white slits. He shook his head and exited the bar, slamming the door as he left.

"Petulant fellow you got there," Nox said. "Who the hell are you?"

"You can call me Julie," the blonde said. "I'm your guardian angel."

Nox let out a sharp laugh.

"Guardian angel? Hell of a job you've done so far."

"You're alive, aren't you?"

"I'll give you that. Why?"

"I've been watching you, Nox. I first found out about you through your job with Donovan."

"You work for Octi?"

"Middle management."

"Then you must know your bosses have a few issues with me."

"I think we're far past the 'few issues' stage. I've never seen such high level interest in bumping off one lowly Independent."

"Mechanic."

"Mech—?" Julie smiled. "You're the last of an honorable breed, Nox. If it were up to Octi, you'd be extinct."

"Which brings us back to my first questions: Exactly who the hell are you and why did you have your boy spare my life?"

"Business is war and promotions are hard to come by. You might say I'm at war with Robert Octi Junior and concurrently seeking a satisfying promotion."

"To his position."

"Naturally."

"And the enemy of my enemy is my friend?"

"Absolutely."

"What do you want from me?"

"I want you to help me discredit Robert in front of his father and the board," Julie said. "They're both on thin ice as it is, but the Old Man's safe. The board won't dare kick him out. Not yet. His son on the other hand..." She winked and leaned into Nox's ear. "Get rid of Robert Junior and I'll be that much closer to controlling the whole damn company. When Robert's gone, the only one standing in my way will be his father, and I have every intention of outliving that dirty old bastard."

"Why should I help you?"

Surprise filled Julie's face.

"I saved your life!"

"You did," Nox replied. "And when I get back to the Big City I have every intention of sending you a heartfelt thank you card. Now, why should I help you?"

Julie sighed.

"I was hoping not to get into this," she said. "You didn't ask me how I knew you would be here."

A chill traveled down Nox's back.

"That's right, Nox. Robert knows about Ellis."

"And Natalie?"

"Of course."

"They killed her?"

"Worse. She was demoted. Natalie had one of the best damn Desertland jobs available. She hung around this nice air conditioned bar collecting tax free tips. Now she's out there in the heat, just like the rest of them. She's lost twenty five percent of her salary and gets no vacation for 3 years. It's fucking inhuman if you ask me."

"Robert did this to her?"

"Yes. But I can correct this injustice, provided I get what *I* want."

Nox considered Julie's words but said nothing.

"Let me sweeten the pot some more," Julie said after a while. "I'll offer you two hundred thousand credits to help me get Robert. I figure that's just icing on the cake. The real incentive will be your chance to get your revenge."

Nox stiffened. She recalled her meeting with Ellis at his gas station. She recalled the bitter look on the old man's face when he noticed Nox's injured hands.

"Revenge...Is that what this is about? Someone hurts you and you have to hurt them right back? First rule of being a Mechanic—"

Nox had finished Ellis' thought: "—don't let emotions cloud your judgment. Do your job like a machine: cold, efficiently, and unemotionally."

Nox turned away from Julie and walked back to the window. The burly red headed Security Guard stood just outside, smoking a cigarette. Another Security Guard was hidden in the shadows by the warehouse. A third, armed with a sniper's rifle, lay on the warehouse roof. Julie had Nox surrounded. Just in case.

"I've made my offer," Julie said. "If you don't want to accept, fine. There are plenty of other people Robert's pissed off that I can look up."

"I refuse, and you bury me with this base," Nox said. "How many more men you got out there?"

"More than enough. But I'd prefer you do this job because you want to, Nox. Remember, I'm not the one who screwed you over and I'm not the one that tried to get you killed... how many times now? I'm certainly not the one responsible for Ellis or his daughter."

"Tell me about the buried base."

A satisfied smile appeared on Julie's face. She reached into her purse and pulled out an old black and white photograph. Nox walked to the blonde's side and took it from her. The image on it was that of a man in his late thirties or early forties. His hair was stringy and disheveled. He wore thick glasses and had an awkward smile.

"Who's the geek?"

"His name is David Lemner. To many he was known as the Demon."

"Demon?" Nox said. She dropped the photograph on the counter. "Looks more like Casper the friendly ghost."

"In his time, he was the wealthiest, most powerful man in the world."

Nox took another look at the photograph. She finally recognized the image before her.

"Oh yeah. He worked with computers."

"That's like saying Shakespeare was a man who just happened to work with a pen."

Julie grabbed the photograph and addressed the man within it.

"This wonderfully gifted individual designed a vast database network that was beyond the scope of anything – *everything*– that came before it. He anticipated changes in technologies decades before they actually happened."

She paused and folded the photograph.

"But most importantly to us, twenty years ago he created the computer system all businesses work on. Even now, a decade after his death, we still use his system. You want to know why?"

"Because they're easy to operate and tamper proof," Nox said.

The smile returned to Julie's face.

"At least so far."

"What about this buried base?"

"As you're no doubt aware, a series of massive sandstorms hit the center of the country and most of the northern continents. It obliterated cities both large and small and took out farms and military bases and nuclear plants and... well, a number of things. Most importantly, it buried an unknown number of top secret research bases that Lemner operated. You see, David Lemner was wealthy and powerful enough to keep the construction, and eventual disappearance, of these bases a secret from everybody. But when he died, rumors of the lost research bases bubbled to the surface. Some of the rumors proved more reliable than others. In time, the largest industries bought into the very real possibility that at least three or four of these bases actually existed. If even one of them could be found, then the secrets of Lemner's research might finally be revealed. The wealth of information buried in these sands would be worth billions."

"Is that the real reason so many companies are out here scavenging?"

"In a word, yes."

"I didn't think there was enough money in collecting all that other shit."

"Oh, there's more than enough of that, too."

"But Lemner's bases are the jackpot."

"Exactly."

"Octi Survey Group 4 found one?"

"Not quite. They found the remains of one of the workers at one of Lemner's bases."

"Who?"

"His name isn't important. He was a low level temp who was trapped in that particular base when the winds first kicked up. He somehow managed to dig his way out and fled. Instead of dying with his fellow workers, he died out here. But he had a diary on him, and Robert spent many hours going over it, looking for any clues that would lead him to the buried base he came from. Robert convinced his father to commit to a costly re-routing of survey expeditions. They were tasked, one and all, to find this base. In the meantime, they scavenged absolutely nothing. Money was bleeding out of the Desertland operation, money his dad kept off Octi Corp.'s books. But Robert Octi Senior's enthusiasm for this project went only so far. After a couple of weeks, he threatened to shut it down. Things were looking real bad for Robert Junior until a miracle happens and one of the search vans stumbles on the base. It was everything Robert hoped for, and more. Ironically, he had *too* much material to go over. His staff had to separate the ordinary programs and equipment from the potentially extraordinary ones."

Julie laid her right hand on Nox's arm.

"And then you showed up," she said. "You hurt him pretty bad, just by doing that. You proved his security, like most everything else in his life, was worth shit. He was forced to pull the plug on the operation, something which did not sit well with dear dad. However, he had already stored a good deal of hardware, so this early withdrawal may prove to be a temporary setback only."

"What exactly is he –is everyone– hoping to find in this base?"

"Come on, Nox, use your imagination."

"I'm fresh out."

"Operating in the business world is not all that different from playing poker. You hide your assets, you bluff, and you bet on having a stronger hand than the other players, whether you actually do or not. As I said before, in the business world, everyone uses Lemner's programs."

"You're not talking about the passkey, are you?"

Julie giggled.

"You have heard some of the rumors after all."

"Refresh my memory."

"It's been said that David Lemner had a so-called backdoor program which worked for all his other programs, an artificial intelligence prototype that scans security features and adapts to them, cracking any security system on *any* computer. With this program you could theoretically break into your competitor's databases. With this program you could erase any outstanding taxes or criminal history. With this program you might even be able to inflate your company's worth or gain inside information on transactions between rival companies."

"Like playing poker with a marked deck."

"Exactly."

"And if you win this particular game, you rule the business world."

"Eventually," Julie said. "*If* such a program actually exists."

Nox considered what Julie said. Her thoughts came with great effort. The effects of the *Go!* pills were wearing out, and she could feel a growing wave of exhaustion wash over her.

"You don't think it exists?" she said. Her words were slurred.

If Julie noticed her weakened voice, she didn't say. Instead, she looked into Nox's good eye and said:

"I'll be honest with you—"

Her words hung in the air like a brilliant sun and time slowed to a crawl. Nox remember the last time someone said those same words to her. It was Donovan, not so very long ago.

The moment anyone tells me they're going to be 'honest' with me is the moment they're about to lie.

"—I think Robert's chasing a fantasy," Julie said. The smile on her face faded, replaced by a look of concern.

"You look pale," she said.

"I'm fine. Go on."

"If you say so. Anyway, even if the passkey did exist, I doubt it could do what people think it's capable of. Oh, it undoubtedly will give you some benefits, but a way to unlock *all* computers? I don't think so. My primary goal is discrediting Robert. Once you help me accomplish that task, feel free to check into what he brought from the base. If you find something, I'll pay good money for it. If you don't, or can't, I want the whole thing destroyed, and I want Robert's dad to know you did it. I want Robert Octi Senior to know his son had you in his hands and you got away."

Nox grabbed at the bar's counter and fought off a wave of dizziness.

"I'll do the job," Nox said. "But there are a couple of things I want."

"Okey," Julie said. There was caution in her voice.

"I want five hundred thousand credits."

Julie's eyes went wide.

"What?!"

"You're middle management. Write it off. Tell your superiors your department needed extra pens and paper clips."

"Very funny."

"You will send half that money to Natalie Howard. You will also find her father's body and arrange its transfer to her. Not that any of you corporate types care, but he was a decorated soldier foolish enough to fight your wars and even more foolish to think he was doing so to protect our freedoms instead of your bottom line."

Nox let out a long cough. The effort of standing here, talking to Julie, was draining the last of her energy.

"But that's old history and I'm babbling. Give Natalie her father back, and pay for a proper soldier's burial."

"It'll take some doing."

"That's not my concern. And I want a signed and notarized document that states Natalie has received both the money and her father. This document is to be made public in the Hall of Records before it's given to me."

Julie's eyes were wide.

"You can't be serious."

"Never put anything in writing, right?" Nox said and smiled. "You're going to make an exception. I won't do a damn thing for you unless I get that document."

"Octi Corp. will not take responsibility—"

"—for Ellis' death? No, of course they won't. And I'm not asking them to. Finesse the language all you want, I don't care. But Natalie receives the funds and her father, and this gift from Octi Corp. *will* be made public, so you can't turn around and take it back. Not without some heavy negative publicity, the type that dips your stock values."

Julie shook her head and let out a sigh.

"I'll do it," she said through gritted teeth. "And the other half of the money?"

"Small bills will be fine."

"I'm sure," Julie said. "I'm afraid to ask. Is there anything else?"

"Yeah, just one last thing. Get me a doctor."

Nox's eye closed and she felt her body slip off the counter and onto the floor.

27

The night's darkness turned to dark gray. The gray grew lighter, and lighter, until it became a sandy brown.

Nox's left eye opened. She looked around, and found she was lying on a cot. She was still in the bar, but neither Julie nor the burly red headed Security Guard were present.

"You're up?" a voice asked.

Nox turned to her right. An old man sat in a cheap fold out chair beside the window. He sucked on a wooden pipe and eyed Nox as if she were a carnival curiosity.

"Who are you?"

"I'm the Doctor," the old man said. "Julie hired me to—"

"Where is she?"

"Gone. She said she needed to get back to the city."

"What did she do, walk?"

"Not in those high heels," the Doctor said and chuckled. "She called in a helicopter and her entourage boarded up and flew off."

"We're the only ones left here?"

"Yes ma'am."

"Ok," Nox muttered. She rubbed her hair. "Got some water?"

Nox recalled the events of the past few days and went over every bit of her conversation with Julie. It felt like a half-remembered dream.

Then again, you were hoped up on stimulants and about to crash.

Nox sat up and examined her body. All the small cuts and almost all the deeper ones were healed. She felt her sliced eye and, underneath the fresh bandages, it too felt almost normal.

"Easy with that, lady," the Doctor said. He handed Nox a glass of water. Nox took it down in a couple of gulps.

"More," she said. "Please."

The old man shrugged, returned to the bar's counter, and poured water into the cup from a canteen. As he did, Nox rose. The *Go!* pills were well out of her system and she felt energized, reborn. She was still alive, and the new day presented so many possibilities.

"You look different, better," the old man said. He handed Nox the refilled glass.

Nox took the water down slowly.

"You're healing up fast. Faster than anyone should."

Nox handed the Doctor the empty cup and smiled. Her next action took the elderly man completely by surprise. Nox reached up and pulled at the bandage around her injured eye.

"What the hell are you doing?" the Doctor asked.

Nox didn't answer. She removed the bandage. As she did, the Doctor's face turned ashen. When the bandage was completely off, Nox felt around her shut eye. It was no longer swollen, though the skin around it was heavily bruised. Very delicately, Nox eased the eyelids apart. She grimaced as a burst of fluids, both clear and yellow, leaked out.

"Jesu," the Doctor muttered.

"Get me a towel."

"Like I'm going to argue with a crazy woman."

The Doctor returned to the bar's counter. He grabbed his medical case and hurried back to Nox's side. From within the case, he pulled out a white hand towel. Nox pressed it against the injured eye, until the white towel was soiled with sticky red and yellow liquids. When it was completely stained, Nox threw the towel to the ground and motioned for another. The Doctor gave her one.

Nox rubbed it gently against her eye and massaged the skin. Similar stains appeared on this second towel, but not as many. When Nox was done cleaning the wound, she dropped the second towel to the ground. Both her eyes remained closed. Slowly, she opened them. As she did, the Doctor gasped. Nox's injured eye, the *destroyed* eye, was revealed. It was there, intact but covered in a thin milky haze. Through the haze the Doctor saw the cornea. It moved to the right and left in perfect synchronicity with Nox's left eye.

"How...?" the old man asked. "It was sliced open, it was drained..."

Nox peered around the bar, as if seeing it for the first time.

"It'll take a while. Maybe one day it'll be fine."

"*How?*"

Nox faced the old man.

"Robert Octi Junior slit the eyeball but didn't pluck it out," she said, as if that explained everything. "Good thing he didn't. Growing another would be some trick."

"But... but how could such an injury heal?"

Nox smiled but said nothing more.

She recalled her earliest days and vague memories of being in a concrete bunker filled with fellow child soldiers. All of them, including her, were strapped to a bed and received injections and experimental treatments.

The procedures involved incredible pain.

She and the others in her group were given doses of experimental nano-probes. The nano-probes, microscopic robots designed to function within their host body and "fix" whatever ailed them, barreled through her veins like a fleet of runaway trains when she first received them. The pain lingered through every second of five very, *very* long days. When the procedure was over, she found herself shipped to Arabia.

The nano-probes proved their worth on that distant battlefield. The microscopic robots healed Nox a number of times, dealing with small scratches to one particularly grisly sucking wound.

Even radiation poisoning.

Nox wondered why the probes were still active in her body. Those prototypes, she recalled overhearing a couple of scientists say way back when, had a limited lifespan. Today, twenty plus years after the Arabian War, they still lurked inside her.

At this moment, she was extremely thankful for that fact.

Though she might never recover perfect sight in her injured eye, she could see through a milky haze and, given the circumstances, some sight was better than none at all. And Nox was eager to see the desert outside. She was even more eager to see the Big City again.

But she was *most* eager to stare into the eyes of Robert Octi Junior.

Sunlight flickered and faded before her.

The Doctor warmed some rations. The Mechanic stood by the bar's counter, her head low.

"You should be in bed," the Doctor said.

"I'll be fine."

"You want some food?"

"Thanks."

Nox's injured eye was very teary and it was difficult to adjust to the sunlight, dim though it was in the early evening. Perhaps, Nox thought, she would need to use a patch. Like Ellis had.

Ellis.

Nox took the rations and shoveled them down. When she was done, she noted a sparkling new leather briefcase lying beside the Doctor's weathered medical bag and pointed to it.

"What's that?"

"Julie left it behind. She told me to give it to you when you were feeling better."

Nox set aside the empty ration packet and approached the briefcase. She opened it and stared at the contents. Behind her, the Doctor let out a low whistle. The case was filled with credit bills. Two hundred and fifty thousand of them, if Julie came through.

"You hit the lottery or something?" the Doctor said.

"Something," Nox replied.

She ignored the money and opened a side compartment. Within it she found a sealed envelope. She opened and unfolded the document within. It was an official Octi Corp. insurance statement directed to Natalie Howard and filed with the Hall of Records in the Big City. The document stated that Octi Corporation regretted the loss of their employee Ellis Howard and noted his body would be delivered to his hometown for a Corporation sponsored burial. A two hundred and fifty thousand dollar check, the amount of his life insurance, was issued in the care of his sole heir, his daughter Natalie.

"Good," Nox muttered. The public proclamation's seal was genuine. The document had indeed been filed in the Hall of Records. Any attempt by Octi Corporation to swindle Natalie or void this public proclamation would have serious ramifications. In the end, it would be in Octi Corp.'s interests to stick to the agreement and count the lost money as a write off.

Which meant Natalie and Ellis were taken care of.

A satisfied smile filled Nox's face. She put the paper away and closed the case. She held on to it and walked to the bar's entrance. The door swung open and she looked out. Parked beside the warehouse was the Octi truck she drove to the base. Her mangled chopper remained tied to the truck's rear.

"You're leaving?"

"It's time," Nox said. She faced the Doctor. "What about you?"

"They –hell, *I*– thought it would take you a lot longer to recover. I told them to come for me at the end of next week."

"Did they leave you a radio so you could call them back, tell them to come early?"

"They were in a rush to go and said they didn't carry a spare. No big deal, they said to sit tight, to expect them by the weekend at the earliest or the beginning of the week at the latest."

"How many rations did they leave?"

"Enough for a week or so."

"How many, exactly?"

The Doctor counted the remaining rations. "Eight days' worth. Plenty. They'll be back way before I'm out."

"We're fifty some odd miles from the nearest rest stop," Nox said, recalling the location of Ellis' gas station. "Could you walk that distance, even with those rations?"

The Doctor chuckled.

"In this heat? Are you crazy? There's no way."

"Exactly."

The Doctor's smile abruptly disappeared.

"Did they leave you anything else? A vehicle?"

"No."

Nox nodded.

"You've been abandoned."

"No."

"I'm afraid so."

The Doctor scratched his head and frowned.

"What exactly are you talking about?"

"I know these people only too well, Doctor, and they're a cold bunch. Their world revolves around profits and loss. They figured I'd drive off in my truck when I was better and not think twice about you. You'd stay behind, not too terribly concerned because they promised you they'd come back. A day would pass, another, and after a while your rations would be low and soon after that they'd be gone. By the time you realized they weren't coming back, there's nothing for you to do but wait for the sands to swallow you up."

The Doctor shook his head.

"It isn't true," he said. "Octi values their employees. They wouldn't—"

"Profit and loss, Doctor. It isn't worth the expense in fuel and personnel to come back for you."

"It...it can't be."

"Believe what you will. You can come with me and live, or wait here for them and die. It's up to you."

Nox exited the bar and walked to the Octi truck. She made a quick check of the truck's engine and underside, to make sure the rig was fueled and ready for the long trip back to the Big City. While searching, she found a freshly planted tracking device. Julie wanted to know where she was.

Fine.

Nox ignored the device and checked her mangled chopper to make sure it was still properly tied down. She found another tracking probe hidden within the motorcycle's engine. Nox removed it. She walked to the warehouse entrance and was about to toss it inside when she spotted the remains of Donovan's robot lying in the shadows. She stared at the robot for several long seconds.

"You started all this," Nox said. She approached the destroyed machine.

Lying inert in the sand, it looked like an overgrown child's toy, busted up, discarded, and now forgotten. The Mechanic planted the tracking device on the robot's remains.

"You've finally become useful," Nox said.

Let Julie think I left the chopper behind.

When Nox returned to the truck and climbed into its cabin, she found the Doctor buckled up and waiting in the passenger seat.

"Fuck them," the Doctor spat. "Fuck them all."

Nox nodded. She reached for the truck's key in the ignition and turned it.

The engine roared to life.

28

Nox drove the entire night and most of the next day. When the sun once again set, she spotted the first rays from the distant lights of the Big City. The truck rumbled across the city limits an hour later and the elderly Doctor missed their arrival. He snored softly in the passenger seat and awoke moments later to find the darkness of the desert's night replaced by intense neon lights.

"Welcome home," the Doctor said and yawned.

"Likewise."

The Doctor popped open an energy drink and guzzled it down.

"Been a while since last I was here," the Doctor said. "Place has changed some. Not for the better."

"You have someplace to go?" Nox asked.

The Doctor shrugged.

"Even when I was here, I never put down any roots. Got all my roots in the Desertland camps. Here? I don't know where to begin." The Doctor said nothing for a few seconds. "I really thought they appreciated my services, you know?"

"Forget about Octi. Focus on the future."

"Yeah. Say, is there a hospital nearby? That's probably the best place to start."

Nox pointed the truck down a large street and drove several blocks before pulling into an oversized parking lot. On the other side of the street was an enormous building shaped like a grounded oil freighter.

"TransCo Oil's Hospital," Nox said. "Largest one in the city."

The Doctor stared at the structure. He was an old man weary and nervous about starting a new life in a new place. He was more than a little overwhelmed.

"A person could disappear in a place like this."

"At this point I'd recommend it," Nox said. "Best to let Octi Corp. think you're still back there at the base."

The words made the Doctor scowl.

"Rotten bastards."

He offered Nox his hand.

"Thanks, Nox."

Nox shook the Doctor's hand.

"Best you don't mention me to anyone, either."

"Yeah, like anyone would believe I treated a woman who could heal her own ruptured eyeball. You gonna tell me how you accomplished that particular trick?"

Nox smiled and released the Doctor's hand.

"Didn't think so," the Doctor said and matched Nox's smile with one of his own. He opened the truck's passenger door and exited the vehicle. Once out, the Doctor stretched.

"Hey, old timer," Nox said before flinging a rectangular package at the elderly man. He caught it and looked it over.

"What's this?" the Doctor asked. He was startled to find a thick wad of credit bills in his hands. It was more than enough to pay for several years of living in the Big City.

"Payment for services rendered."

"I can't take this."

"Of course you can. Thanks for everything."

The Doctor nodded.

"Thank you for taking care of *me*," the Doctor replied. The smile returned to his face. Whatever unease or fear he felt was gone. He waved to Nox as he crossed the street and headed for the hospital.

When the Doctor was gone, Nox shifted the truck in gear. Julie was tracking the truck's movements, of course, and had to know the Mechanic was back in the Big City. Like the Doctor, Julie probably thought Nox would take longer to recover and arrive later in the week. Hopefully, her premature arrival messed up whatever plans Julie had in place for her.

Nox drove the truck to the opposite end of the hospital and parked inside a large parking zone.

She unloaded her chopper and dragged it into the motorcycle parking area. No one would notice it there, at least not for the remainder of this night. Plenty of time.

Nox then walked to the main entrance of the hospital. Beside it was a pharmacy. Nox entered the store and picked up a bottle of aspirin, an anesthetic, *Go!* pills, and gauze. Beside the counter she found a rack of sunglasses. She picked one and noisily dropped all the items she collected onto the counter. The crashing sounds awoke the young cashier. She eyed Nox's stash before examining the Mechanic's bruised face.

"Emergency room's through the main doors, friend."

Nox stared at her through angry eyes, until she was certain the cashier was good and uncomfortable with her presence. All the better to remember her visit, should anyone ask.

"If I wanted the emergency room, I would have gone there," Nox finally replied. Her voice was heavy with sarcasm. "Are you gonna sell me this shit or what?"

The lady shook her head. Rudeness was all too common in the Big City, and the teller was nothing if not a Big City gal.

"Fuck you too," she cheerfully replied. She rang up Nox's items and took her money. When she handed the Mechanic her change, she added: "And have a nice fucking night, asshole."

"Thank you," Nox responded. The edge in her voice was gone, as if it never existed. She pocketed the change. When her hand emerged from the jacket, it carried another wad of bills. She handed these to the lady behind the counter.

"What's this?"

"A tip," Nox said.

"Tip?"

"Take it."

"I don't know what you think I am, but—"

"Please. I let my temper get the better of me. Have a good night."

Nox put the sunglasses on and grabbed her paper bag. If all went well, this side trip to the Pharmacy would create enough confusion to hide the fact that she brought the Doctor in from the desert.

When Julie checked up on Nox's path back into the Big City, she would find the Mechanic stopped at this Hospital's pharmacy and used up some of the undoubtedly marked bills given to her to pay for these drugs. Any other monies used by the Doctor in this area would, hopefully, be attributed to Nox as well.

Good luck, Doctor, Nox thought. From here on in, he was completely on his own.

Nox smiled when she stepped back into the parking lot.

It was the first time since she returned from the desert that she noted the acrid smells emanating from the Big City. Only now did she realize how much she missed it, and how close she was to never coming back. The place wasn't much, but it was home, and there were so many things to do before the night was over.

Nox weaved in and out of the streets of the Big City seemingly without purpose or destination. In reality, she had both. She stopped before stores and bars and clubs and exited the truck, distributed more money, and was off once again. The night wore on, and most of the money Julie left her was spent. Nox kept a little, for later. By that time, she hoped, no one would care where the bills turned up.

On impulse, she brought the truck within a couple of blocks of the Salvation Brokers Building. She stopped at a red light and eyed it from the distance.

The building, never much to begin with, was a burnt out shell. The Salvation Brokers sign hung limp on the sidewalk, its lower right corner still nailed to a charred post.

This place sure went to hell, Nox thought.

She pressed down on the accelerator and continued her nocturnal journey.

At three in the morning, Michael Remor, Security Guard Fourth Grade at the Octi Plaza Building, made his final rounds for the night. He yawned while the elevator took him down from the top floor to the lobby and yawned once again when the doors slid open. He stepped into the lobby and walked around the repair crew's equipment.

The mess they left behind was ghastly, even if most of their equipment was covered beneath a large canvas sack.

How much longer would they need?

Michael had no idea. Though the damage to Donovan's office was extensive, a good deal of time had passed and it seemed very little progress was made in the repair work.

Maybe it's in Octi's interest that the repair crew take their sweet time. After all, the more time wasted, the higher the expenses. You could take these expense figures to your accountants and lobby for higher tax breaks. Hell, you could squeeze the insurance companies for more money as well.

No matter what happened, Octi Corp. always came out ahead.

Michael Remor sighed. *Wish I did.*

He walked to his post, a dark wood octagonal desk set in the middle of the lobby. It was elegant and functional and faced the enormous glass panels that lined the entry to the building. When he wasn't watching the monitors before him, Michael stared outside and wished he wasn't locked in this glass prison. He eyed the Octi Plaza's enormous parking lot and, beyond it, First Avenue, one of the Big City's primary thoroughfares. Across the street were Octi's competitors, the other buildings housing other Big City companies.

Competition between companies was always fierce, but Octi Corp. was winning. Rumor had it that old man Octi was intent on renaming First Avenue after himself, a particularly satisfying poke in the eye to all those competitors surrounding Octi Plaza.

Could you imagine? The Security Guard thought. *To get to your buildings, you have to travel through Octi Avenue. Oh, the humanity! And what's next? Could old man Octi work on getting the entire business district named after himself? If so, why stop there? Why not re-name the entire city?*

"Octi's Big City," Michael said and chuckled.

He reached for his cup of coffee and leaned back in the chair behind the monitors. He watched as a dozen different camera views cycled through the monitors. He saw the parking lot, the lower garage, the inside of the elevators, several empty hallways, and, finally, the lobby itself. At that point he turned to the camera and waved at himself.

Over the course of the next hour, he saw the lobby and the other familiar images whisk by maybe a hundred times. And each time, he saw the same: Nothing.

Again Michael yawned. He was so very tired. Without meaning to, he closed his eyes.

When he re-opened them, he lurched forward. He looked at his watch and was relieved to see that he dozed off only a couple of minutes.

Good thing, too. His shift was ending in the next half hour, and if his replacement were to find him sleeping, he was done.

Michael stretched and rubbed his fingers through his hair. He felt a faint rumbling in the lobby and wondered if that was what had awoken him.

The outside traffic, he thought, must be building early. *Real* early.

Michael rose from his chair and walked to the glass doors leading outside. He looked past the parking lot and at First Avenue but saw no traffic.

"Huh."

The rumbling grew with each passing second. Somewhere out there a vehicle, a *very* large vehicle, was moving closer.

Perhaps, Michael thought, the rumbling was coming from a truck delivering cargo. Large trucks weren't allowed in the city during the day, so naturally all deliveries were made at night.

Michael remained by the door while the rumbling increased. He was curious to see this approaching monster.

It didn't take long.

In the distance and at the end of the road, he finally saw it. It was a dark truck without a cargo payload. It moved up the street very quickly.

Michael's eyes narrowed. The truck ran through a red light and for a second Michael spotted the Octi Corp. logo on its side. He didn't recognize the vehicle's exact model, but, based on the size, he was certain it came in from outside the Big City. Perhaps from the Desertlands.

It roared along the street and, without slowing, squealed into the Octi Plaza parking lot.

Michael swallowed.

The truck's lights lit up the lobby. They were blinding. The roar of the truck's engine caused the window panels to vibrate.

Where are you going?

Michael watched in fascination as the truck approached, closer and closer. She had to slow down to park real soon, right?

Right?

Michael's eyes went wide. The truck wasn't slowing at all. If anything, it was speeding up, and Michael was standing directly in her path!

The truck's horn blared several times, like a warning from hell. The noise shot through Michael's body and kicked up some primal instinct within him. The security guard jumped to the side.

Just in time.

The Octi Corp. truck rammed through the glass paneling, sending hundreds of pounds of jagged shards all over the place. The truck barreled forward, obliterating Michael's mahogany post. The monitors and octagonal desk were reduced to rubble and still the truck plowed on. Brakes were applied and the tires locked in place. The truck skidded along the marble floor, leaving behind a heavy black skid mark, and rammed the worker's tools. Still it slid, ultimately crashing against the elevator doors.

In the distance, an alarm blared and the lobby's fire sprinklers came. A stream of water rained down over the rubble.

Michael found himself curled up in a fetal position besides the shattered front entrance of Octi Plaza. There was no more roaring, no more shattering crystal. With the exception of the distant alarm and the splash of water, all was relatively quiet.

Michael sat up and looked at the heart of the Octi Plaza lobby. He couldn't believe the devastation.

The Octi Corp. truck had demolished the lobby and its front end was wedged into the elevator doors. Dust and debris were everywhere.

"Holy shit," Michael said.

The truck's passenger door swung open. A lone figure, a woman, stepped out and calmly jumped to the floor. She noted the damage to the lobby while approaching the cowering security guard.

For a second or two Michael thought about reaching for his gun, but didn't bother. He spotted it lying some thirty feet away, closer to the truck's driver than to him. How it got there, he would never know.

The driver of the Octi Corp. truck spotted the weapon and leaned down to pick it up.

"Oh God," Michael muttered. He closed his eyes, fully expecting this crazy woman to shoot him dead. Instead, he heard the driver's voice.

"You OK?"

Michael opened his eyes. The driver stood directly before him. The woman was very tall and *very* muscular. She had short, jet black hair and blue vertical tattoos over her right eyebrow. She wore jeans and a dusty shirt, and there were cuts and bruises over almost all her exposed flesh.

The woman emptied the cartridges from Michael's handgun, made sure there wasn't one in the chamber, and offered the weapon back to the security guard.

"I...I'm fine," Michael managed. He took the gun and replaced it into its holster. "What...what happened?"

"Came to make a delivery," the truck driver said. She reached into her shirt pocket and pulled out a piece of paper.

"See that the old man gets this."

Michael took the paper and unfolded it. He read its contents.

YOU KEEP FUCKING UP.
LOVE AND KISSES,
              NOX

Michael folded the paper. The unreality of the situation threatened to push him over the edge.

"You...you're Nox?"

"You heard of me?"

"Who hasn't? What you did to the fortieth floor...it was really fucked up."

Nox shrugged and walked away. Michael followed. He waved the paper.

"Is this it?" Michael asked.

"What do you mean?"

"This note. Is this all you wanted the old man to read?"

"What are you, a literary critic?"

Michael stopped walking and let out a fractured laugh.

"I am no literary critic," he said and pointed to all the destruction around them. "I suppose all this is enough of a message."

"Subtlety was never one of my virtues," Nox said before walking off into the night.

29

Robert Octi Senior arrived to find, for the second time in as many weeks, the parking lot of his Plaza filled with fire trucks, ambulances, and police vehicles. Even more annoying was the large group of reporters that lined the street and took pictures of the latest Octi Corp. misfortune.

Octi swore.

It would cost him even more to keep this new story from leading the evening news. He didn't even want to think what he'd have to tell the board about *this* particular misfortune.

His limousine crawled through the masses of gawkers and professionals filling the parking lot. Behind the tinted windows of his limousine Robert Octi Senior watched a heavy duty tow truck strain to pull one of his Desertland big-rigs from the lobby of his beloved building.

Octi swore once again. He knew what the bizarre vision before him meant. It explained why his son wanted to see him this early in the morning, and why he was hesitant to fully brief him over the phone.

"Would you like me to leave you by the lobby door again?" Octi's driver asked, remembering the last time Octi arrived to find this circus at his building's doors.

"Fuck no."

"Are you sure, sir? I thought you said it was good for morale that the boss walk about the wreckage and look like he's in charge."

"Just take me to the fucking private lot."

The driver fought hard not to snicker.

"Yes sir."

The limousine headed for a metal door at the side of the building. It opened as the vehicle approached and closed immediately after it entered. The limousine's lights revealed a private underground parking lot that held only a handful of available spaces. The driver parked the car in the space closest to Octi's private elevator and next to a shiny red sports car.

Octi snorted when he stepped out of the limousine. He recognized the car parked next to his, for he bought it for his son's thirtieth birthday.

On days like this, he wondered why he bothered.

Robert Octi Senior sat behind his desk and read and re-read what was written on that single sheet of paper Nox left him. Standing at the foot of the desk was his son. The younger man looked very ill at ease. After several seconds of deathly silence, Octi folded the paper. His eyes were red and his right hand shook.

"Nox," Octi spat. "You had her. You had her and you let her go."

"Dad, I don't understand. Nagel told me Nox was—"

"Don't attribute your failures to others," Octi hissed. "You didn't feel Nox was a sufficient enough threat to our organization to *personally* check on her corpse? How many times have I told you *not* to delegate so damn much?"

Robert closed his mouth and stared at the floor.

"I had high hopes for you, Robert," Octi said. "I gave you all the breaks, even when we were losing money on all your idiotic pet projects. But you failed me each and every fucking time."

"I've tried to do the best—"

"And that's the saddest thing, isn't it? I *know* you're trying your best. I know everything you've done, every single screw up you've made, has been performed while 'doing your best'." Octi paused and sighed. "Family is family, but business... business is everything."

A single tear rolled down Robert's cheek.

"Please sir, I beg you..."

Octi tore the paper into small pieces. He leaned back in his chair and stared at the ceiling, as if searching for divine inspiration. Instead, he found that annoying popcorn ceiling pattern that went out of style decades before. Tomorrow he'd get the workers to strip the popcorn and repaint the ceiling some bright, colorful pattern. Yes, that would make things much nicer.

The anger dissipated and Octi's cold stare returned to his son.

"Against my better judgment I'll give you one last chance to redeem yourself. You brought back fifty tons of shit from that desert base. I'll give you one week and one week only, to find something among those crates that makes this whole fiasco worth my while. Understood?"

"Yes sir."

"Find it quick," Octi said. He turned his chair around and stared out at the Big City. He didn't bother watching his son exit the room.

Down below, Octi personnel were busy chatting with the news media and offering subtle bribes to bury the stories they planned to report. Nox watched them work the crowd and wondered if she too could collect a few bucks by posing as a reporter.

Let's get serious.

Nox worked her way through the crowds, keeping her head low and drawing as little attention as possible. She found an abandoned broom leaning up against a wall outside the lobby and grabbed it. She swept away a few shards of glass just outside the building and used a tow truck as cover to enter the lobby itself.

Thankfully, the various security guards were busy dealing with the crowds and didn't pay much attention to another person carrying a broom. Nox headed to the deepest part of the lobby and opened a door leading to a stairwell.

Nox found what she was looking for on the Plaza's second floor: A computer station. It was an information station, standard equipment for buildings of this size. Nox tapped on the monitor and a bright green screen with the Octi Corp. logo appeared. Below it were several lines of information.

Welcome to the Octi Plaza.
It is our hope your stay here is productive.

"It will be," Nox said. The green screen faded, replaced by another.

If you need information on our various departments, please press here.
For information on staff, please press here.

Nox tapped on the second line. A list of Octi personnel filled the screen. Each name was followed by information on where their offices were located.

Nox noticed Donovan's name was no longer there, but she wasn't looking for it.

The person she was looking for had an office on the forty
fifth floor.

The office was large and tastefully furnished. An oak desk
lay at the rear and over it was a lush Johansen oil painting of a
barn and meadow. To Nox's untrained eyes, it looked like the
genuine article. To either side of the painting and desk were
bookshelves lined with legal tomes.

It took Nox several minutes to find the office safe.

At first she thought it might be hidden behind the
Johansen. But that would be way too obvious. Instead, Nox
checked the legal casebooks and found a couple of them were
phonies. When she pulled them aside, she found the small wall
safe.

Nox took a few minutes to examine the safe for security
measures. She found and disabled a couple and felt
comfortable enough to pick the lock itself.

A siren flared up and died down the street, a jet airplane
rumbled as it lifted off. The silence of the very early morning
took over. Then, a slight click was heard and Nox smiled. She
found the final security measure just inside the safe's door. It
was a small trigger and a loose wire. To the untrained eye,
they looked like nothing more than parts of the safe's locking
mechanism. The loose wire could have been anything.

It wasn't, of course.

Nox slowly pulled the wire out, until it was fully exposed.

"Nice," she muttered.

The Mechanic took a small aerosol can from her pocket
and sprayed the wire. A dull white foam completely covered it.
Once done, Nox let out a relieved breath. Had she missed this
wire and touched it while opening the safe door, she would
have been electrocuted.

Nox opened the safe and searched it. She found and
removed several documents. At the back of the safe she found
a small package.

The smile crept back onto her face.

Nox took the package to the oak desk and risked turning
on a small lamp. She opened the package and found three old
and worn computer disks.

Jackpot.

Nox took the package of old disks and put the other
documents back in place. Afterwards, she closed the safe and

eyed the office to make sure everything was where it was supposed to be.

She then reached for the lamp and was about to turn it off when she spotted a photograph on the corner of the desk. It was a professional quality black and white picture of a just married couple engaged in a tender embrace. They both smiled for the camera, a young couple eager to begin their shared life.

Nox recognized them both. Robert Octi Junior held the beautiful blonde Julie very close.

"Should have held her a little closer," Nox said.

She shut off the lamp and exited the room.

30

Robert Octi Junior took a deep swig of rum, swallowed, winced, and belched. He hit the brakes and his five hundred thousand credit sports car veered wildly to the right. The cat that wandered into the middle of the road was lucky its reactions weren't quite as badly impaired. It scampered away intact and disappeared into a bush while the car skidded to a stop right over the path she just crossed.

Robert clenched his teeth and stared at his bottle of rum. It lay on its side on the floor of the passenger's compartment, spilling and staining the car's one of a kind carpeting.

"For fuck's sake," Robert groaned. He grabbed the bottle and capped it.

Dark thoughts floated through the young executive's mind. His whole life was spent trying to prove himself worthy of the Octi name yet time and again he failed. Both himself *and* his father. Despite each failure, he moved on to bigger and bigger projects.

This time it'll work, he'd tell himself. And when the latest project inevitably blew up in his face, he'd dust himself off and find the next big thing to tackle. At some point, something *had* to work out, right? Right?

Robert Octi Junior was many things but he wasn't stupid. He was only too aware of what everyone whispered behind his back.

You wouldn't be here if it wasn't for the fact that you're Octi's son. If you were like everyone else, you'd be out on your ass.

Well, Robert thought, *I'm* not *like everyone else. I'm an Octi, and I'm richer than you are and much better than you are. And you know what? I* will *succeed. Sure I've taken some hits, but I've got what others don't: I know I'm right. I've got clarity of vision and my decisions, in the long run, will prove me right. History* will prove me right. Besides...

"...I'm the decider," he whispered. There was a slur in his voice.

Fuck them. Fuck them all if they don't see what's right in front of their noses.

Robert pressed down hard on the accelerator and shifted the car into gear.

Fuck them all.

The warehouse district's security was beefed up after Donovan's robot went wild. The short electrified chain link fence that used to circle the perimeter was replaced with one that rose a full five feet higher. The extra security was not so much to keep out curious civilians or industrial spies, but rather the media.

Robert Octi Junior's sports car skidded to a stop next to the guard gate. The guard, an elderly man with an elliptical paunch, eyed the car and its occupant and noted the pungent smell of alcohol in the breeze.

"This is a restricted area," the guard said. "You can't enter."

"Do you know who I am?" Robert said.

"No sir. Nor do I care."

Robert's face turned red.

"I don't have time for peasants," he yelled.

"Son, it's late. Why don't you go home, sleep it off?"

"I'm Robert Octi Junior."

The guard's mouth shut tight. He squinted hard and looked down at the occupant of the car. He suddenly stepped back. His lips twitched nervously as the expression on his face turned to complete shock.

"Recognize me now, asshole?" Robert muttered.

The Security Guard tried to say something, but couldn't. Instead, he reached for the button next to the guard gate door. The gate rose and Robert shifted the car into gear.

"You're fired," Robert said. The sports car's tires squealed and the vehicle sped into the district.

The guard wiped sweat from his face and sat back into his post.

"Thirty years," he whispered. His body slid down heavily on the chair. "Thirty years."

The guard thought of his wife, of his son, and of their young family. Times were tight, no more so than now, and though this job wasn't much, it provided some security. That was over. All because he didn't recognize—

The elderly security guard spotted the approaching shadow from the corner of his eye, but his reaction to it was slow.

A single bullet tore through his heart, killing him instantly. No more worries, no more fears.

Robert Octi Junior slammed on the brakes. His sports car skidded to a halt in the parking lot in front of Warehouse 23. The lights around the warehouse were off and the place was quiet. In fact, Robert thought, it look abandoned.

Where is everyone?

Robert frowned. At the very least there should be no less than an army of technicians inside, sorting through all the shit brought in from the Demon's Desertland base. Were they taking the night off?

This thought angered Robert even more. His ass was on the line and his people were on break. No *fucking* way.

Robert exited the sports car and marched to the entrance of the warehouse. His head was on a pivot, moving back and forth while searching in vain for any technicians or security staff.

When he reached the door leading in, he found it ajar. The anger within him, already barely contained, turned nuclear. He pushed the door fully open and darted inside.

"Where the fuck are you guys?" he yelled.

Not there. The interior of the warehouse was as devoid of life as the outside. Robert's only company was the hundreds of crates brought in from the Demon's Desertlands base.

"Hello?" Robert yelled. His word echoed in the distance.

Fuck me.

Robert wandered deeper into the warehouse. He was alternately shocked and angered by the fact that no one – *absolutely no one*– was here. But, by the time he neared the rear of the warehouse, his anger was gone. The place was simply *too* empty. Someone should be here. The emptiness was...creepy.

"Hello?" Robert repeated. He no longer yelled. There was an unease in his voice. The back end of the warehouse was drenched in inky shadows and Robert felt alone and vulnerable.

At first slowly, then faster and faster, he retreated. He passed several columns of boxes and crates and the only sound he heard was that of the heels of his limited edition Arceli shoes clicking on the concrete floor. His eyes scanned the shadows as he progressed while his mind went wild. He feared imaginary monsters lurking behind every black corner. They tensed in their shadowy lair, jagged muscles coiled while sickly tongues licked sharp teeth. They waited for him. They waited to move.

"Just my imagination," Robert said. The brittleness of his voice came as a surprise. *I'm above all this,* he thought.

I'm above all this.

The words offered him a little courage, and Robert slowed his hasty retreat.

"I'm above it all," he said, as if it were his new mantra.

But just as he got a grip on his fears, Robert spotted a pair of shining red eyes glowing from the shadows beside one of the many crates in the area. The image was so surreal that it took several seconds to register. Once it did, Robert let out a screech and lost control of his movements as well as his bladder. He fell heavily on his ass and a sharp pain flooded his body. Tears ran down Robert's face as he desperately crawled from those evil red eyes. The only thing between this foul creature and the young executive was a puddle of urine.

"Please, don't," Robert begged. Though he spent much of his professional career sending others into dangerous, even deadly situations, up until this very moment he had never experienced such mortal fear first hand.

Tears streamed down Robert's face as the red eyes watched. Their gaze was unblinking and cold. They did not move, they did not blink. They almost seemed...

Frozen?

Despite his fears, Robert stopped crawling away. The pair of red eyes remained exactly where they were, completely immobile. Robert watched them for several more seconds before getting up on his knees.

The ghastly pair of eyes remained stubbornly in place. Robert stood now, staring them down. A minute passed, and then another, yet the eyes didn't move. Not even an inch. No living creature could stay that still. And if it wasn't a living creature...

"...then what the hell are you?"

With great hesitancy, Robert moved forward, circling the puddle of urine, until he was at the edge of the great shadows and just a couple of feet from the glowing red eyes.

"What the hell?" Robert said.

It took a moment for his eyes to adjust to the dark shadows. When they did, he made out a rectangular shape attached to the pair of red...*lights?*

Robert leaned in some more, until he was directly in front of the lights. Though his instincts still screamed to run, curiosity got the better of him.

Shaking hands reached out and very hesitantly touched the source of the lights. The object was larger than a shoe box but smaller than a Domination game. Heavier, too. Robert pulled the box out of the shadows and into the light. When he finally had a good look at it, he gasped once again.

It's a bomb.

Robert slowly, extremely cautiously put the box on the ground. He then pulled back at the speed of light. In a fraction of a second the junior executive was running to the warehouse exit. He made it only halfway there before something heavy smashed into the side of his face. The young executive's legs folded under and he crashed to the floor, blacking out for an instant.

When he once again opened his eyes, he was relieved to see Nagel standing over him.

"Nagel," Robert said. Blood dripped from his mouth and one of his molars was loose. Despite the pain and fear, he felt embarrassed. Would Nagel realize he pissed himself? How could he possibly miss seeing...? Maybe the shadows—

"Thank the Gods," Robert said. He tried to get up, but was too dizzy. "Someone is trying to blow all this stuff—"

Robert abruptly stopped talking. Nagel held a handgun and pointed it directly at the junior executive.

"What the hell are you doing?"

A serpentine smile appeared on Nagel's face.

"I found a better paying job," Nagel said. "Consider this my two-week notice."

Nagel showed Robert his other hand. In it was a small silver cylinder. At its top was a large candy red button. Robert recognized the device. It was the Octi Corp. Dash 3000 Detonator. There was little doubt it was linked to the explosive Robert just found.

"You bastard," Robert said. The extent of his personal bodyguard's betrayal was brutally clear. "Back at the base, you were the one that let Nox go."

Nagel nodded.

"What's your plan? Are you trying to ruin me?"

"No," Nagel said. He cocked the gun and smiled. "I'm going to kill you."

"Wait!" Robert pleaded. He reached into his coat pocket and with trembling hands removed the worn diary the Octi survey crew found so many weeks before. "We can make a deal! This has to be worth something to you!"

Robert tossed the diary toward Nagel. The bodyguard let it fall to the ground at his feet.

"It describes Lemner's passkey, Nagel," Robert continued. "You know that. It'll help you find it!"

Nagel let out a laugh. He gave the diary a vicious kick that sent it flying into the shadows. The smile on Nagel's face turned sinister.

"I don't need it," Nagel said. "Or anything else here."

"You... you already have it, don't you? You have Lemner's passkey?"

The smile remained on Nagel's face.

"After all I've done for you... How could you?"

"It was easy."

Nagel lifted the detonator.

"Don't!" Robert yelled.

But Nagel pressed the button.

Robert closed his eyes, expecting the world to erupt.

It didn't.

When Robert opened his eyes, Nagel stood in the very same spot. He let out a sarcastic laugh.

"Did you really think I'd blow this place up with *me* inside? Do you think I'm as stupid as you are?"

Nagel's laugher died down.

"There are eighteen bombs hidden throughout the warehouse. I just set off every one of their timers, Robert. *I've* got five minutes to get out of here. *You* get to stick around and see them explode. Up close and personally."

Nagel lifted the handgun and aimed it at Robert's leg. Robert felt his chest tighten.

He wants to cripple me...leave me here to die.

Robert closed his eyes and turned away. If his bladder wasn't already empty—

The sound of a gunshot filled the empty warehouse.

Robert winced and let out a yelp. He expected to feel the intense pain of bullet shattering bone. Instead, he heard the roar of the gunshot echo throughout the warehouse until it faded away. When the sound was gone, Robert realized he felt no pain. No pain at all.

Robert slowly opened his eyes. He was surprised to see Nagel lying on his stomach on the floor. Standing a few feet behind the bodyguard's corpse was Nox. She held a smoking handgun.

"Hello again," Nox said.

The Mechanic walked to Nagel's side and picked up the bodyguard's gun. She examined the detonator and, realizing she had no use for it, tossed it aside.

"W... why?" Robert gasped.

Nox eyed the young executive.

"Speak up," Nox said. "Got some ringing in my ears."

"Why did you save me?"

"Did I?" Nox replied.

Robert rose.

"Look, what I did to you back in the base..."

"Don't remind me, you vicious little shit."

Robert swallowed.

"Nox," Robert muttered. "We can still make an arrangement. You could work for us."

Nox chuckled.

"Sure. You've got at least one opening," Nox said and pointed to Nagel's corpse. "I suppose you could use a new bodyguard."

Robert ignored Nox's sarcasm.

"I meant it when I said you would make a good Octi Corp. employee!"

"You're still trying to peddle that shit? Sorry, Robert, your dental plan sucks."

Robert swallowed hard. He clenched his fists.

"Then go ahead, get this over with. Kill me!"

"If we stick around much longer, I won't have to," Nox replied. "Let's go."

"You...you're taking me away from here? Why?"

Nox didn't answer and Robert felt a deep shiver.

"Oh no... You want to take me away, to torture me, right? Do to me what I did to you? Well you can go to hell! I'm staying here!"

Nox grabbed Robert by his shirt's collar and pulled him close to her.

"I'm not interested in torturing you, you fucking jackass," The Mechanic snarled. "In fact, I don't plan to ruffle a single hair on your pretty little head."

"What?"

"That's right, Robert. I'm going to let you *live*."

31

Robert exited the warehouse first, followed closely by Nox. Robert's feet dragged as the two walked past the junior executive's sports car and past the warehouse parking lot. When they were a safe distance away and standing behind a large metallic trash dumpster, Nox motioned Robert to stop. She then ordered the young executive to sit. Robert wearily eyed the Mechanic.

"What's this all about?"

Nox leaned against the dumpster and put her gun away.

"It's time for some clarity," Nox said. "Nagel wasn't the only one working against you. Hell, he wasn't even the *closest* person to you that was planning your latest spectacular failure."

"Closest? What are you talking about?"

"I'll bet you're curious who's been screwing you, in more ways than one. She planned it all, your entire downfall. Not that it required that much effort. She's a hell of a combination of beauty and brains, if you don't mind my saying so."

"What the fuck are you talking about?"

"I'm talking about your wife. Julie Octi."

Nox expected Robert to take a swing at her, but instead found all fight was gone from the young executive. He stared at Nox with barely focused eyes.

"Julie?"

"When Donovan's robot failed to take me out at my apartment, Julie used the opportunity to get me after *you*. Why not? I was furious with Octi Corp. At that point, I was willing to do anything to destroy you. She fed me bits and pieces of information and directed me to your Desertland operation and closer and closer to the Demon's base. It was after I broke in and was captured that she overplayed her hand. She had Nagel and that security guard fake my death for your benefit. If she could pull such heavy strings to save me while I was at your complete mercy, it meant she was deep into your operation. I figured she knew *everything* that was going on."

Nox paused and smiled.

"She probably knew more about it than you did."

Robert's hand came to his mouth and he let out a gasp.

"She's the one!" Robert said. "She has Lemner's passkey!"

"That'd be my guess."

Robert wiped sweat from his forehead and muttered a series of unintelligible words.

"Cheer up, Robert," Nox continued. "It wasn't personal. She was just trying to get ahead, like all good middle management types do."

Robert had enough. His eyes bulged and, finally, he rushed Nox. The Mechanic easily swatted the young executive to the ground.

"Pay attention. Because this was supposed to be one of the last scenes in Julie's little play."

"F...fuck you," Robert mumbled.

Nox leaned down and faced the junior executive.

"Your father is on your ass both because I'm still alive and because your Desertland operation hasn't yielded much of anything. So here you are, desperate to placate the old man by fixing either of your two biggest problems. Dealing with me would take time and plenty of hired help and isn't work you could do on your own. Therefore, your only move was to return to this warehouse and personally oversee the search through Lemner's material. You're hoping that luck will finally be on your side and you'll find something."

"You're so goddamned clever."

"So you get here and –surprise!– that crazy bastard Mechanic Nox is waiting for you. She's tracked you down and, after killing your staff, puts a bullet through your head. And why not? You tortured the fuck out of her back in the Desertlands. It makes sense I'd want some hot and juicy revenge. After killing you, I rig up a series of explosives and blow your warehouse sky high, sending all of Lemner's wonderful equipment to hell before fleeing. Now, who do you suppose was to present this particular fairy tale to your father?"

"Nagel."

"Exactly. Nagel sets up the explosives. Nagel takes out your staff. Nagel was set to kill you. But when Nagel shows up later on at Octi Plaza, he blames *me* for all of *his* actions. And who would counter his version of the story? You're pushing daisies and Nagel is clever enough to eliminate any warehouse district witnesses. In fact, the only one left is me, and I highly doubt your father would give me a chance to explain myself. It won't be too terribly long before either the police or your father's head hunters catch up to and bump me off. That leaves Julie and Nagel with a very clear path to seniority within Octi Corp. The only one standing in her way is your old man, and I'm sure she's already figured out how to deal with him."

"I...I don't believe it."

"Keep telling yourself that. And while you're at it, don't forget Julie has Lemner's passkey. With the passkey at her disposal and your father gone, the sky's the limit."

Robert closed his eyes and covered his ears with his hands. He looked like a child that couldn't bear any more schoolyard bullying.

"So much effort, just to get a better job."

The Mechanic sighed. The warehouse stood before them, dark and empty. Nox looked at her wristwatch.

"Won't be long now," she said. She reached into her jacket and pulled out a tan mailing package. She dropped it on the ground before Robert.

Robert reached for the package and opened it. Within, he found two micro-recorders and two micro disks. Written on the disks' sides and in black marker were the following words: *Donovan Conversations.*

"What is this?" Robert asked.

"My complete conversations with Donovan," Nox replied.

"You're...you're just going to give them to me?"

"That's right. It's all I had on Octi Corp."

"Just like that? You must think I'm really stupid, to believe you'd just give away such a valuable commodity."

"You're right, I *do* think you're really stupid. But I'll leave it to your tech boys to verify the fact that these are the original recordings. As for copies, you'll just have to take my word I don't have any."

"The word of an Independent?"

"I'm not an Independent, Robert. I'm a Mechanic." Nox gave the young executive a cold, hard stare. "And I've had enough of you, your wife, and your father. You guys deserve each other."

The Mechanic turned and walked away. She managed a dozen steps before the warehouse erupted. A great ball of fire rushed into the sky before burning out. The explosion left a thick cloud of black smoke. Any firefighters who weren't at the Octi Plaza would soon be heading here.

Nox looked back at Robert one last time. The young executive remained sitting on the ground, holding the Donovan conversation recordings. Nox shook her head and continued walking.

In the distance, the sound of the sirens grew into an ugly wail.

32

The *Yoshiwara* **was** empty except for Catherine, the bar's owner. As she did early every morning, she cleaned the filth left over by the previous night's guests. Broken bottles littered one corner of the bar, vomit another. It was an incredible mess, but Catherine couldn't complain. Bringing in the local bands proved a stroke of genius. Despite the noise and the extra hours of work, she turned a profit, even after a couple of weeks.

Only problem was that she was so damn exhausted from the effort.

Catherine sighed and alternately worked the floor with her mop and broom. It would take a couple of more hours before she could finally get some sleep. Then, a few hours later, it was time to open the bar and start the process all over again.

Yes, she was making money, but the personal cost was high. At some point, she reluctantly realized, she would have to ease back on the hours of operation or switch to the old format, at least on alternate days. If only, Catherine thought, she made enough to hire help. But it would take a lot more profit to get to that point and, in the end, she really didn't mind switching to her old format.

Catherine let out a laugh.

She actually missed her old clients. If they knew...

She scooped up a broken beer bottle and dropped the glass in an over-stuffed trash bag. She tied the bag's top and dragged it to the back of the bar. Once there, she opened the door leading to the outside alley. When she tossed the bag into the oversized metal trash container and turned to re-enter the bar, she was startled to find a figure standing before the bar's rear door, blocking her entry. She reached to her belt for her mace, but the figure was quicker. She grabbed Catherine's hand and held her tight.

"Easy," the woman said. "I'm not here to harm you."

Her voice was weary, the sound of someone who, like her, hadn't slept in a long while. For the first time Catherine noticed the bruises on her face and head, at least those visible on either side of her jet black hair.

"Ms. *Prestigio*," Catherine said. The woman released her.

"I never formally introduced myself," the woman offered. "The name is Nox. I'm a veteran of the wars. Like you."

Catherine stiffened.

"How did you know?"

"The tattoo on your right upper arm."

Catherine looked at her arm and spotted the small insignia. A pair of dice. Six by two. Intel Ops. The tattoo was with her for so long she had forgotten all about it.

"It's not as visible as yours," Catherine said and pointed to the three vertical blue lines tattooed over Nox's right eyebrow. "Please tell me you didn't scare the living shit out of me just so we could have ourselves some girl talk about the bad old days?"

"Going through that shit storm once was more than enough," Nox said. "But I am interested in your expertise. There wasn't a computer you couldn't handle back then, right?"

A sly smile appeared on Catherine's face.

"Not a one. Why?"

"I've got a job for you," Nox said.

"That's a switch. A Mechanic hiring someone for a job?"

"How did you know I was a Mechanic?"

"That first night you showed up a guy named Donovan came to see you."

"And how did you know *that*?"

"The news vids the next day announced his death. I figured you and he agreed on a job and he double crossed you. Instead of running and hiding, you came right back at him in his home turf. You confronted him in his office. You took care of him."

"I offered him a chance."

"I'm sure you did. Anyway, I don't know of any Independents out there with balls big enough to take on an Octi company man. That's why I knew you weren't one of them. Did Donovan deserve what he got?"

Nox thought about that for a while.

"The man was responsible for the deaths of several... Independents. He hired them for a bogus retrieval job. He nearly got me killed, too."

"Then he had to be stopped."

"There were consequences."

"There always are. By the way, the name's Catherine. What can I do for you?"

"Can you link up to deep 'net?"

Catherine whistled.

"What you're talking about is illegal. Everyone had to give up that kind of data mining back in '34."

"I pay well."

"Someone once told me money wasn't everything."

"What kind of asshole would say something that stupid?"

Catherine laughed.

"Will you do the job?"

Catherine motioned to the door.

"Step into my boudoir, madam," she said.

The computer was hidden away in a dark corner of the basement below the bar. It was an ancient machine, the type that, outside of newly discovered Desertland bases, you didn't find anymore. To an uninformed observer, she looked like so much obsolete junk. To those who knew better, she was a Terran IV.

Clunky, but hardly worthless.

Catherine sat in front of the ancient machine and pressed a button.

"It'll take a minute to warm up."

"I've got plenty of time."

"What do you want me to do once I'm inside?"

"Establish a link to the Government Computer Network."

Catherine's head shot back.

"First it's deep 'net and now it's the GCN? Don't get me wrong, Nox, I always did like challenges, but this is borderline crazy. If the GCN's security gets even a whiff of our presence, we're in some really deep shit."

Nox reached into her pocket and pulled out a wad of credit bills. She dropped them on the table, right next to the computer. Catherine eyed the money and smiled.

"What's life without risk, right?" She reached for the money. "With this kind of cash, I can *really* cut back on band nights."

"Either that or get a better pair of earplugs."

Catherine pressed a series of buttons and various screens, both deep 'net and hacker links, appeared on the monitor. Catherine felt the old excitement build, that unique feeling of slipping unseen into forbidden zones while raiding others' restricted playgrounds. It was a unique thrill, one her guest was unlikely to share.

"This will take me a bit," she said.

"As I said, I've got time."

33

Outside, the rising sun sent a wave of brilliant light throughout the Big City. A flock of birds flew by, their bodies perfectly framed against the deep blue sky. It was a perfect morning, but Julie Octi wasn't aware of it. She sat behind her desk in the dim fluorescent light of her office. Her eyes were focused on the vid unit on the far side of the room.

On it, a pretty young reporter spoke into a microphone. The reporter stood before the charred remains of an Octi Corp. warehouse. Firefighters and police circled around behind her, barely acknowledging her presence.

"Octi Corp. Warehouse 23 on the West Side Docks went up in flames at approximately five in the morning. Early word from authorities is that an as yet unidentified body was found within the rubble. Several other bodies, all Octi Corp. Security Staff, were found outside the warehouse and in the immediate area. Investigators will hold a news conference at two this afternoon to state their findings, though early word is that all deaths were the result of foul play. Further—"

Julie's telephone rang and she pressed a button to mute the vid unit. She grabbed the phone.

"We have confirmation that Nox returned to the Big City," a man said. "The bills you gave her are starting to show up all ov—"

"Thanks, but I already knew that," Julie said, cutting the man off. "She did park her truck in our fucking lobby, you know."

There was silence on the other end of the line.

"So...Do you still want us to follow the cash?"

"What do you think?"

Julie slammed the phone down.

I'm working with morons.

Despite it all, a smile worked its way onto her face. She was lucky: Everything worked out in spite of Nox's premature return to the Big City. For Julie's original plan was much more elaborate, but it hinged on her assumption that Nox was cunning, not deranged. The trackers in Nox's truck were meant to give her a head's up of when the Mechanic returned to the city. Julie figured Nox would dump the truck and lay low to lick her wounds before trying anything against Robert. The money she gave Nox would serve as a secondary tracker, allowing Julie to follow Nox's movements while inside the city.

Eventually, Julie figured Nox would use some of the money to buy weapons, which in turn would be used against Robert. Once she had the inventory of Nox's purchases, she would steer the Mechanic toward Robert and make sure Nox took care of him in a place of *her* choosing and in front of several well hidden cameras. The video and inventory evidence would be unimpeachable evidence proving Nox coolly planned and carried out the cold-blooded execution of the young executive. Any moves against Nox would be fully justified.

All nice and legal.

But Nox arrived in the city much faster than anticipated and rammed her truck into the Octi Plaza's lobby. Clearly the torture Robert inflicted on Nox was too much and there was no telling *what* the Mechanic would do next. The more complicated plan was hastily simplified. Nagel was ordered to take out Robert in a way that cast the blame on the crazed woman.

She chuckled and eyed the vid unit's monitor. Images of the burnt out warehouse filled the screen.

In the end, everything worked out *very* well indeed.

She shut the vid unit set off and rose from her seat. She stared at the Johansen oil painting for a few seconds before pressing a button on the desk. The painting slid off to the right, revealing a large window and the world outside. It was the first time in a while that Julie appreciated the beauty of a new day. And why not? Today was *her* day. It was the beginning of her new life.

A far, far better life.

She turned from the window and approached her bookcase. She set aside the fake books and exposed the wall safe. After entering the combination, she opened the safe and reached inside.

The satisfied smile on her face abruptly disappeared.

She pulled the documents out one by one and, as she did, her anger and despair rose. It didn't take long to completely empty the safe. It didn't take much longer to realize the Lemner disks were gone.

Julie's face turned bright red and her eyes bulged. She fought back a wave of fury.

Nagel, you bastard. You're the only one that knew. You fucking double-crossing...

She threw the documents back into the safe and slammed the door shut.

"Fuck."

Julie took a deep breath and, after a few moments, calmed herself down. Now was not the time to lose control. She considered her options and, after a few minutes, the smile returned to her face.

There were ways to get back at Nagel.

Julie straightened her clothing and hair.

Devious ways indeed.

She exited her office and walked to the elevator.

Robert Octi Senior stared out of his office window. Most of the firefighters at Octi Plaza were gone, though there remained a sizeable contingency of investigators and media in the parking lot below. The cost to keep them quiet still annoyed the hell out of him. So much so that he barely heard the door to his office open.

"Honey?"

Octi found Julie standing at the office's threshold. He waved her in and sat behind his desk. The cushions enveloped his elderly body, allowing him to forget his pains, both mental and physical, and focus on the blonde beauty's face. Tears smeared her mascara.

"I heard about Robert," she said and sniffled. Her white handkerchief was stained with dark make-up. "I'm so sorry."

"What about him?" Octi replied. His voice was even and emotionless.

The sadness in Julie's face turned to surprise.

"By the Gods," she said. "I thought you heard. Robert was... Robert was found dead in the West Warehouse. He was... he was killed, and I know who did it."

The expression on Octi's face remained stubbornly neutral.

"Really?" he said.

Julie wiped away a fresh cascade of tears.

"It was that Independent Donovan hired. Nox. I think...I think she's working with Nagel. That's how they got so close to us. That's how Nox survived her capture in Lemner's base. But the worst thing is that I'm sure they have Lemner's passkey!"

Having played her trump card, Julie released another round of tears. From the corner of her eye, however, she noted the elderly Octi's reaction. Or rather lack of one. Julie sensed something was very wrong.

I can believe the old bastard doesn't care about his loser son. But the program? Maybe he'll care about other *things.*

Julie wiped her tears away and composed herself. She offered Octi a seductive glare.

"We no longer have to hide our relationship," she purred. She thrust her chest out, offering Octi a generous view of her cleavage.

Still no reaction.

Octi sighed.

"Robert isn't dead," the elderly man said.

For Julie, the world turned upside down. She felt like she was in a foreign place, a reality similar but completely alien from her own.

"But...but the news," Julie began. "I saw the report."

"They found *Nagel's* body inside that warehouse," Octi said. "That asshole son of mine came whimpering back here an hour or so ago. He told me you and Nagel screwed him from the start. Nox saved him from *your* boy before washing her hands of us. Dumb bitch actually gave up the Donovan conversations. She's a Mechanic all right, all honor and no brains. No wonder her kind doesn't exist anymore."

"What...what about the truck? Why did she crash it into the building?"

"To flush you out, Julie dear."

The expression on Julie's face, if possible, turned even paler.

"It... it can't be."

"You want proof?" Octi asked. He reached into the desk drawer and pulled out the Donovan conversation recordings. He waved the disks and recorders in the air and allowed Julie a good look before putting them back. "Nox played her hand well, if you ask me. She exposed Octi's internal rot while assuring me there was no need to waste another blue cent hunting her down. The board'll like that, at the very least."

Octi's seething eyes contemplated his daughter-in-law and mistress.

"You look confused, Julie. Out of sorts. Would you like me to clarify something? Should I go over this once more?"

"...no..."

To this Octi chuckled. Julie looked up.

"This...this is some kind of trick."

"I'm afraid not," Octi said. "I have to give it to you, Julie. What you did to my son... It was fantastic. I've never seen such incredible planning and execution. I'll be damned if I wasn't impressed. You made Robert look like the rank amateur he is. If everything had worked out, there's no doubt you would have easily –*easily*– replaced him on our board."

The skin on Julie's face was bone white.

"Robert's gone now, of course," Octi continued. "Given his failures and...well, once word got out about this situation, no one would respect him anymore. You can't do business with someone like that. It's a real shame I had to get rid of my own flesh and blood, but with this latest fuck up, he gave me no choice."

"You... you killed him?"

"Hell no. I fired him. I'm certain other companies will be interested in picking him up and mining him for information on our operations, but I doubt they'll rely on what he has to say all that much. A loser will always be a loser."

Octi shook his head. *Such a shame.*

"Anyway," Octi said. "As of an hour ago, that's old news, and I'm not one to dwell on nostalgia. So tell me, Julie, where is Lemner's passkey?"

"I had it—"

"Come on, Julie. Where is it?"

Julie sat in the chair before Octi's desk. She shook her head.

"I was... I was planning to bring it to you this morning."

Octi let out a laugh.

"Don't bullshit me. You were going to keep that program to yourself. What was the first thing you planned to do with it? Get the goods on me? Use it to get me taken off the board?"

"No, it was nothing like—"

"Where is it?!"

"Please, Robert, I—"

"Where. Is. It?"

"Someone stole it from my office."

"Who?"

"Nagel. It had to be. He's the only one that knew."

Octi sighed.

"He's dead, Julie."

"We need to search his house, his car, any place he's been! The disks will turn up. They have to!"

"Oh yeah, that's just what this company needs. Another wild goose chase."

"But—"

"Don't worry, Julie. We'll have some staff –a small, easy to hide staff– search Nagel's home and office. Maybe we'll get lucky and Lemner's passkey will turn up. On the other hand, Robert always bragged about how clever Nagel was. He was the brains of that outfit, you know. My son was the one with all the stupid ideas and Nagel implemented them. I have no doubt Nagel was clever enough to hide his treasure where it can't be found."

"What about us," Julie said. "What about... what about me?"

"You're through, Julie. You meddled too much in my personal business. I can't forgive your failures, just like I couldn't forgive my son's. For all your scheming and all your dirty little tricks, you failed. The Lemner venture is over as far as I'm concerned. Get the hell out of here. *Now.*"

Tears, genuine tears, formed in Julie's eyes. She rose, but her legs could barely hold her weight. She stumbled to the door leading out of the office.

"Julie," Octi said when she opened the door.

Julie stopped and faced her former boss, lover, and father-in-law.

"My son's out there somewhere. He'll be looking for you."

34

With each passing minute, Catherine's confidence in successfully cracking into the GCN grew. The screen before her flickered and flashed with bits of information, text, and graphics. Some lasted only seconds, while others forced her to pause and examine subroutines and arcane security measures.

After four straight hours of work, she leaned back in her chair and let out a satisfied grunt.

"Nox."

Nox was instantly at Catherine's side. The Mechanic stared at the information on Catherine's monitor.

"I've managed a small, superficial entry, not unlike poking a needle into a whale's belly," Catherine said. "But from here, we can watch the data stream pass by. Bank transactions, news, emails, streaming videos and music, and porn. Lots and *lots* of porn."

"Can you add an entry?"

"Depends. What and where?"

"The police networks," Nox said. She unfolded a piece of paper and handed it to Catherine. "I want this addendum leaked to all the news networks."

Catherine read the note and whistled.

"Whoa," she said. "I'm a damned good computer jockey, if I do say so myself, but if I try anything like what you're asking, we *will* be discovered. Five minutes after that, the police'll break through the bar's door, and they won't be here to enjoy the questionable pleasures of our live band."

"You can do it."

"I wish I shared your optimism, Nox. We can put out spam or virtual graffiti, but there's no way I can mimic a legitimate police report."

"You can," Nox insisted. "You just need the right tools."

Nox pulled the package of disks she robbed from Julie earlier in the morning. Catherine frowned at the obvious age of this material.

"What the hell is this?"

"Your ticket inside the GCN."

"These things are ancient. Do they still work?"

"We won't know until we try."

"You mean *I* won't know," Catherine said and winked. "Let's see if I have a disk drive for these relics."

Catherine searched through several cabinets before finding the proper drive for those old disks. She plugged the drive into her computer and hit a series of buttons.

"The drive works," she said. "Now let's see if the disks do as well."

Catherine inserted the disks into the drive. After a few seconds her computer screen went blank, and seconds later instructions on entering the government network appeared.

"Holy shit."

Catherine pressed several keys and examined the information before her.

"What is this, Nox?"

"What do you think?"

"It's...it's some kind of a back door entry key. Like...like..." Catherine let out a gasp. "No fucking way. Is this...is this Lemner's passkey?"

She faced Nox. Her eyes were wide open and her breath heavy.

"Where did you get this?"

"Can you do what I'm asking?"

"Are you kidding?" Catherine said. It was hard for her to contain her growing wonder and delight. "But, Nox, what you're asking for is...it's nothing. With this program we could do *anything* we wanted! We could skim money from any bank. We could get legit deeds for any number of properties. We could infiltrate all the industries and make off with their most well-guarded secrets! We could, we could—"

"Rule the world," Nox said. "I've heard it all before and I'm still not interested. That program cost many good people their lives. It almost cost me mine." Nox pointed to the piece of paper she handed to Catherine moments before.

"Just get that addendum into the proper channels," Nox said. "That's all I want."

Catherine nodded. A warm smile formed on her face.

"Snowflakes in August," she said.

"What?"

"Looks like there are some good people left in this world."

Static filled the vid unit's screen, followed by the image of a handsome young reporter. He smiled and read from the teleprompter.

"...in business news, the Stock Markets turned bullish, with the top ten major companies reporting strong earnings. Ironically, the one company that has not benefited from this increased prosperity is the once golden Octi Corporation."

The news anchor faced another camera. Serious reporting required a closer shot.

"In a stunning development, new evidence submitted to the police has cleared Claire Donovan, wife of murdered industrialist Jason Donovan, of her husband's death. This new evidence, still under seal within the Big City's Police Department, points to responsibility for the industrialist's death on Octi C.E.O. Robert Octi Senior."

The image of the reporter was replaced with footage from in front of Octi Plaza. Several police officers led a handcuffed Robert Octi Senior out of his building and into a waiting police car. The elderly executive's face was both indignant yet defeated. He knew there was no way to undo the damage of this broadcast.

He knew he was done.

"Reacting to this shocking news, the board of Octi Corp. convened an emergency session within the past hour," the reporter continued. "It has been confirmed that they have unanimously ousted Robert Octi Senior from his own company. Board members are currently voting on a replacement. In another shocking twist, Robert Octi Senior's son, Robert Octi Junior, once groomed for this job, is no longer a member of the company and could not be reached for comment."

The police car carrying Robert Octi Senior drove away, and the image on the screen cut to the reporter in the studio. His right hand came up to his ear.

"I'm receiving word that the board of Octi Corp. just concluded their latest vote. Cindy Patterson is standing by just outside the boardroom..."

The image on the screen changed once more. Standing before the door leading into the Octi Corp. boardroom was another reporter. She eyed the camera and said:

"This is Cindy Patterson, reporting from within Octi Corporation. I am able to confirm..."

The door beside her opened and Charles Lambert stepped outside. Beside him was Brinkman and closely behind the two were the rest of the board. Brinkman's smile was a mile wide as he stepped before Lambert and patted him on the shoulder. He then faced the vid unit's cameras and said:

"Ladies and gentlemen, I present to you the new C.E.O. of Octi Corporation."

The rest of the board members applauded.

"We value your leadership and have faith in you," Brinkman continued. "And let me just add, we're with you all the way."

Lambert acknowledged the complements by shaking the man's hand. The applause from the other board members grew.

Lambert took in the adulation for an appropriate amount of time before motioning his board to quiet down.

"It's a new day for Octi Corporation," Lambert told the crowd around him. "I promise I will make you proud. Even more importantly, I promise to make you rich. Very, *very* rich."

Laughter and more applause.

Lambert waved to his board before walking to Cindy Patterson's side. He offered her, and the vid unit camera, a triumphant yet serious smile.

"Hello, Cindy," Lambert said.

"Congratulations, on your appointment, Mr. Lambert."

"Thank you."

"May we ask a few questions?"

"Certainly."

"Mr. Lambert, Octi Corp. has taken what can only be described as some serious hits these past weeks. What words of encouragement can you offer your investors in these tough times?"

Lambert took a few seconds to consider the question, as if grappling for a significant enough answer.

"Let me be clear: Change is coming," Lambert finally said. "The old ways of doing business are over but we can –we will– right this ship."

"How?"

"We've initiated a top to bottom review of all our research and technical properties. We expected to find plenty of waste, and have already dealt with much of it. But we've also found some diamonds in the rough; projects we feel will help Octi Corp. rise from the ashes."

"Can you offer our viewers any preview of these so-called diamonds in the rough?"

"Well, many of these projects are top secret," Lambert began. "But there is one I think will make a definite impact in the very short term."

"Sounds exciting. Can you tell us more?"

Lambert nodded. He stared directly into the cameras.

"Within the next few days, Octi Corp. will unveil the next generation of automated robotic security. Frankly, I was surprised to find the previous regime so casually discarded such a sophisticated, fearsome machine. Next week, we're going to formally unveil her and you're all invited for the test run." Lambert offered the cameras his brightest smile yet. "I want a *big* crowd around to see what this baby is capable of."

35

Nox strolled on the wooden pier. The day was bright and the sun was dazzling in the cloudless sky.

Nox held Lemner's disks and tossed them, one after the other, into the salty water before her. They would be quickly lost in the mud and filth. Within an hour or two, the information stored on them would corrode in the polluted, acidic sea, along with the dreams of all would-be tyrants.

When she was done ridding the world of Lemner's passkey, Nox continued her walk and eventually reached her destination. It was the *Shoreline Choppers*, a repair and reconditioning garage. Like all the structures on the boardwalk, it was a rusted warehouse. Its front doors were wide open and Nox gazed within. A couple of grease monkeys worked on her beat up motorcycle.

They told Nox they'd get the motorcycle back in shape in another week or two. They couldn't promise any miracles, but Nox's chopper, even on the best of days, was never all that good to begin with. Nox didn't care. As long as the cycle started after a few tries and took the Mechanic where she needed to go, it was all she could ask for.

A smile filled Nox's battered face.

She looked forward to taking that ride.

THE END

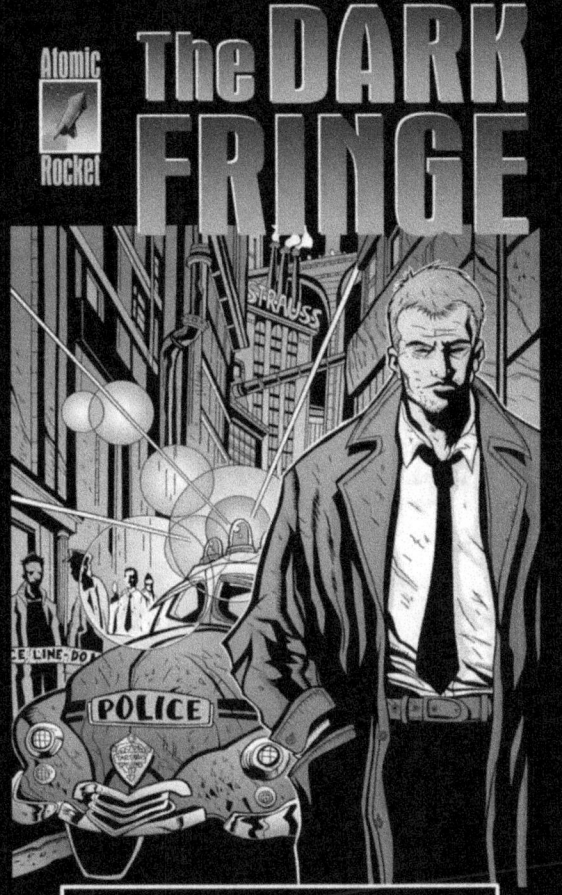

From the grittiest corners of a dark metropolis...
...to the coldest reaches of outer space...
...and all those uneasy places in between...

SHADOWS at DAWN

E. R. Torre

Fourteen tales of Mystery, Suspense, and the Fantastic.

Visions of a dead actor haunt a lonely young man...
Fate leads him on a journey to the man's home town...

E. R. TORRE

HAZE

It started with Blood...

...see how it ends.

Return once more to the world of
The Dark Fringe.

COLD HEMISPHERES

E. R. Torre

An elderly Hitman's most dangerous job
Is the one he can't complete.

HER NAME IS NOX. HIRE HER, AND SHE WILL GET
THE JOB DONE...

E. R. TORRE

MECHANIC

CORROSIVE KNIGHTS 1

...CROSS HER AT YOUR OWN RISK.

For over two hundred years a deadly secret has been kept.
A secret that could shatter the delicate peace between two
galactic empires and result in the death of billions...

CORROSIVE KNIGHTS 2

THE LAST FLIGHT
OF THE ARGUS

E. R. TORRE

That secret is about to be revealed.

Arizona, 1925: A Sheriff makes a discovery in the fiery desert
that changes everything.
Bad Penny, the Present: On an idyllic island army base, a
hidden menace is about to be unleashed...

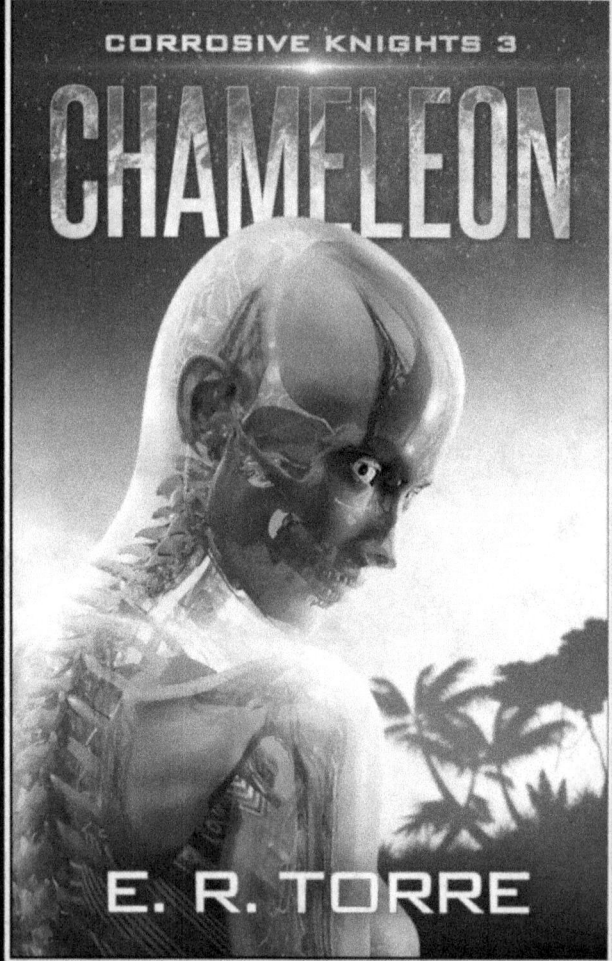

CORROSIVE KNIGHTS 3

CHAMELEON

E. R. TORRE

For the seven passengers of a military transport helicopter,
the next twelve hours could signal the end of mankind.

Nox the Mechanic is back and this time she faces
a threat that could destroy all of mankind...

CORROSIVE KNIGHTS 4

N O X

E. R. TORRE

A threat she carries in her own blood...

Centuries ago, an unstoppable enemy
forced humanity to flee to the stars.

CORROSIVE KNIGHTS 5

GHOST OF
THE ARGUS

E. R. TORRE

Today, humanity will take the fight to *them*.

A scavenger on a lost planet
carries a terrifying secret...

CORROSIVE KNIGHTS 6

FOUNDRY OF THE GODS

E. R. TORRE

What lies beneath the desert sands
within the Foundry of the Gods?

CORROSIVE KNIGHTS 7

LEGACY OF
THE ARGUS

E. R. TORRE

ertorre.com

Atomic Rocket

Science Fiction, Mystery, and Suspense

www.ingramcontent.com/pod-product-compliance
Lightning Source LLC
Chambersburg PA
CBHW071144260626
47162CB00003B/918